Fool

RED PUDDLE PRINT

marylawrencebooks.com

Copyright © 2026 by Mary Lawrence

All rights reserved. No part of this book may be reproduced in any form or by any means without the prior written consent of the Publisher, excepting brief quotes used in reviews.

Red Puddle titles are available through Ingram, local booksellers, and Amazon.

ISBN: 978-1-7347-3611-3 (softcover)

ISBN: 978-1-7347-3612-0 (eBook)

First Red Puddle Print Trade Paperback Printing: March 2026

10 9 8 7 6 5 4 3 2 1

Printed in the United States of America

Cover Designer and Interior Formatting by Damonza

Fool

MARY LAWRENCE

Red Puddle Print

To Rose and Manon

A fool uttereth all his mind: but a wise
man keepeth it in till afterwards.

PROVERBS 29:11

The Provocateur

CHAPTER ONE

London, October, 1541

A MAN OF MY stature must have twice the wits if he is to survive amongst men twice his height. That is not to say that I have had fewer opportunities afforded me. Nay, decidedly not. My shortcomings have merely coloured the cards of fate that I have been dealt. And while others may have folded, I have played on.

So where must my tale begin—this one of courts, and queens, dissemblers, and fools? Should I bore you with tales of my youth? Of being raked out of a dung heap as a babe at Thetford Priory? The monks raised me and taught me to read and write, then tossed me out after I was discovered with a farmer's daughter behind a wheel of Wensleydale.

Instead, I shall take you to Whitehall where our sovereign, King Henry, fat as a stuffed boar and about as lively, delights in his new child bride, Katherine Howard.

I am a titled fool of the court, a stage monkey, a ninny chosen to charm the lords and ladies with my antics, my juggling, my wit. Indeed, my awkward presence alone is enough to incite laughs and jeers and set anyone in a better humour. However, a dwarf must have more about him than his appearance.

I was popular with the ladies. I had a handsome face once; women could gaze on that and forget the rest. They could hide me beneath their skirts where I could tease and pleasure them, none any the wiser of a little tryst, as they supped or stood in the halls of Whitehall, gazing out a window overlooking the Thames.

Such boasting. It will do me no benefit now, and only make me sad for what I have lost.

So let us travel to a room in Whitehall where a chambermaid folds linen as I partake of the enticing nectar of her fragrant neck. She giggles as I nibble, when suddenly we hear voices at the door and the sound of a latch being lifted. A hanging tapestry of Saint John offers cover for me—a relic from Cardinal Wolsey's collection, purloined by our king after His Grace's demise. Moths have eaten through the paps of an angel, affording me a risqué view of the room. Surprised by the sudden arrival, my sweet paramour straightens her bodice and smooths down her skirt.

"I've never seen a chambermaid so cheered to be folding sheets," says a man upon entering. I glimpse his black Canterbury cap and silk gown with marten tippet and realise it is Archbishop Cranmer, complaisant vassal of the king's clerical needs. He is followed by a young cove, of the king's court, for I recognise the fellow, though he is not of great usefulness. "Go child, we need this room for conference."

My pert little chambermaid curtseys and gathers the linens into her basket, flashes a glance in my direction, then hurries to the door. Archbishop Cranmer sees her out while the scatty-eyed fopdoodle takes in the room.

"And so, John Lascelles," begins Cranmer, crossing the room to sit at a table. He settles in a cushioned chair, the motes of dust rising to float in the sun streaming through a mullioned window, then props his elbows and touches his fingertips together in a prayer-like gesture befitting a man of his ilk.

Meanwhile, the dust from the tapestry dances in my nostrils, cueing me to sneeze. I wrestle the urge into submission, at least for the moment.

"You have my attention and your request for privacy. You have alluded to knowledge regarding our sovereign's new queen. But tell me, why should I believe you?"

"Sir, my sister Mary lived with the young queen before she ever was groomed for such office, of course. They shared quarters in the ladies' dormitory at the Duchess of Norfolk's house at Lambeth."

Archbishop Cranmer lifts an eyebrow. His upper lip quivers and the lad knows he has managed to capture his audience's full attention. "Continue, John Lascelles," says the archbishop.

The young man steps closer to the desk. "When it was announced that Katherine Howard would be the next queen, I encouraged my sister to seek service with her." His eyes grow wide, in mock imitation of his sibling. "'I will not,' said she. 'But I am very sorry for her.'"

"Sorry?" queries Cranmer.

"I, too, questioned—why? 'Katherine is very light in behaviour,' said she."

If being light of character is so opprobrious then I should float away and live my life in the clouds.

Archbishop Cranmer studies Lascelles with sombre eyes. "Tell me more," he prompts, leaning forward in his chair.

"It was common gossip that the young queen had encouraged the attentions of her music master. Then, when she lost interest in him, she indulged her affections on Francis Dereham."

"The queen's private secretary," says Archbishop Cranmer, astonished.

I, too, share his astonishment. I'd seen this Dereham leave the Queen's quarters on occasion but assumed his purpose was nothing untoward, for I was unaware of any history between them. Although, as I think on it, I do recall seeing a smirk on the fellow's face once and wondering…

"For a hundred nights and more, Frances Dereham climbed through her window and she entertained him in her bed, not caring that her roommates could not sleep for all the noise the two made behind the drawn bed hangings."

Ah, the folly of youth and reckless abandon! I nod in commiseration, suppressing a chuckle, when the dust from the tapestry distracts me, reminding me of my place. The dust, that meddlesome antagonist, wheedles up my nose, twirling and wiggling, causing my face to contort in the most violent attempts to suppress its antics. The silence that follows this last tidbit is interminable. If I am found standing behind the tapestry, it would not be advantageous having heard such incriminations against our fair queen.

Finally, Archbishop Cranmer speaks. "Do you swear to this?"

"I would rather die telling the truth than live with its concealment."

Ho, words to endear oneself to a man of such office. Such a wily fellow this John Lascelles.

"Why did you not seek me before now?" questions Cranmer.

Lascelles drops his gaze in a show of humble regret. "I have been wrestling with my conscience."

Archbishop Cranmer sits quietly, weighing the import of this knowledge.

"Sir, you may ask my sister for her account. She has said she would speak it."

The archbishop stares across the room in reflection. I hold

my breath, worried about disturbing the silence or his thoughts. I am nearly blue before he speaks.

"Will you sign a statement swearing to the veracity of this information?"

There is no hesitation on the part of the newsmonger.

Cranmer stands and walks out from behind the desk. "What you have told me does not flatter our young queen's character. Such dubious morals could lead to behaviour unfitting for a queen."

The archbishop sees John Lascelles out the door, then calls for his assistant. "Summon the Lord Chancellor and Edward Seymour. They must come at once."

The door closes and I listen for Cranmer to return to the table. He does not. He must be mulling over the possible consequences of Lascelles' words. I steady my breath, praying that in this silence he does not hear me breathing. If I can remain hidden until he abandons the room, then I might escape unnoticed, saving myself for another day. Oh, to be ignorant. By pure accident, I am now informed. I should have allowed myself to be caught fondling the chambermaid rather than surreptitiously hide, because if I am caught, in their eyes I would be a possible intrigant.

After a long minute, the archbishop exits. He must be impatient waiting, or, more likely, he knows better where to find the two men. Then again, he may be paying a visit to the garderobe. I have no interest either way. I only want to find a way out.

I step from behind the tapestry, scanning the room for a possible escape other than the obvious door. There is no connection or passage to a second room. Nor do the windows offer a possible egress; the yard below is very far. I may be a monkey, but I am not the climbing kind. I consider what to do when suddenly, the latch rattles. I dive behind St. John again.

Through my spy hole, I see the Lord Chancellor, Thomas Audley, following Cranmer back into the room. Close behind is the Earl of Hertford—Edward Seymour.

"It is not to say that she has made the king a cuckold with Francis Dereham, but why would she grant the fellow special office if she didn't take an interest in him?" says Audley, resplendent in his marten-trimmed gown. He is of fair snout, by some measures—a handsome fellow, low-born like me. Low-born like Thomas Cromwell and Cardinal Wolsey—all men made by the king and alas, also unmade and sleeping for eternity under flagstone.

"Your lordship," says the Earl. "It is incriminating, a possible scandal may be imminent. We must think to protect our sovereign."

Cranmer is again sitting at the table. "I agree, but our king is deeply in love with this one. It may be dangerous to introduce such doubt."

"It may be more dangerous to keep this queen in office with her family's ideas of quelling the reformation." Methinks Thomas Audley says this for Seymour's benefit. Seymour would love nothing more than to see the Howard family tumble. Especially his Privy Council rival, Thomas Howard.

Seymour says, "We have all benefited from the king's reforms."

The archbishop does not reply to this, but when he rose to power after being favoured by the Boleyns, he continued the policy laid down by chief-minister Cromwell to dissolve the monasteries, thereby putting an end to the corruption that was believed to run rampant amongst the clergy. Instead of sending our English money to the Pope to line his pockets, Cranmer and King Henry could keep it to line theirs. The enormous acreage and spoils of religious properties were divvied up among men of favoured status such as Audley and Seymour.

"I will have to consider how best to introduce this worm of doubt to our king. It could turn on me. The king will not appreciate being told that he has been cuckolded."

"No, Your Grace," agrees Seymour. "But if you know information that may have import to his reign, and you say nothing, then you are in a precarious position should he later learn of it. How would you explain your secrecy to our king?"

The archbishop strokes his chin in consideration. It is then that the dust of the tapestry resumes worming its way through my nostrils, tickling just under my eyes. If I should pop out my eyeballs to suppress this urge to sneeze, so be it, I shall deal with that later. I hold my breath, reciting twelve Hail Marys in my head. I swear I will never ravish another maiden (at least for a day) if sweet Mary delivers me from this sternutation.

My preoccupation is so complete that I fail to think that it might not be a sneeze that would give me away, but my pointy-toed shoes. Suddenly, the tapestry is whipped aside, revealing Archbishop Cranmer staring down at me.

I let slide an involuntary fart.

"Who is this?" he cries.

"It is the king's fool," replies Edward Seymour.

"Rake," says the archbishop, snatching me up by my collar and pulling me to my toes. "What do you mean spying on us?"

"Your Grace, I was not spying."

"Standing silent behind tapestries is not spying? You insult me, little man."

Audley walks to the door and speaks to a guard outside, then joins Cranmer's side. "You cannot trust him. He is Kronos, a court fool, practised in gossip and mischief."

"I swear I will not say a word. This is none of my concern," I say.

"Pah!" exclaims Audley. "To let him go with a sworn silence is as effective as sending him off to tell all."

A quick rap at the door is answered by Seymour. Three burly guards cross the room. Their menacing manner alone reduces me to quivering like chicken fat on the king's platter. The archbishop releases me to their custody.

"Your Grace," I start. "I was not here to spy. I was merely hiding until you left."

Archbishop stares at me stone-faced.

I swallow back a lump in my throat. "I was with the chambermaid before you came in."

An uncomfortable silence follows. I am hoping that the archbishop realises my intentions are completely self-serving and base.

Seymour shakes his head. "I would not trust a man of his character to keep his tongue."

"Then perhaps we should keep it for him," says Audley.

What followed has changed my life forever. I can hardly think on it without trembling. I endured, yes, but the cost to me was more than my mutilation. They burned out my tongue, and set fire to my soul along with it.

The glowing poker neared my face, my jaw was pried open, and a plume of steam and boiling blood rose from my mouth. God did comfort me in my suffering because I passed to black so that I couldn't recall each interminable second of my pain.

When I finally come to, I am stripped and left for dead in a stinking back alley. The sky pisses on my pathetic person and I wallow in the rain and rotting filth of London, thinking how once again I am tossed into the street.

It is only fitting that the mud should be my shroud.

The Novice

CHAPTER TWO

ALL STORIES HAVE a beginning—as do all lives. *Once upon a time* begins with a mother's final push thrusting a child into the world. A world indifferent to yet another mewling mouth seeking to find its place among a multitude of others just as needy and just as expectant. There with its scowling face, clenched eyes and fists, the necessity to breathe air instead of fluid. Live—and a story unfolds.

Stories build incrementally, then become full with the passage of time. Is it not true of lives? Threads of days become months, become years, which are woven into a tapestry. Mayhap the tale might be pleasing. The tale might be simple, an ease of prediction satisfying, but hardly revolutionary. Then, there are tapestries and lives that dazzle. Their threads shimmer and are appreciated by those who know how to see.

Which tale is this? That is for you to decide.

But I know what I am about.

Imagination fleshes out my earliest years because I have no mother, no father, no siblings to inform me. Eventually, though, memory dispatches my fantasy.

What must my mother have thought when she first laid eyes

on me? Did horror squelch her maternal instinct to push my nose against her teat? What woman would allow my half-baked self to suckle her breast? Ha! Show me a woman so forgiving.

Brother Trelli said I was found one sharp March morning when the wind blistered the noses of monks hurrying to their morning devotion. My voice—blessedly lusty—bellowed forth, piercing the stolid oak door and stone walls of the priory. The monks stopped. They listened. They queried each other's puzzled faces.

"'Tis a cat," concluded Brother Gregor, the priory's cantor, a man who should recognise the difference between the yowling of a human and that of a beast. He hurried on, leaving the rest of the good monks to freeze in further debate.

Their discussion was brief, for a timely, frigid gust penetrated their homespun and spurred them on to the sheltered nave where they commenced their prayers. But the continued wails haunted their meditations. Brother Dowser could bear it not. Before his last *ave* faded in echo, he sought a kitchen lad to assist him in finding the insufferable feline and scare it away.

They threw open the door onto the fallow garden, crunchy underfoot with frost, and listened for direction. Nearby, the limbs of an apple tree mournfully creaked. For a few blessed moments they enjoyed the quiet of the dormant grounds.

"I heard it too," said the boy, noticing the perplexed look on Brother Dowser's face. "I thought it a cat in the midden fending off a rat."

The monk looked in the direction of that corner of the grounds hidden behind a wall and an ash tree still skeletal despite the change of season.

"They must have come to terms because I hear it no more," said Brother Dowser.

Satisfied, the two turned back for the door where a kitchen

fire blazed and pottage burped in cast iron kettles. They had taken no more than a step when again the caterwauls commenced.

Without a word, they hurried across the chequered plots to the ash and rounded the corner of the stone wall to the pit that held such filth as to make them retch upon reaching it.

"God's tooth!" cried the lad, who received a hard look from the monk.

There, on top of the pile, screamed the object of the raucous.

"Whoever did this took the added misery of planting the babe squarely in the middle," said Brother Dowser, quickly signing the cross.

The lad, expecting to be asked to wade through the glop and slurry, retrieved a long-handled fork leaning against the wall then removed his shoes.

"Fish him out of there, boy. A greater reward awaits you in heaven."

If the boy had his doubts, he kept them to himself and stepped to the edge of the pit, hoping to reach the turd-covered creature without having to venture knee deep in nasty. He extended the long handle of the implement and gingerly slid it under.

But humans fall as naturally as birds fly. He hoped to dislodge me but I rolled onto the tines, face down, swallowing a muzzle of waste—surely portending my future when undesirable things would be shoved in my mouth.

Persist, though, they did, and for their efforts they got a brown-caked, misshapen raw dough of a babe in return.

They christened me Ivo after the patron saint of abandoned children, but they called me Kronos after the Greek god for time who castrated his father (I would never stoop so low), thus separating heaven from earth. Odd for good Christian men to scour the Hellenic pantheon for a name. Perhaps Ivo was too sacred;

after all, there was something unsanctimonious about my abandonment and perhaps they wanted to mark me thus.

No effort was made to find my mother. Nor did the monks peddle me to one of their tenant farmers which would have destined me to a life of drudgery—scything barley, mucking stalls, or digging trenches in the low-lying fens.

Instead, they cared for and nurtured me and for that I am grateful. They bent my fingers around a quill and taught me to write, though my attempts to copy scripture and perhaps work in the scriptorium proved disappointing. I possessed neither the patience nor the ability to sit for hours scribing faint lines, or mastering a steady hand, or training my eye for the beauty and balance required to accomplish even one line of text. Eventually, they accepted my failings and sent me to the kitchen to assist Brother Trelli and work in the potager.

How far I have come since then, only to find myself lying in the stink, lapsing between consciousness and pesterous memory. My thoughts tumble backward remembering my youth spent working by Brother Trelli's side, abiding by the Benedictine rule of prayer and duty—*Ora et labora*.

I chopped vegetables to feed fifteen monks and as many lay brothers and toted pails of peelings to the compost. I scrubbed the stacks of pots and trenchers left after every meal. And when my daily chores were done, I kept up my education and read with avid interest the writings I found tucked away in the dim recesses of the priory's library.

The monks with failing eyesight could not easily read the blurry cover of what I had my nose buried in. When asked, I would quote a passage or one of the Benedictine rules and they would nod, pleased with my humility and industry. They did not know that hidden inside the covers of Saint Augustine's

Confessions were Catullus's bawdy poems about fucking Lesbia—
"she who is juicier than a grape."

Contemplating lewd verse occupied most of my thoughts but
one day, Brother Trelli told a story that encouraged me to ponder
man's darker inclinations; those pricks of devilment and aggression that we all have and work so diligently to subdue or hide
from one another. He took some pleasure in relaying disreputable
scuttle on occasion and I was eager to hear it. I realised then that
my relationship with God would be a tenuous one because for all
of my confessions, and attempts to stay in His good grace, I do
crave a good story. And isn't that why you are here?

One day, as Brother Trelli and I returned from collecting walnuts
from a nearby stand, we neared the great door of the nave, and
before passing through he pointed to a patch of ground beside
it. "A prior was murdered there," he said.

"A murder at Thetford Priory?" I asked. This was news indeed.
Our placid, mundane environ suddenly became interesting.

"'Twas quite long ago," added Brother Trelli. "Long before
we were born."

Hoping for a recent account of murder, I was disappointed
that it had occurred during the days of yore, when our Benedictine
monasticism was better known for its decadence than for its
godly achievements. Brother Trelli pushed through the door and
held it open for me.

"There once was a Prior Stephen who came from Savoy
across the channel. A man ill-suited for the office, but nonethe-
less appointed. Not long after, he sent for his two brothers from
France. The night they arrived, the three commenced to drinking
and the prior forewent evening Vespers and Matins the following

morning. Indeed, the three brothers spent their days and nights in drunken stupors, cavorting and pleasuring themselves with innocent village maids."

This got my attention. A debauched prior at Thetford? Village maids—seduced and raped? I could no more imagine our own Prior Ixworth, that dour-faced martinet of doctrine, looking at a woman, much less touching her. The entire subject of the opposite sex was almost entirely avoided at Thetford.

Brother Trelli set his basket of walnuts on the table. "Tales of their misdeeds circulated amongst the brethren. It was a source of terrible consternation and embarrassment." He disappeared into the pantry and rummaged about, emerging with a hammer and bowl.

"At the time, there be a Welsh monk in the brotherhood named de Charun," he said upon his return, handing over the items. "Brother de Charun took issue with Prior Stephen's behaviour. When de Charun confronted the prior, the prior threatened to send him back to Cluni from whence he came. The Welsh monk raged, 'It is not I who must leave—but you!' Their fiery words alone should have smote them dead on the spot if God had been listening."

Brother Trelli began slicing onions for the evening meal, his stout fingers making quick of the chore. I moved myself down the board to prevent my eyes watering, took a walnut from the basket, and cracked it with the hammer.

"One night, the Welshman stole into the kitchen and took a gutting knife," continued Brother Trelli, dumping the onions in a pot. He held up the knife as if it was de Charun's weapon and pointed it at me. "He slipped it up his sleeve, no one the wiser for what mischief he had in mind. That night, just before Matins, de Charun lay in wait outside the great door for the three to return from their night of revel.

"Meanwhile, the monks rose for their night office and gathered for their prayers as usual. They had nearly finished their bleary-eyed recitation when their susurrations were interrupted by shouting. With sighs of resignation, the brothers shook their heads and ignored the cries, for they had grown accustomed to their prayers being disrupted by the three drunken men. For good measure, they commenced to pray for their prior's soul—for what else could they do?

"It would have been another night in a long string of others similarly spent, but de Charun entered the nave. He walked up the aisle, past the monks to the rood screen, his robe glistening with blood.

"'I have finished the prior,' said he.

"The monks rushed outside and there lying on the ground was their prior—a look of surprise forever frozen on his face."

I held the hammer mid-air, contemplating the thought of murder on these hallowed grounds. I was so amazed that my grip loosened and the hammer clattered to the table. "What became of the prior's two brothers?"

"They fled the priory. Never to be seen again."

"And Brother de Charun? What happened to him?"

Brother Trelli shrugged.

"He was not reprimanded for murder?"

"The priory keeps its secrets."

Brother Trelli merrily took up a pitcher and added water to the pot. How could these reticent and peace-loving brothers commit debauchery and murder? Such misdeeds are the transgressions of commoners and men outside the fold—not the doings of Benedictine monks. I picked up the hammer and brought it down on a walnut, sending shell fragments scattering. What other confidences were buried at Thetford Priory?

"We take the vow, but we are just men," said Brother Trelli.

"And, as men, we struggle with mortal desires. We are not immune to the pull of sin, but we strive to reject those impulses and live in God's grace. Every one of us has lied, we have all coveted. We, as mortals…sin."

Are we, as monks and servants of God, whose life work is to think first of Him, given more allowance than others? Are we held namely to His standard rather than the institutional laws of man? To me, it appeared so. Our bevy of transgressions are our own free will. In the end, He will hold us accountable. But if we love Him and ask His forgiveness, what transgressions are we capable of in this life that we will not be held accountable for, in the next?

CHAPTER THREE

W ITH EFFORT, I roll onto my back and open my eyes. Reeds surround me, reaching up to a leaking, black sky. A whiff of the putrid Fleet places me on its banks, its water spoiled with flotsam of broken chairs, waste from tanneries, entrails from market, kitchen scraps, and skat of the human kind. I have no strength to crawl and escape this foul bed, so in effortless surrender, I continue living in my memories…

I never questioned that another life was possible for me. At Thetford, I was no better and no less than any other brother. True, there was a hierarchy in the priory, but because we were one in our love of God, we did not suffer the same challenges of the secular world. We did not marry or have to provide for children. Our family was the brotherhood.

In my thirteenth year, Brother Trelli and I were in the woods collecting mushrumps, as was our habit after days of spring rains, when a caravan approached. A man riding a donkey led the way for a covered cart followed by a second filled with several men and women singing in good cheer. They were on the road headed to Thetford village.

Upon seeing us, they stopped and asked if they might rest in these woods for the night. The sun had begun to fall below the tree line and the road would soon be difficult to follow.

"It is monastery land," answered Brother Trelli. "You are welcome here. The brethren will not trouble you for just a night of rest."

A man hopped down from the second cart and looked long at me. "Do you juggle?"

I stared back at him.

He made a motion with his hands. His wrists bent and it looked as though he was tossing invisible objects in the air. He stopped, tilted his head, questioning whether I understood.

I looked at Brother Trelli for explanation, but just as fast, the fellow went to the covered cart and retrieved three wooden balls painted with yellow and blue stripes. Without a word, he commenced to tossing them in the air where they circled easily, never coming to rest in either hand. He kept them spinning and the colours blurred into a green ring. His deft ability intrigued me. Then he tossed the balls ever higher and completed a turn without dropping a single ball. Finally, he caught each one and swept his arm across his waist in a dramatic bow.

"Juggling is a skill you should learn," he said. "You might entertain kings and queens someday."

I gaped in surprise. "How would I learn…"

Brother Trelli pulled me on without letting me finish. "Come, Kronos. It is time to return to our tasks."

We trudged back to the kitchen in silence, each of us lost in thought. Brother Trelli pondered adding mushrumps to the evening's stew, and I wondered about performing for the king and his court.

Here was a possibility that had never occurred to me. The thought of living beyond the walls and rules of the priory was tantalising to a boy whose only excitement were the naughty books he kept hidden during *Lecto Devina*.

I had assumed the outside world would be hostile—especially for someone like me. The brethren had been kind not to abuse me for my physical appearance, but couched in their acceptance of me was a warning. The secular world was sinful and it could be cruel. They told stories about those with impairments less obvious than mine who had suffered mistreatment through no fault of their own. As a result, the brothers' protection had filled me with gratitude. I dared not take it for granted, and perhaps that was their intent.

However, I began to think about my life of labour in their gardens, *ora et labora*. Of cleaning meat off the bones of chickens, and hauling pails of refuse to the midden heap—the one from which I had sprung—all for a pallet on which to lay myself down at night. The monotony of years spent at Thetford Priory stretched before me, like the vast sea which I had never seen but had only heard of.

The man in the caravan had afforded me a glimpse into another world. One that might welcome a man such as me. Could my physical affliction, in actuality, be my *gift*?

Later, after Brother Trelli had left the kitchen, I snatched three apples from a basket and practised tossing them into the air to make them circle. I spent most of my time running after the dropped fruit and had the misfortune of getting caught by Pinter Pender, a novice a few years my senior.

"Ye piddling about bruising the brothers' apples?" he said. What God gave him in height, He had taken away in wit. Pinter Pender always straightened his spine when addressing me; I suppose to remind me of his physical advantage, since he lacked a mental one.

"I've finished my chores. What is the harm?"

"There's harm when ye waste food."

"It is still edible," I replied, taking a bite and swallowing.

Pinter strolled around the kitchen as if he was lord of it. He stopped to study the row of ladles on hooks, then considered the small stool near the hearth where I often sat to tend the fire which cooked our food. I grew impatient for him to leave, but I stood by, waiting for him to move on.

Finally, he spoke. "I found a string in a book in the library." He plucked the twine from the shelf. "Much like this," he said, showing me the spool. "Someone is keeping their place, so as not to lose it."

I said nothing, unsure what he was playing at, but my mind ran in different directions.

Pinter sniggered. "'Tis the same string you use to truss a goose."

"The kitchen is not the only place where there is twine."

"I found it in a forbidden book."

"If the book is forbidden," I said, "how did you find the string hidden in it?"

He blinked, momentarily flustered. "You put it there to hold your place."

"I would not be so sure," I said, attempting to deflect his accusation. "Others might question how you discovered it."

Pinter started to speak, but his jaw clamped shut as he thought better of it and his face flushed an unflattering shade of rust. He returned the twine to the shelf and with a final pinch of his lips, he left.

Whether he caught me reading Catallus or Sappho, or juggling, I expected Pinter would find a way to expose my insincerity sooner or later. At prayer he'd cast a knowing sidelong glance at me, and I didn't doubt that he spent more time planning how to disgrace me than he did thinking about glorifying God.

For weeks, I abandoned ancient Greek whores for Mary Magdalene and Tamar—at least when there was a possibility I could be caught. If necessary, Brother Trelli's piece of twine would remain in that forbidden book until the arrival of the four horsemen of the apocalypse.

But I continued to practise my juggling, taking care to keep it secret. Turnips fit my hands with a comfortable weight and unlike apples, no one noticed a dent in their skin. I kept them in my pockets so that when I went to the garden or midden heap to dump scraps, I could hide behind a hedge and snatch a moment to learn my new interest. Over time, three turnips successfully juggled became five. I could fall to my knees and stand without dropping a single one.

A few months later, while Brother Trelli and I were kneading bread, he said, "Ye would be better served in prayer, Kronos." He glanced at me through his tangled brow as dense as a bramble thicket. "I see your preoccupation. 'Tis a frivolous waste of time."

I froze in confusion. Did he mean juggling or the time I spent reading Sappho in a quiet carrel and imagining my mouth on a woman's breast?

I slapped the dough against the board waiting for him to clarify.

"You think no one has seen you. But I have. Word will spread, and you will have to answer for your indiscretion."

I swallowed down the lump in my throat. Perhaps it was better to admit the truth than deny it. "I know it is a sin," I said, carefully. "But I struggle to control my desire."

Brother Trelli looked up from his bread.

"I am wicked," I continued, hoping by admitting my

transgression I would be spared public humiliation. "I shall go to confession and do penance for my indiscretion."

Brother Trelli considered me before picking up his dough and dropping it onto the board. "I will not stop you," he said. "You must make peace with your conscience. Nothing good will come of your obsession."

I remained silent, the embarrassment of being caught more upsetting to me than my actual sin.

"The man in the caravan put a worm in your ear," he continued. "But such frivolous amusement with fruit does not serve God."

I blinked, realising that I had misunderstood his concern. I went back to kneading my dough, relieved he was referring to my juggling and not Lesbia's paps. "Brother Trelli, I meant that the thought of performing for the king inspires me." I was being honest.

"You trust the suggestion of a minstrel more than God?" Brother Trelli shaped his loaf and plopped it on a board for the oven. "Kronos, you are nearly old enough to decide whether you want to become a novice."

"Brother Trelli, I do not wish to become a brother." My temerity surprised even me. There. I had said it. I had admitted my heart.

Brother Trelli studied me for what seemed like half a day.

"Life outside these walls is not painless. Especially for one such as you. Here, you are protected," he continued, reiterating the usual warning. "You have no experience out there." He made a gesture towards the brick oven, but he meant the greater world. "Cruelty and suffering are commonplace and it is beyond anything you have ever known."

"I know that I am at a disadvantage," I said. "But I do not believe God has called me to the life of a monk."

"Oh yay, he has," said Brother Trelli. "It was by God's grace that you survived a winter's night on the midden heap and were rescued."

I began shaping my loaves of bread, digging my fingers into the firm dough to divide it. Why God allowed me to be placed on top of a pile of filth said more about Him than it did me.

"You are still too young to understand, but in time you will come to know."

I agree that with time comes discernment. I had reached an age, though, where I felt conflicted. In truth, the only experience I had with the outside world was what I had been told. Dreaming of adventures beyond the safe confines of cloistered living seemed sinful. Later, it would become deliciously so. At first, the twinge of disloyalty, even ungratefulness, made me pray all the more. Still, when I caught a glimpse of life outside the monastery walls, it filled me with unsettled feelings that were impossible to ignore.

But Brother Trelli's warning had pricked my resolve. Perhaps what he said was true and he did me a service reminding me of my place. I had pinned my hopes on a dream of leaving Thetford Priory—perhaps this was a dream as elusive as the ones that disappear when you wake in the morning. They are real in your head, your heart quickens and your senses prime, but imagination is as fragile as a whisper. Then, when your aspirations are deflated by another, whose intents, they think, are well-meaning, you lose affection for that ill-bearer. Where once was affection, there is resentment. The loyalty I had for Brother Trelli faltered and soon I found working in the kitchen had become complete drudgery.

One day when the sun nipped at the last droplets of dew,

Brother Ulric, the apothecary and infirmarian, found me in a patch of blooming herbs staring at a dragonfly on my hoe. He peered at me over his spectacles—the rims so round and small they outlined the lucent blue of his irises. He broke off a branch of purple flowers, and their sharp scent thus released caught my attention.

"Do you know what this is?" he asked, handing me the branch.

"Brother Trelli flavours his stew with it. But nay," I said, shaking my head.

"'Tis hyssop. I make a syrup from the leaves to soothe sore throats and chest complaints."

He withdrew a small knife and began sawing off more stems, releasing a distinct smell into the air. I laid down my hoe and helped him gather enough to fill his basket.

"I'll use these to make a decoction."

I queried what he meant by that.

"A decoction allows me to extract the plant's essence. I can show you if you are interested."

I looked towards the kitchen, hesitating, wondering if I'd be missed. Anything seemed more interesting than spending another moment helping in there.

"I won't keep you from your chores, but I could use some help in the infirmary today. Ask Brother Trelli if he could spare you."

With enthusiasm I had long forgotten, I ran to the kitchen and found Brother Trelli in a rare moment of ease, sipping brew and ruminating over the kitchen ledger. I quickly tempered my excitement, not wishing him to quash my hope to escape my duties, if only for an hour. Asked as a favour to Brother Ulric, he would likely grant my leave.

"Brother Ulric wishes my help in the infirmary," I said.

Without lifting his gaze from his numbers, he said, "You? He has no one else to assist him?"

His brow furrowed in thought as I had no answer.

"Go then," he said, after a moment and waved me away. "Do his bidding and return before prayers to watch the bread bake."

I tripped in haste getting back to Brother Ulric, who was waiting patiently in the kitchen garden, admiring the pastel blooms on some climbing beans. He smiled as I neared.

"I can stay until Nones," I said, taking his basket to carry.

I followed him through a door off the garden into a room filled with shelving. Labelled jars lined the entire length of these shelves, taking up every available space. Next to a window was a simple writing desk with a modest shelf of books on the wall. All about were bouquets of herbs dangling from the rafters. Compared to the heady smell of incense in the nave, or the culinary creations of Brother Trelli, this was a delicate mash of earthly scents, one taking precedence over another depending on where I stood.

No doubt my slack-jawed, goggle-eyed self amused Brother Ulric. Perhaps he had forgotten what it was like to first enter the pharmacy. I knew every square foot of space in the kitchen and could have performed my tasks blind-folded. Here was a new opportunity afforded me.

He had me leave the basket of hyssop on a board cluttered with crockery, including bowls of fragrant herbs waiting to be made into concoctions or poultices. A breeze wafted through the open windows causing dried pieces of minced spearmint to swirl on the table as if they were performing a gentle dance.

"First, we must attend to the brothers in the infirmary. Fill this pail and bring the ladle to give them drink."

I fetched water from a barrel outside the infirmary, then followed Brother Ulric into a larger room. I'd visited before, but my mind had been distracted by pain and fear. I had never stayed long, being blessed with good health for most of my life. Now it was as if I saw the room for the first time.

A subdued northern light shone through high windows. Partitions separated cots on the opposite wall, giving a bit of privacy to the infirmed. A small chapel at the far end was empty but stained glass surrounded its periphery, allowing light to colour the floor in motley shades of red, yellow, blue, and green.

A mournful creak of a door drew my attention. In doddered Brother Giles, an elderly brother who had spent the last five years in the infirmary. Ailing brothers or those in need were dismissed from their duties and a small attached chapel allowed them to continue their prayer and meditations, but they rarely left the infirmary. Giles struggled to close the weighty door behind him.

"A walk in the inner cloister, Brother Giles? The angelica is in full bloom, did you see?" asked Brother Ulric.

The old monk's stooped posture prevented him from lifting his gaze. With some effort, he tilted his chin and with undisguised surprise stared at me. "I took a short stroll," he said in a whispery voice. "I could smell the angelica." A white cataract clouded his left eye, but the other distinguished my stunted height. "Is that the Kronos with you?"

"It is," said Brother Ulric. "He has been kind enough to help me with a few tasks." He paused, watching Brother Giles totter forward. "Kronos, can you help Brother Giles to his chair? You can find me once he is settled."

I went to Brother Giles, but he refused to take my proffered arm. Though his spine curved forward so that his face was level with my height, he would not lean against me or rest his hand on my shoulder for stability. After a few wobbly steps, I reached for his arm to steady him and with surprising force, he jerked it away.

"I am well capable," he wheezed. His weathered face took on a menacing expression.

I attributed his petulance to old age and the frustration that came from trying to maintain some dignity while his body failed him, but I also sensed an underlying dislike of me. Nevertheless, I accompanied him to his cubicle, ready to throw myself before him if he should lose his balance. At least I could soften his fall.

I held his chair while he eased himself down, dropping the final few inches. I started to cover his lap with a blanket, but just as I unfolded it, he snatched it from my grasp. He fussed about, pulling it across his lap and up to his chin, all the while huffing like an irritable horse. Once his breathing slowed and he settled, I asked if there was anything else I could do for him.

He sat there motionless as if thinking about his answer. I straightened. Perhaps he hadn't heard me. I was about to repeat myself when his reply came with petulant overtones. "Leave me alone."

CHAPTER FOUR

Brother Giles was the first person whose dislike of me I attributed to my appearance. I'd treated him with patience and respect, believing my compassion for his feeble, aged body would be met with a shared commiseration for, or at least an understanding of, my own physical limitations. For neither of us were adonic specimens of men. Ingrained in him were misgivings that no manner of kindness could unwind. My physicality challenged his bounds of acceptance. Decline was the natural result of aging, but there was nothing natural about my condition. And, being an adolescent, I was becoming more sensitive to lingering stares and the perceived hint of disgust in anyone's reaction to me.

Despite my unease around Brother Giles, I helped in the infirmary whenever I could. The change of routine attracted me and when one day I proved useful to Brother Ulric during a medical crisis, I knew I would not have to work in the kitchen forever.

A scything accident had slashed a layman's calf, resulting in a gaping wound. He was carried to the infirmary on a litter and at Brother Ulric's direction, I cleared a table and gathered the implements he needed to stitch the man's wound. My presence of mind served in the moment, and even Pinter Pender could not fault my response. Even though I assisted well enough to impress others, it was not enough to improve my reputation in Brother Giles's opinion.

In spite of the old monk's resistance and probable protests, however, Brother Ulric desired my service more often and he thought me well suited to working in the infirmary. I heartily desired to be done with my kitchen duties and to leave the service of Brother Trelli. One day while I was collecting peas, Brother Ulric crossed the garden to the kitchen. I heard him address Brother Trelli and hurried over to crouch beneath the window outside the kitchen to listen.

"It is altogether rare for a boy to possess such presence of mind under pressured circumstances. The priory would be better served if he could work in the infirmary," said Brother Ulric.

"Kronos is familiar with the routine of the kitchen."

"I am certain that you can find someone else to assist in the kitchen and garden. Lay brother Windrow's boy is of an age to serve. He comes from a hardworking and pious family."

"I do not wish to teach someone new. Besides, Kronos is better suited to working here."

"Brother Trelli, eventually you will have no choice. Soon Kronos will become a novice and you will be forced to find someone to take his place. Why not now, while Kronos can show the boy his duties?"

"Kronos will never become a novice," answered Brother Trelli.

"Why would you say that?" answered Brother Ulric. Assuming the reason was my physicality, Brother Ulric quoted, "The Lord sees not as man sees: man looks on the outward appearance, but the Lord looks on the heart."

"It is not his appearance that will keep him from the

brotherhood," said Brother Trelli. "It is his desire. He does not wish to serve God."

"At his age, did you know what you wanted? His mind thirsts for knowledge. He has grown bored toting scraps to the compost heap."

"Don't be fooled. He shall tire of changing sheets in the infirmary."

"I will teach him what I know. If he does not become a novice, he could continue his studies in London. He has the intelligence to become a physician or an apothecary."

"Brother Ulric, you have lost your good sense. It is wishful thinking that Kronos would ever be accepted in either of those professions. The secular world would be less accepting of his dwarfism."

"I disagree. There are those who will recognise that his intellectual capacity is not impaired by his condition."

"We can no more pretend that his appearance doesn't matter than we can deny the sun setting at the end of a day. Here, we may see his mind before his body, but the priory is not London."

"Why do you wilfully hinder his advancement? If he should not succeed, so be it. But let me give him skills that may prove useful in his life."

Quiet lengthened between them. I held my breath hoping Brother Giles would release me from the kitchen. I'd grown so bored I could scarce abide another day.

"Give me time to consider," he said, at last. "Send me the Windrow boy so that I might speak with him."

I scurried away from the window and busied myself with pulling skirrets in the garden. Did I want to learn the medicinal concoctions Brother Ulric was prepared to teach me? I brushed the wet soil from the long taproots as I considered this. True, that delightful tingle of curiosity stirred within me, but in all honesty,

I did not know what I wanted. What boy knows his destiny at so young an age, especially one such as me? I suspected even then that it was not so much a desire to find one profession that spoke to my heart, as it was being given the opportunity to experience something new.

The next day, after making the morning bread, Brother Trelli sat me down.

"Brother Ulric has asked that I give you leave from the kitchen so that you may assist him in the infirmary," he said, sitting across from me.

My eyes settled on the powdery fingerprints of flour on his shoulder where he'd scratched. I waited for him to continue.

"How interested are you in learning his methods to heal people?"

I wasn't going to admit that I was uncertain about learning the ways of an infirmarian. Here was an opportunity to try something new. I couldn't deny that getting out from under his scrutinising eye appealed to me.

"I see it as an opportunity to help Brother Ulric," I said, careful to keep my gaze on his shoulder should he read in my expression any hints of insincerity.

He waited for me to explain myself.

And waited.

Finally, he spoke. "You would be entrusted with the lives and well-being of the infirmed and elderly."

"I understand that," I said.

"You will learn things that can save a man's life…or end it."

My eyes met his. The solemnity of this struck me.

"It is an education that you must take seriously."

Having disparaged the time I'd spent practising juggling, had he come to think of me as thin-witted? Did he think me only capable of frivolous antics with no ambition? I might not desire to become a healer someday, but I certainly understood the gravity of what I was about to learn. Did he think I would use it to ill effect?

"I shall do my best to please Brother Ulric."

The bells rang for Terce and Brother Trelli got to his feet. "You will show the Windrow boy your tasks and oversee that he understands his duties. Once he is efficient, you have my blessing to assist Brother Ulric."

I applied myself to Brother Ulric's teaching, and for several months I only visited the priory's library to read medical and botanical texts. Catullus and Sappho called to me from the shelves, but I resisted their siren song. The infirmary was as busy as the kitchen, except there was a steady stream of people coming through the doors instead of food.

Brother Giles kept his good eye trained on my whereabouts. He didn't have to say a word for me to feel his distrust. His withered body stiffened whenever I was near, as if primed to defend himself should the occasion arise. He never offered me pleasantries and eventually, I stopped offering him mine. He saved any kind words he could muster for Brother Ulric. His inexplicable animosity reminded me that I should expect this kind of treatment should I ever leave the monastery, for Brother Giles was the embodiment of intolerance.

His dismissive manner hardened me, and rather than rile at his distrust, the worm of his resulting unease burrowed under my skin and laid eggs. Perhaps I shouldn't be trusted. God had created a strange character in me. Perhaps His intention was to irrevocably label me—my destiny was to endure people's suspicions.

I wondered if people thought my physical deformity was a reflection of my soul? Why else would God create me thus if not to warn others of a lurking, perfidious morality? Did they think one caused the other? And it seemed with Brother Giles that the harder I tried to forget or ignore his underlying revulsion, the more entrenched his belief that I was evil.

My education with Brother Ulric evolved from learning basic decoctions for curing chest maladies and skin eruptions to the more involved techniques of distillation and crystallisation. I learned about medicines whose application had to be carefully administered to prevent adverse effects. One of these was a powder Brother Ulric gave in small quantities to Brother Giles when he had difficulty breathing.

The first time I saw Brother Ulric use it was when he spied the elder monk sitting in the infirmary cloister with his hand on his heart, his head bobbing as he struggled to breathe. His pallor had never been sanguineous, but it was even more pale than usual.

"Go to Brother Giles. Comfort him until I get there," he told me.

I knew there was little I could do to console the old monk as his resistance to me made even my approaching him a source of discomfort to the man. I called to him as I left the herbarium.

"Brother Giles!" I shouted, waving my arm as I loped through the garden. "Brother Ulric is coming." I reached him standing shakily, as one knobby hand gripped his walking stick and the other waved me away between gasps for air. "He is coming," I reassured, glancing anxiously toward the infirmary. The old monk's panic ruffled me.

At last Brother Ulric arrived with a cup of potable. "Drink this, good friend. It shall ease you." He held the cup and tipped it between Brother Giles's thin lips as the old man sputtered, the liquid dribbling down his chin.

We stood back to observe the old monk's reaction. Ulric placed a hand against Giles's neck to feel his pulse, and bent to look into his one good eye. "Ah, it shall help your humours flow. Take ease, breathe deep."

As I stood by, avoiding eye contact with the elder monk, my mentor's drink began to take effect. Brother Giles's frantic gasps eased. Soon, his breathing normalised and a small flush even tinged his pallid cheeks.

Brother Ulric's shoulders dropped in relief. "Let us get him to his pallet, Kronos."

Between the two of us we supported Brother Giles through the walkway to his bed. The old monk was too weak to object to my help.

Once he was settled, I asked Brother Ulric what he had given him.

The infirmarian led me back into the herbarium and showed me the leaves of a plant drying on a tile in the sun. He took a leaf between his thumb and forefinger and ground it into a light green powder. "Purple beardtonge. A small amount mixed in ale will stimulate the pulse. The humours rise to the surface of the skin and it becomes easier for a man to breathe." He blew the fine powder into the air and wiped his fingers on the front of his habit. "It is a potent remedy and care must be taken when administering it."

Later, he placed his compendium on the study desk and motioned me over. He pointed to an entry of an herb showing a detailed drawing of the plant. The flowers looked like drooping pink bells, and it had large musty-green leaves with serrated edges. I recognised the plant as one I'd seen growing in the shade of the herb garden.

"It is lovely," I said, running my finger over the drawing.

He closed the book beneath my interested gaze. "It is never to be meddled with. Certainly, not until I say you are ready."

I blinked up at him.

"Beauty can be deceptive," he said, and the corner of his mouth turned up in irony. "Too much can have devastating effects."

I've since come to learn that beauty can be dangerous, indeed.

My thoughts flit to the lovely Bess. Ah, Bess—my first, unwitting obsession. Because of you, I changed my life course. My affection for you endures—you slip through my memory and beguile as expertly as our king's latest infatuation—Queen Katherine. But if what John Lascelles says is true, our moonstruck king shall have his heart crushed by Kat's delicate foot. Then what? How shall he be contained?

I wince, feeling my jaw throb in excruciating pain and I jolt back into the moment, laying in the mud and weeds of the Fleet. Where shall I end? I will die if no one finds me. What a hopeless and sorry thought that this is how it will end. I open my eyes to the dark around me then snap them shut, preferring the memory of Bess of my dreams. But I am dashing ahead—my domitable Benedictine upbringing demands patience and discipline…

The art of compounding ingredients demanded my respect. I paid close attention to Brother Ulric's methods and asked questions. Brother Ulric indulged my fascination and gave me his crumbly-paged herbal to study. He must have felt hopeful he could disprove Brother Trelli's assertion that I would never serve God. My interest must have led him to think that even if I chose not to become a novice, I might still choose a life caring for and healing the infirmed.

Was becoming a physician my intention? Ha! I've already mentioned that my love for new experiences is motivation enough in my life. I still practised my juggling when no one was looking.

In truth, I longed to see the world beyond Thetford Priory's walls. Until then, I'd never travelled any farther than the grain fields abutting the property's borders. When villagers had sickness or a broken bone, they were brought to the infirmary for treatment—Brother Ulric rarely left the grounds.

That changed one day when Pinter Pender rushed into the herbarium. He pointedly ignored me even though I was difficult to miss, sorting through bunches of herbs and tying them. "Brother Ulric, the Steward of Kenninghall has requested you to come at once. An illness threatens the entire household."

Brother Ulric's brows raised in alarm. "Where is the messenger?"

"Outside the gate. Prior Ixworth has forbid him entry."

"Kronos, go to the stable for two horses. You are coming with me."

Before I could reply, he hastened through the cloister garden towards the great gate, leaving me momentarily flustered. Pinter Pender turned heel and I stood motionless, wondering what possible illness could endanger an entire household? Immediately, the scourge of black death came to mind. I shuddered, thinking of the possible consequences of assisting Brother Ulric on this mission. But I had no choice in the matter.

I found the ostler humming to himself while grooming a chestnut gelding. The horse nickered softly, enjoying the tune as much as the attention. "Brother Ulric needs two horses saddled. We leave for Kenninghall immediately."

The horseman ran his eyes down my person. "You? You shall accompany him?"

I swallowed, and his eyes followed the lump in my throat. "Aye."

"Have you ridden before?"

"Nay, I have not."

He blinked, keeping what thoughts or misgivings he had to himself.

I left, uncertain what to do, and returned to the pharmacy. Brother Ulric was gathering jars and medicants and placing them in satchels. "Prepare yourself, Kronos. It may be a long night."

"What should I do?"

"Fetch bread and water, Kronos. And bring an extra smock should it rain."

I stuffed it all, plus a blanket, into a leather pannier and carried it, along with his satchels, to the stables. The liveried rider who had brought the steward's message would accompany us back to Kenninghall.

"It has been years since I've been that direction," said Brother Ulric to the liveryman.

The ostler helped him onto his mount and secured the satchels, while a stable boy held the bridle of my horse.

"Hold her steady while I help him in the saddle," directed the ostler.

My ride was slightly smaller than theirs. It side-stepped expertly once it sized me up. Getting atop the beast took some hefting on the part of the stableman, and with me clawing myself up, I finally managed to sit astride the animal. The stirrups were hitched up, but there were no notches short enough; a last-minute fix was required to accommodate my short legs.

Finally, we ambled along a path to the road; Brother Ulric and the liveryman easily managed their steeds while I yanked the reins when my horse saw sumptuous grass to nibble. Once on the road, the liveryman's horse broke into a canter. Brother Ulric's did the same and some unspoken signal prompted my horse to follow suit. I clung to its mane, terrified to be so far off the ground and fearing what might happen should I fall. I dared not yell or curse, though I had plenty of oaths at the ready if only I wasn't in the presence of Brother Ulric. At the sight of an open field with a gentle hill, our chaperone departed the road, slowing his mount to a walk, which allowed me to collect myself and, more importantly, my wits.

Brother Ulric turned to me as I rode up beside him. "I see you have managed to stay on your horse."

"Aye," came my reply, trying to hide my trepidation and discomfort. My tailbone had taken an unkind beating courtesy of this wooden saddle.

"If I may," said Brother Ulric. "You must fight the urge to tightly grip the horse with your legs. Soften your spine and move with the animal. It will make for a smoother ride." He then left me, following the liveryman at a trot up the hill.

A trot seemed the most unpleasant of paces. My resistance to the jostling further exaggerated the assault on my tailbone. I was grateful when they resumed a canter for, eventually, I learned the horse's rhythm and began to ride more comfortably.

The birds had gone to roost by the time we arrived at Kenninghall Palace. The handsome brick structure stood against a paling amber sky, presenting a stately presence in the lush countryside. We arrived in the courtyard of a building resembling a letter 'H' with two long wings extending north to south from a central great hall. Two stable boys emerged from an extensive brick mews and crossed the yard to hold the bridles while we dismounted. The messenger and Brother Ulric managed the task expertly, while I clumsily slid to the ground with one foot still caught in a stirrup. Brother Ulric was already at the manor's entrance by the time I met up with him.

We remained outside only briefly while the steward was summoned. In those few minutes I marvelled at the sheer expanse of grounds, rivalling the scope owned by Thetford. The orderliness of the estate spoke to the wealth of this nobleman; every shrub or plant was pruned and groomed. No unkempt rogue of a tree or bush had surreptitiously insinuated itself into this landscape.

At last, our guide arrived and bade us enter. The man was older than Brother Ulric, dressed in a fine scarlet doublet—the colour of the household's livery. His manner was as polished as the buttons down his doublet. As I followed behind, my jaw dropped at the splendour of the manse. We passed richly appointed rooms, presently all vacant, but I envisioned them filled with lords and ladies, their privileged laughter echoing off the high ceilings. This was my first experience seeing how a nobleman lived. Although stately, the manor exuded a warm, intimate ambiance. My shoulders dropped; my inexperience was not questioned. Leaving the formal rooms behind, we walked through a series of service rooms, passed a deep sink where a lad scrubbed pots, then a room filled with cupboards from floor to ceiling. We then entered a hall leading to an area of bed chambers, simple in appointment, presumably occupied by the manor's help.

Finally, we emerged into a more decorated hallway and stopped beside a door. The steward knocked.

A maidservant answered, her weary expression indicative of exhaustive attendance at least since the previous evening. Her small eyes and sallow skin reminded me of black currants plopped in custard. A smell of sweat and stagnant air wafted past and I must have squinted in distaste as her eyes caught my impudence and she stiffened.

"I am Margaret Barlowe. My Lady Bess's mistress." She

allowed our entry, standing aside, her eyes scrutinising every inch of me. Drapes hung over the windows to keep out the sun and a single burning candle provided a small and ineffective orb of light. A bowl of water sat at the bedside and my eyes travelled the short distance to our patient—a girl, not much older than me. She lay in a feverish state, the covers kicked to the foot of her bed.

Brother Ulric and I stepped forward, observing her cheeks as red as apples and her hair damp with perspiration. Her eyelids flickered. She seemed unable to open her eyes and cared not a spit who was staring at her.

"How long has she been like this?" asked Brother Ulric.

"Yesterday she told her father that her head throbbed and she had lost her stomach from the pain of it. She had not the strength to do her duty as the children's nurse and governess."

Lady Bess was unaware of my roving eyes, and I studied her with impunity. Her cheeks still held the fullness of a young girl's face, but beneath her sodden smock her breasts hinted at womanhood. My compassion for her illness did not squelch the stirrings inside my hosen.

Here was a girl, the first lovely one I had ever seen. A twinge of shame reminded me of my impertinence, but it wasn't enough to stop me from staring. The monks had tried their best to model a life of celibacy and service to God, but I knew at that moment choosing such a path would require more restraint than I could ever possess.

"Is this the first she's suffered from this malady?" asked Brother Ulric.

"Aye, she's never taken so ill," replied Barlowe. "Her father is John Holland—the duke's secretary. Her proper name is Elizabeth, but everyone calls her Bess."

Ah Bess, it is no longer Catullus's Lesbia for whom I lust—but you.

Though the room was comfortably warm, Lady Bess began shivering as if a sudden chill swept through.

"Kronos, cover her with blankets," said Brother Ulric, as he riffled through his satchel.

While the maid spoke with Brother Ulric, I went to the foot of the bed and hesitated, taking one last, lingering look at the shape of her body before pulling up the blanket. I tucked it close to her sides, inhaling her scent and tasting it on my tongue to remember like a cat.

Brother Ulric shook a small jar and removed its waxen seal.

"Kronos, support her head."

I moved to the other side of him and slid my hand beneath Lady Bess's neck. Bess's eyes partly opened as I cradled the back of her head, tilting it forward as Brother Ulric tipped the contents into her mouth. My fingers burned from the touch of her skin, making me wonder whether it was the effect of her fever or my inchoate desire.

Brother Ulric peered down his nose at her, his spectacles glinting in the candlelight. "My lady, you must swallow. This will help you."

She struggled with the liquid, but, with encouragement, got it down her throat. I laid her head upon the bolster and returned her arm under the blanket, letting my hand linger.

"What have you given her?" asked the nursemaid when I stepped back.

"A tisane from a meadow plant. It shall break this cycle of fever and chill. Once her body is calm, we can better determine what ails her."

There was nothing more to do but sit and wait. Barlowe left briefly and returned with two servants, each carrying a chair that they placed near the window for us.

"Might we get a kettle of boiling water?" inquired Brother Ulric.

Margaret Barlowe lifted an eyebrow, as if puzzling out the reason behind the request.

"For a poultice," added Brother Ulric.

Without comment, the nursemaid disappeared out the door, leaving us to wonder if we had perhaps insulted her. But she soon returned with a kitchen boy toting a steaming kettle of water. She set an empty bowl and spoon on a table for us.

"Kronos, fetch my satchel," said Brother Ulric. He poured water into the bowl, then added cider from a bottle. I helped stir the mixture as he added oats until the consistency met his approval. A couple of drops of oil of peppermint were added to help clear her sinuses.

"Apply a compress, Kronos," said Brother Ulric as he put away his bottles, then handed me a linen cloth.

I soaked the linen and wrung it enough to apply to Bess's forehead without soaking her linens. At least now the pleasant scent of mint took precedence over the stale air.

In time, the tisane settled her racking chills and fevers and the compress aided her breathing. She fell into a comfortable sleep and, with that assurance, we left her in Barlowe's hands and went to have a meal of boiled mutton with the servants.

As I followed Brother Ulric, I had a second opportunity to study my surroundings. I'd never seen such fine tapestries and intricately carved wood panelling. By comparison, Thetford was more utilitarian, though I'd heard the Abbot's quarters were richly appointed. A small army of attendants bustled about, cleaning, fetching pots, guarding doors, glancing at Brother Ulric, then noticing me—some stopping in their steps to gawp. I was so familiar to the monks that they never had cause to scrutinise me, so this sudden interest I found unsettling.

The palace was the home of the third Duke of Norfolk, Thomas Howard, military commander, lord treasurer, and the king's most trusted councillor. Apparently, his wife, Elizabeth Stafford, was a sharp woman with a tongue to match. She was a lady-in-waiting to Queen Catherine of Aragon and was gone to court enough that the care of their three children was mostly left to young Bess, whom the children adored.

"Have any of the children suffered from this malady?" asked Brother Ulric as we finished our meal of mutton.

"Children are not our concern," replied one of the men.

"Nay, they have been healthy from what I know," replied another.

"And where is the mother?" inquired Brother Ulric.

"She has been summoned from Whitehall in the event that she must find another governess to replace this one."

After being shown our quarters, we returned to Lady Bess's chamber where the girl slept restfully, breathing at ease. It was late to the eve and Brother Ulric dismissed me to find what sleep I could. He would seek me later to take his place so that our patient would have one of us present during these crucial hours.

Though weary from our travel and responsibility, I slept fitfully, my mind imagining fanciful scenarios with the lovely Bess. She did not even know of my existence, but she was already intimately familiar to my imaginings, her mouth on mine, her hands gripping me where no one else had. I did with her to my heart's desire and she returned the favour and then some. I startled when Brother Ulric's hand shook me awake and was glad for the thick wool blanket to hide my tumescence.

"'Tis one the hour, you must keep watch on the girl until

morning. If she relapses into a feverish state, give her more tisane. I have left the bottle on the table."

✧

I made my way through the dark halls of the palace, a small candle guiding me. The rooms were still and silent, though an occasional guard looked up from his station to observe me pass. Just the thought of being alone with her warmed my blood and hastened my step. I could gaze upon her with no hesitation or embarrassment, no notice of my prolonged stare. I would soon be attending her—alone.

However, upon entering her chamber, her nursemaid stirred on a pallet at the foot of her bed.

She raised up on one elbow and peered at me. "Oh, 'tis you."

I closed the chamber door, aware of her keen black currant eyes watching my every move.

"How does she fare?" I asked, going to Bess. I cast off my immodest thoughts and assumed an official mantle. "Does she sleep soundly?"

"Oh, aye. Brother Ulric's potion seems to have worked. She sleeps as soundly as I can ever recall. You may return to your bed."

"Brother Ulric has asked that I stay while he sleeps."

"Surely if she is sleeping without issue these past hours, there is little sense in depriving anyone else of rest."

"My master has asked it of me. It is his request that I must honour." How dare she deny my opportunity to watch Bess?

She sat up and set her jaw. "I am her mistress and as you can clearly see, we have no need for you here."

"My master knows best in these matters of patient care. He has demanded it of me."

"You will lust after her," she said. Her face took on a spiteful countenance. "Your kind cannot be trusted."

Her words stunned me into silence. She assumed my character was suspect—not because of any history between us, but because of my congenital malformity. I had given her no cause to mistrust me, and I had been careful to disguise my interest in Bess. Or so I thought.

I tried reasoning with her. "If she should relapse, then I am able to attend to her, and I would be responsible for her life. If a problem should occur, you would be remiss in having dismissed me."

"Your master has already instructed me to give a dose of the tisane should she require it. I see no need of your sitting here leering at my Lady Bess."

"You are making a mistake," I said.

"No greater than letting you stay. Leave now. Or I shall have you removed."

I was accustomed to being denied—I lived in a Benedictine monastery. But I had never been treated with such blatant disdain by a woman. She had insulted my honour. And, lurking beneath her words, I recognised her contempt for my physical person. I was not completely surprised by her mockery, but in matters of the care and wellbeing of another person, my appearance should not matter.

I glanced at lovely Bess in deep slumber—oblivious to our quarrel; however, I could see that I would not convince Margaret Barlowe to reconsider. Against my better judgement, I said not a word more. I left the lovely Bess in the care of her truculent nursemaid.

CHAPTER FIVE

"**S**he refused me."

"Lady Bess refused you?" asked Brother Ulric, waking the next morning and rising to sit on the edge of his pallet.

I had returned from Bess's chamber with the intention of alerting Brother Ulric of the maidservant's refusal to let me stay. In fact, I had put my hand on his back to wake him, but thought better of it seeing him sleep so peaceably. After a long day of travel, neither of us needed to spend the night arguing with an irascible wench. Instead, I crawled onto my pallet and somehow managed to stanch my anger enough to fall into a much-needed sleep.

"The nursemaid Barlowe. She would not allow me to keep watch over her lady."

Brother Ulric put on his spectacles. "Why ever not?"

"She said I was not needed. That Bess slept soundly and she thought we should take advantage of her improvement and get our rest."

My master rose from his pallet and sat on a bench to put on his shoes. "We must go at once to see if she is well."

I dutifully followed him through the halls of Kenninghall to Bess Holland's chamber and stood aside as he rapped on the door. Around us, the sounds of servants encroached on the early morning tranquillity.

Nursemaid Barlowe cracked open the door, wavering whether to open it wider.

"It is imperative that you allow us entry. We have a duty to Mistress Holland."

Her gaze fell to me and the vein in her neck visibly bulged. I thought she might try to explain herself, but reluctantly she stood aside and let us enter.

Lady Bess looked a flower of beauty laid upon a crisp linen pillow. Her face had lost the worried scowl of pain and sickness. A healthy flush rouged her skin and her general look of comfort eased our concern. Brother Ulric exhaled in relief. How could any man not revel in such a sight? Even he must have fallen under the girl's bewitching spell.

Her eyes opened at the sound of us and she turned her head to calmly look upon us as if it were the most natural occurrence to see a monk and a dwarf in her bed chamber. I should have looked away in modesty but the colour of her eyes reminded me of the moss growing along the forest floor where Brother Trelli and I used to pick mushrumps. It was a green rich with life. I could not look away.

"Lady Bess, you are improved this morning," said Brother Ulric.

She smiled, her lips like rosebuds, pert and teasing. "I have you to thank?"

Her grudging protector, the nursemaid, stepped between and pushed a pillow against Bess's back to help the girl sit.

Brother Ulric smiled. "You must thank the Lord our God, for all good deeds come through Him."

"You are His servant, are you not?"

"We are both His humble servants. I am Brother Ulric of Thetford Priory, and this is my apprentice, Kronos."

Bess looked past Brother Ulric to find me. No distaste or judgment influenced her. Her expression was as smooth and untroubled as a pond in January. Perhaps Brother Ulric's insinuation of my status impressed her. Certainly, hearing him refer to me as his apprentice bolstered my confidence.

"You travelled a distance. I am grateful for your good care."

"The distance is not so far, Mistress Holland," said Brother Ulric. "It is in the priory's interest to attend to the duke's wishes."

"It was the duke who sent for you?"

I wondered why she was surprised. Surely any master of a storied estate such as this would have been informed and then sought help for the governess of his children.

"In truth, it may have been your father," said Brother Ulric.

Her shoulders slumped as if this news was expected and perhaps disappointing.

Brother Ulric dispensed with the immaterial and asked after her health. When did she first feel ill? How would she describe the pain in her head? Was it a fever or a chill that first unsettled her?

Bess answered evenly, recalling a general malaise that she sought to overcome through force of will. "Children care not if you feel dozy. It is beyond their comprehension." She examined a lock of her hair then smoothed it down. "There is no one to take my place should I fall ill."

"No one is suitably educated to assume her teaching duties," added the nursemaid.

"How many children do you care for?" Brother Ulric asked.

"There is nine-year-old Henry, and Mary is eight—a dear, sweet girl. Thomas is nearly six." Bess sat immodestly in bed, her smock untied at the throat. Though its thin linen was no longer damp, I could make out the contours of her breasts.

Again, prudish Margaret Barlowe insinuated herself to pull a blanket up to Bess's shoulders and gave me a stern look.

Before Brother Ulric could continue, we heard voices in the hall—a woman ordering a servant to ready her writing desk. The door latch lifted, startling us with its unapologetic clamour and a woman strode into the room with an arrogant lift of her chin.

She wore a dove gray velvet gown trimmed in blue braid with a matching gable hood. An impressive strand of pearls looped from her bodice halfway down her stomacher. The forepart of her kirtle was a matching blue damask. I was in the presence of nobility.

I followed Brother Ulric's lead and bowed my head in greeting. When I looked up, the woman was staring at me. Brother Ulric made our introduction.

She did not bother to tell us who she was, nor did she comment on my presence. I felt myself dismissed and disappearing into the background. I was of no concern or import.

"It appears I have been summoned here under false pretences," she said. "Bess looks the vision of health." Her head snapped to Brother Ulric. "I was told she was in a serious way. I travelled all the way from London."

Bess's gaze focused on the bed coverlet.

"She *was* quite ill when we arrived," said Brother Ulric. "I gave her a remedy which seems to have settled her condition."

"Then, she must return to her duties. I see no need to delay."

Brother Ulric spoke. "Another day of rest would benefit her."

"Nonsense. The children need a governess. There is no one else capable of handling them."

"My lady, I caution that her return to good health may be

short-lived. It is possible she could relapse without additional rest. I advise letting her regain her strength in full."

"What authority have you in Kenninghall? Did my husband give you permission to make this decision?"

"My lady, I have not spoken to your husband."

"Of course not, because he is not here. He sent me home to manage this while he sups with the king and licks his Majesty's boots." Disregarding our stunned expressions, she continued, "Come, this has been a convenient hiatus from responsibilities, but there shall be no more lolling about." She swept her gown behind her as she turned and walked towards the door. Stopping partway, she addressed Brother Ulric over her shoulder. "You may return to Thetford. We have no further need of you and your…" She seemed unable to find a word for me—"…charge."

A strained silence followed the click of the latch. Brother Ulric spoke.

"Mistress Holland, we have not determined the cause of your malady. It appears the duchess believes you are well enough to return to your duties. Let us pray that this is the last of your illness. We shall abide by her wishes and return to the priory." He bowed his head in respect to Bess and her petulant nursemaid and made the sign of the cross.

My heart hurt wondering if I would ever see Bess Holland again. I drank in her face, then bowed in respect to Bess, foregoing acknowledging the old wench who stood glowering at me.

On the road back to Thetford, Brother Ulric kept a steady pace since we were not pressed by time or a setting sun. I studied the countryside, its bramble hedges, its vast tracts of soggy lowland, the clouds stretching in endless tracts of rippled white against a muted blue sky. My master kept his thoughts to himself, as did I. Neither of us were inclined to comment about our visit to Kenninghall, our encounter with Duchess Norfolk, or her abrupt dismissal of us. Likely, we were consumed by the same subject, but for different reasons. Brother Ulric must have wondered about the source of Lady Bess's ailment and I simply wondered about Lady Bess. However, as we neared the last stretch of road, the infirmarian stirred from his contemplation to share his observations.

"It is that time of year when people suffer from bouts of ague. Lady Bess's intermittent fever then chills mimics cases of swamp fever that I have observed. I gave her the tisane of meadowsweet to mitigate her fever and it worked well. It is the same tisane I use to treat ague. If one matches the proper treatment to the symptom, and there is no recurrence, we can narrow down the possible cause of illness.

"However, the disease is characterised by periods of relatively good health then a sudden onset of chills," he continued. "If I hadn't been in such a hurry to reach Kenninghall, I could have brought extra tisane to leave with her should my theory prove correct."

"You had little information when you were sent for," I said, reassuring him. "Is that all the possible illnesses associated with chills and fever?"

"There are other, sometimes short-lived miseries that can present with similar effect." He gave his ride a pat on its neck and the horse knickered softly. "I suppose time will be the best indicator of what ails her."

"I could return with more tisane if you think it helpful," I offered. The idea of seeing Lady Bess again quickened my heart.

"Nay, we shall wait. There is no sense in wasting the remedy if that is not the cause of her illness."

We rounded the bend and the gray slate of the nave's roof reflected the sun like silver platters that I imagined decorating the duke's cabinets. Though I wished I had spent longer in the company of Bess Holland, I could not ignore a sense of relief at seeing the priory again. Here, I knew my place and was comfortable in it. The questioning glances and suspicious looks at Kenninghall didn't beset my every move. Brother Trelli had been right when he said the world could be unkind.

Life in the infirmary returned to its expected routine. I cared for lay brothers and monks who came through the door with strained ankles or oozing gashes. Brother Ulric taught me what poultices to make for a myriad of maladies, and my knowledge of plants and remedies grew. I even administered tisanes and dosed Brother Giles, ignoring his resistance. I spent time studying the compendium of plants my master was compiling, and on the rare days when the infirmary was quiet and I had completed my tasks, my thoughts drifted to Lady Bess.

She was ever on my mind. The time I had spent watching her in the throes of sickness deepened my familiarity with her. I had scrutinised the full breadth of her person, reading from every inch of her body the generosity, the guileless compassion, the angel that she was. She was magic. Who could know her without falling under her enchantment?

Months passed with no word from Kenninghall. Eventually, I came to the conclusion that I might never see her again. I questioned Brother Ulric about his diagnosis of ague.

"Her malady may not have been ague, lest she would have relapsed by now. For cert, I have been wrong before."

"She could be suffering, and we may not know it," I said,

voicing a worry that had been niggling me for a few weeks. "Would it make sense to visit her again? Just to assure her good health?"

"The duchess requires her to take care of the children. It is possible that if she is unable to fulfil her duties, she may have been replaced. For all we know, she may no longer be at Kenninghall."

I had not considered that her presence at the manor may have been so tenuous. A monk was never tossed aside because he was no longer capable of his duties. His tasks were amended to suit his ability until a time came when he was sent to the infirmary to live out his days, cared for, but never disposed of. At Thetford, lives were cherished.

One warm, summer day, Brother Ulric sent me into the garden to collect valerian. Across the way, Brother Giles strolled along the circumference path, his walking stick tapping the tiles underfoot. I avoided him, seeking an alternate way to reach the plants I needed. I had snipped several stems when I heard a feeble cry.

The old man lay sprawled on the path, face down.

"Brother Giles!" I ran through the garden, trampling poppies and Brother Trelli's patch of primulas to crouch beside him. He hated me touching him, but I grasped his shoulder and turned him over. Blood ran from his nose and he gasped for breath. He had likely broken his nose, but was having an episode of troubled breathing in addition. I wiped his face, then shouted towards the herbarium. "Brother Ulric!" Not getting a response, I reassured the old monk. "Brother Giles, lay you still. Do not try to move, I must go for help."

I hurried to the pharmacy, but Brother Ulric was not there. Nor was he in the infirmary. I was torn between returning to Brother Giles or finding my master. My indecision could very well end the old man's life.

Perhaps I should treat him with beardtonge like I'd seen

Brother Ulric use. Going to the shelves, I looked through the jars of ingredients under the planet Saturn, easily laying my hands on the green powder, knowing exactly where it was kept.

What was the proportion of powder to ale? Brother Ulric's warning repeated in my head—'Too much and you could kill him.'

But leaving him on the pavement in his distressed condition did him no service.

I prepared the dosage and brought it to Brother Giles.

"Drink," I encouraged, supporting his head so he could swallow. An inordinate amount of blood ran into his mouth and he sputtered as he choked it down.

Though I knew he inwardly recoiled at my touch, I laid his head in my lap and patted his back. He had never shown me a single kindness, yet I felt compelled to ease his suffering.

A minute passed and his spluttering ceased. He quieted. The remedy had worked.

CHAPTER SIX

"DID I HEAR my name?" called Brother Ulric, appearing at the door of the refectory. He stepped outside, followed by several brothers and, at the sight of me, hurried over.

Brother Ulric knelt beside Brother Giles and felt his wrist. "He's alive, but his pulse is quite weak. Let us get him inside."

A litter was brought and Giles was lifted onto it. His eyes had rolled up under his lids and his limp body showed no sign of life.

"What happened?" asked Brother Ulric as we carried him to the infirmary.

"I was collecting valerian when I heard him cry out," I said. "He must have tripped. I found him lying on the path. I thought he'd broken his nose. There was a lot of blood on his face and he had difficulty breathing so I tried wiping and clearing his nose but he couldn't sit up."

"You did what you could. We must clear his passageways as best we can," said Brother Ulric, as I trailed behind.

I followed the brothers inside and bowls were swept onto the floor to prepare a table to lay him on. I readied a small basin and selected a cannula the correct diameter to feed up his nose.

Brother Ulric found a bladder to attach and instructed Brothers Medford and Dowser to sit him up so he could begin suctioning Giles's nostrils.

A copious amount of blood ended in the bowl.

"I need the long cannula for his air passage, Kronos."

As I crossed the room to the shelving Brother Ulric suddenly shouted, "He's turning blue! Get me a knife! Kronos, bring me a knife! He can't breathe. We must lay him flat. I'll have to insert a cannula."

"In his mouth?" asked Brother Medford.

"In his neck!" answered Brother Ulric.

I'd never seen this last chance effort to save a man before. I quickly found his sharpest blade; a thin one he'd used to remove small growths from people's backs and necks.

While others turned away, I looked on. Brother Ulric ran a finger down the old monk's neck, finding an indentation between a large lump of cartilage and a smaller. He made a horizontal incision, exposing a yellow membrane underneath. "One more cut," he said, under his breath, then sliced the tissue to create a hole. I handed him the copper cannula.

Without hesitation, he pushed the metal into Brother Giles's neck, then placed his lips over the end and sucked. "It's in the passageway," he said, holding the cannula in place. He then breathed a couple of quick puffs, pushing air into the pipe. The old monk's chest expanded and Brother Ulric watched to confirm his breathing.

"He is extremely weak," said the infirmarian, addressing the awe-struck brothers surrounding him. "With rest he may recover, but I am uncertain."

The brothers crossed themselves and lifted their eyes skyward. Prayers of thanks slid from their lips and I expected the mention of Brother Ulric's miraculous intervention to be excitedly discussed for the next several days.

As the noticeably pale monks began filtering out of the infirmary, Pinter Pender, having heard all the commotion, planted himself in the doorway. "I found something on the path where Brother Giles fell," he said, holding up a glass bottle. "Does this belong to you, Brother Ulric?"

The monks stopped and turned their heads in interest. The infirmarian looked up at the proffered bottle, then glanced at me.

Pender came forward and handed the bottle to Brother Ulric. "It appears empty," he said.

Brother Ulric examined the bottle, confirming that it was, indeed, empty. He turned to me, a concerned look on his face. "Did you use this on Brother Giles?" he asked.

"I thought it would help."

"You failed to mention it."

"I was going to, but—"

"But you did not," said Brother Ulric.

I was aware of the monks looking from Brother Ulric's troubled face to mine. Were they searching for signs of malice, traces of deception, ill intent?

"You do not know the correct proportions," he said. "Why would you chance giving him this without proper knowledge?"

"He was struggling. I sought to ease his suffering."

"You tried to poison him!" said Pinter Pender.

Brother Ulric pinned him with a terse look. "Leave us, Pinter."

The novice gave me a smug look, as Brother Ulric pulled me aside.

"You have stepped beyond your bounds, Kronos. I have never properly trained you in administering this."

"I'd seen you use it on similar occasions."

"True, you had seen me. And do you think that by watching you are now expert? It is not your place."

With a final, baleful glare, Brother Ulric returned to Brother Giles, leaving me to endure the harsh stares of the remaining brothers. I stood, chapfallen, unsure what to say, what to do. Brothers Medford and Dowser exited along with the others, leaving me with Pinter Pender as the last to leave. The novice couldn't resist one last parting comment. "You never liked the old monk, did you?"

I immediately left for the scullery. I couldn't bring myself to help with Brother Giles, nor did I want to tend the other monks in the infirmary. Brother Ulric barely looked up as I walked by.

As I scrubbed out the remains of my master's concoctions, I wondered if he would dismiss me from his tutelage. What is the worth in having an apprentice who takes chances with the lives of his fellow monks? Granted, Brother Giles had not much life left in him. Should I have stood back and let him flail like a fish on land? I thought I was doing him a kindness.

I set the last bowl aside to dry then dumped the tub of water in the yard outside. I lingered a bit, admiring the oaks at the edge of the woods. Taller than the nave and monastery itself, they stretched their limbs to the sky, inviting the divine to descend upon their branches. Other places as divine as this existed outside this monastery. I did not have to let Thetford Priory be the limit of my world.

My lungs filled with the smell of earth and breeze. I closed my eyes and reminded myself that some might see my physical limitation as a gift. The man on the donkey with the caravan of performers had suggested I might juggle for kings and queens someday. Why not follow a different path? Why not embrace this body that God gave me?

As if my thoughts had conjured an opportunity, I heard the rhythmic beating of hooves strike the ground at a gallop. A horseman appeared out of the woods rigidly formal and disciplined. He was dressed in the livery of Kenninghall and the Duke of Norfolk.

I dropped the washtub and ran after him to the great gate of the monastery.

By the time I arrived, he had dismounted and was already speaking to one of the monks.

Brother Denton looked at me. "Summon Brother Ulric. He is needed at Kenninghall."

"He is tending Brother Giles. The old monk had a spell." I declined more detail.

The messenger spoke, "Kenninghall is threatened with an outbreak again." He levelled his stare at Brother Denton and said without delicacy, "The duke is the king's most favoured advisor. His wellbeing is more important than the life of an old monk."

Always circumspect, Brother Denton said nothing to this.

"I'll take you to Brother Ulric," I told the messenger.

He followed me through the cloister to the infirmary where Brother Giles was surrounded by a small group of monks standing over him, praying. I stood aside for the messenger to enter, not wishing to be the first person my master saw when he looked up.

"Brother Ulric," the messenger said, "Mistress Holland has taken ill again. We do not know if it is the same malady that afflicted her before, but you must return to Kenninghall at once. It is feared this will take her life…and mayhap others."

I could see Brother Ulric's conflicted thoughts furrow his

brow. My eyes dropped to the elderly monk whose complexion had turned from blue to its characteristic ashen pallor.

"Kronos will go."

I looked at Brother Ulric, astonished. What could I do to prevent Lady Bess from dying? Why was he entrusting the care of Lady Bess and all of Kenninghall to me?

"Kronos, you must leave at once."

"Master, I—"

"Take the tisane as before and only give it to her if she is taken with fever and chills." He turned back to Brother Giles and said over his shoulder, "Take whatever else you think you might need."

The responsibility filled me with dread. I hoped I would be of some service to Kenninghall, but what if I failed? What if Lady Bess died under my care?

Perish such thinking, my chance to see her again was at hand.

I could be her champion.

The time and scenery flew past as if I dreamt it. The messenger had left with the assurance that I would follow within the hour and while I secured the needed medicines and my own effects, my horse was saddled and ready. I had no intention of waking from this sublime sweven until I was standing in the courtyard of the duke's distinguished residence. Then I might panic, questioning my ability and the faith invested in me. Determined, I pushed the thought out of my head and rode the mercurial beast I'd been given with an inexplicable confidence even the gelding didn't question. Sometimes confidence is simply the suppression of doubt.

As the miles passed uneventfully, I saw myself giving the

tisane to Lady Bess. She, like a sleeping beauty, would wake from her torpor. She would see me and whisper, "'Tis you. I've walked the edge between life and the death and you have delivered me from an eternal slumber, Kronos." I would thrill at the sound of my name, then touch my lips to hers. The heat between us would meld our bodies into one.

But stop!

I reined in my steed and pulled it to the woods, where I slid off the saddle and quickly took care of my lust, spewing it over the ferns near my knees.

I fell against a tree, spent from my imaginings.

A sort of dreamlike state befuddled me, and I slid down the trunk of the tree, consumed with thoughts of Lady Bess. I did not imagine her succumbing to whatever malady afflicted her, but instead, imagined her in a state of robust health, with me as her paramour. If thoughts could make it so, then my wish for her recovery would sustain her until I arrived at Kenninghall. She could not possibly leave this earthly realm without my seeing her again. I felt myself recovered enough to feel the swell beneath my hosen once again and was reminded of my mission by the sudden realisation that my mount had wandered off.

I shook off my ruminations and cursed myself for my indulgence. I could little afford this oneiric dereliction beneath a tree. Now I had to manage mounting my horse without a stableman to assist me. My ride was happily snorting through the undergrowth, unaware of my predicament. There were no boulders or rock walls on which I could stand. I took the reins and led my gelding deeper into the woods, past buckthorn and trees with massive girth until I found an oak with limbs low enough for me to reach.

I threw the reins over the lowest limb, looped them around and commenced to climbing. I'd never been a tree climber for obvious reasons—my legs were too short to swing and hook over a branch—but I scrabbled and cursed until I got myself onto a branch high enough to drop myself into the saddle.

As I peered down at the horse's rump, I realised just how high I was. The tree afforded no ideal height from which to gently lower myself. I must let go and fall, hoping that the beast didn't startle when I landed. If I should miss, I could be trampled or dragged through the forest.

It was my poor luck that I was alone with this problem. I couldn't waste any more time contemplating; Lady Bess needed me. From my perch, the target on the horse's back looked disappointingly small. I spoke quietly, hoping to calm my mount as much as myself. With a final prayer, I let go and dropped from the tree with my legs spread wide and my eyes squeezed shut against the twigs threatening to gouge them out. The fall took interminably long and with a solid whump, I landed against the pommel which maliciously pinched my bollocks.

Alas, my horse did what I feared it might. It reared up and pulled against the reins looped around the branch, snapping it free. The limb fell and struck the horse's flank and the beast took off through the woods at a wild pace, the branch still caught in the reins and flogging its haunches.

I grabbed its neck and buried my nose and fingers in its mane as the branch flailed beside us, alternately striking my leg then the horse's hind quarters. Low branches threatened to club me no matter how low I crouched. The descending night added to my fear. I needed to take hold of the reins and tighten them and I had to do it now. As I lifted my torso to reach up the horse's neck, I spied, too late, a stone wall. My mount leapt, and though I clung to his extending neck, it was no use. I was free of my horse. That brief realisation of falling and the inability to do anything to stop it lasted painfully long. My side hit the wall and I slid to the ground, the air knocked out of me.

⁕

I don't know how long I lay there. When I blinked up at the dusky sky and cursed my horse, I heard no sound of its fading gallop. I was battered and bruised. And very alone.

Gingerly, I lifted one arm and then the other. Thankfully, my legs were not useless. However, when I sat up, a trickle of blood ran down my cheek. A wound to my temple and its sharp sting warned me from touching it further.

Where was the road? With a sinking feeling I realised my horse had run deeper into the woods. I would probably never find it. Without my pannier of remedies what good was I to Kenninghall and to Bess Holland? How could I possibly cure her?

I'd come too far to turn back and get another horse. But the single most important reason for continuing was my desire to see Lady Bess. I knew I'd be a fool to show my face at Kenninghall with nothing to offer, but I simply could not refuse an opportunity to be in the same room as her.

I brushed myself off and began walking in the presumed direction of the road. My body ached with each step but at least there were no broken bones. There might be a trail of blood from my head wound, but I could move body and limb.

As I tramped through the woods, I decided that once I reached Kenninghall, a selectively-worded version of my story would not be as despicable as telling them the full account.

This time of year, the difference between night and day was as if a drape had been drawn. If I got to a road, at least it would lead me somewhere. Despite my uncertainty, I picked up my pace.

It seemed I had walked for half the night when I came to a

break in the woods. A well-trodden path stretched in either direction. I set an uncertain course and with some distance I might come to recognise where I was, but traversing on foot is different from sitting on the back of a horse. A distant hill viewed from a saddle disappears when traipsing by foot.

If I had gauged my progress correctly, from where I had parted with my horse, it would take another couple of hours for me to walk to the duke's manse, if indeed I was pointed in the right direction.

Without the comforting steady clop of a horse beneath me, the murmurs of woodland creatures sounded like the din of malevolent animals. Theirs was a secretive communication that unsettled me more than the ungenial silence of the nave when I passed through it on my way to the infirmary. I distracted myself by singing chants in imitation of the monks. My voice warbled softly at first as I tested my lungs against the night, then seeing it was not loud enough to drown the wild imaginings surrounding me, I crowed with abandon, daring the terrors and phantoms to spook me with their stirrings.

An inkling of futility still seeped into the rare silence when I ran out of chants and was trying to remember a new one. I trudged on, determined, when I heard the snorting of horses and men's voices. I looked over my shoulder and caught a glimpse of rushlights approaching.

My inclination was to think them highwaymen and footpads. Who travels at night but those who prey on stragglers like me?

I had reached a part of the road that was carved out of a hill with steep embankments on either side. Scaling them was inconceivable, so I looked for a boulder or shrub that could give me cover. Alas, the section was sadly free of any such landscape. I had no choice but to stand aside and hope that they ignored me.

The orb of light grew with the advance of horse and riders.

I squinted, trying to see, and realised these men were neither rogues nor deceits; they were men of gentle persuasion. Their fine leather boots squeaked in their stirrups. The plumes on their flat-caps rippled in a light breeze. I knew I must bow as they passed and I hoped they saw no disrespect in my diminutive size. These were men who could find insult if watched too long, and could have you whipped for a silent fart.

The plod of hooves neared and I swept off my cap and bowed as low as my bruised body allowed. A statue could not have been more still. Their steady pace slowed and the men's conversation came to an abrupt stop.

"What creature is this?" asked one of the riders.

"It looks to be a boy."

"On the road, in the woods, deep and dark?"

They halted just in front of me. The older, more lavishly dressed of the four, spoke.

"Boy, what say you to this night time stroll? Know you that wild boars will tear off your leg and chew it for dinner?"

I straightened, glad for an excuse to no longer stoop. "My lord, I am headed to Kenninghall. The good duke's manse."

A response came after a long hesitation.

"The duke's household called for one such as you?" His puzzlement coloured his voice. His most noticeable feature was a long, prevalent nose, which he now took the time to look down.

He saw that I was not a boy, but something less.

"I come from Thetford Priory," I said. "Mistress Elizabeth Holland has taken ill. I am Brother Ulric's apprentice, Kronos."

"Kronos?" he said, with a derisive snort. "Kronos what? Or there is no surname given to a creature such as you?"

"I was named by the brothers of the priory. I had no say in the matter."

"Odd bit of wit for these Benedictines."

I couldn't agree more, but thought it best not to say so.

"And you chose to walk instead of ride? The good lady might be dead by the time you make it there on foot."

"It was not by choice. My horse spooked and left me in the woods."

"Ah. You were thrown?"

"I was, my lord. It is not so easy to hold one's water for a long journey. Remounting is a challenge for me, so I climbed a tree and dropped myself into the saddle. My ride did not like my technique."

The lord snickered, allowing the others to join him in a good smirk.

"I see no satchel of medicines for your endeavour. How do you expect to be of service?"

"I have what I need up here." I pointed to my head. "I may be small, but my thoughts are as big as the next man's."

The corner of the lord's mouth turned up. He glanced over his shoulder at a liveryman then said, "Kronos, luck is your mistress tonight. You shall ride with us to Kenninghall."

Before I could blink, I was hoisted onto the back of a horse, and I clung to a retainer for the remainder of the journey. During our ride, I was privy to the conversation of these notable men, and inferring from their discussion, I realised that I was in the company of the third Duke of Norfolk, himself—Thomas Howard. I would suffer from whatever jibe they hurled at me, for I understood that I was in the presence of a great man. Of course, I knew not then, what I know now, so I cannot be faulted for naïveté at the innocent age of fifteen.

CHAPTER SEVEN

L UCK *WAS* MY mistress that night, although I wish it had been Lady Bess instead.

We arrived at Kenninghall in the small hours. One window glowed in welcome, but from the outside, the palace sat in doleful silence, its inhabitants and internal workings slowed by night's stifling hand.

I was helped down and led inside then escorted to Bess Holland's quarters. The resistive nursemaid from before visibly recoiled at the sight of me. I can't say that her displeasure wasn't reciprocated by my own at seeing *her*. I was as good as they got this night, so she would have to content herself with glaring at me from across the room.

"Good eve," I said as politely as I could manage.

She did not return the greeting, but muttered an oath under her exasperated sigh.

A small stand of candles burned close enough to Lady Bess that I could see that her face was damp with sweat. She appeared semi-delirious from her malady. Her eyes rolled beneath their lids, and her lips mouthed words only she, in some abstruse state of being, understood. Without my assortment of remedies, what could I do?

"We must get her fever down," I said, deciding on a course of action. I drew back the bed covers and instructed Margaret Barlowe to bring fresh water so that we might cool her brow.

"I will not leave my maid," she informed me.

The state of Lady Bess had alarmed me to the edge of panic. "Then you would let her die rather than leave her alone with me?" The woman's distrust rankled, and I saw no reason to be evasive. I took issue with her obstinacy, attributing it to a reflexive mistrust of my person, though the monks always cautioned me against making such assumptions. Before she could defend herself, I went to the door and called for a servant to fetch the water.

"The matter is settled," I said. "If you insist on staying, then you will help me find fresh cloths to mop her sweat."

My outburst curbed her further objection. Perhaps it impressed on her the need for cooperation. Without another word, we left, together, to find a cloth that could be torn apart.

She led me to a room where linens were stored and found a sheet waiting to be mended.

"This will do," she said, ripping off a good portion. "It shall not be missed."

A basin of water awaited our return and Barlowe tore the sheet into smaller squares to wipe and dry Lady Bess's body. She began unlacing the front of Lady Bess's smock and before she could glower at me, I turned my back, allowing her to proceed without consternation. Besides, a silver plate on a table provided me with an adequate reflection to watch. I pretended to admire its ornately carved edge. For cert, I was worried for the lady's health, but I was not immune to the thrill of seeing her in a state of undress. I might never have the opportunity again.

As I considered what course to take, I remembered a poultice that might draw out her fever. It was simple to do, made of ground mustard—a herb the kitchen would certainly have.

"Can you send for mustard and flour?" I said, my back still turned.

"She is too unwell to eat," replied Margaret Barlowe.

"To make a poultice. Brother Ulric taught me."

Margaret Barlowe wrung out the water and began dabbing Lady Bess's chest. Her patience gone, she said, "Why is *he* not here? Why were *you* sent? It was Brother Ulric who saved my lady the last time—not you."

I turned to address her disapproval and she quickly covered her charge. "He could not leave the priory," I said. "He sent me in his place."

"He sent you without any medicine?"

"My horse threw me then ran off, taking my pannier and the remedies with it."

"And you still persisted?" she said, incredulous. "What use are you without your remedies?"

"Lady Bess needs help and my master has taught me well. We are wasting time in argument when we could be doing more for her."

The nursemaid clamped shut her mouth. She dropped the linen in the bowl of water and stalked out the door. Again, I was left to wonder after the woman's abrupt leaving.

I stood beside Bess and peered down at her face with fresh beads of perspiration forming at her upper lip and temples. I could think of nothing else to do but take up the linen rag and continue trying to cool her. What if she did not improve? Apprehension churned in my gut, and the burden of her well-being fell upon my now slumping shoulders.

How ludicrous to have thought I could be of any use. My urgent desire to see her again had made me a fool. Perhaps I should have returned to Thetford for more medicine and a fresh horse. But if I had left and taken the time to get medicine and to return, would it have been too late?

I had not come to a conclusion when the door opened and Margaret Barlowe entered. She placed the ingredients on a small table along with a mortar and mixing bowl.

"There is more mustard should you require it."

She took the washrag from my hand and vigorously dunked it in the water, wringing the cloth with such relish that I wondered if it was my neck she was envisioning twisting.

Leaving Barlowe to tend the lady, I set about making the poultice. I started with one part mustard to two parts flour, whisking them together then adding water. When the mash was the right consistency, I spread the paste on a swath of linen and directed Barlowe to spread open our lady's smock so that I could lay it across her chest.

The nursemaid's lips pinched as she reluctantly exposed her lady. I expected her to snatch the remedy out of my hand and apply it herself, but she stood aside with a pained expression on her face.

For as many times as I had laid poultices on the sick in the infirmary, I couldn't help but be acutely conscious of my every move while attending Lady Bess. Barlowe's watchful eye imbued the mundane act with added weight. I called on my better celibate angel to guide me.

If the poultice was applied for too long, the mustard could burn her skin. The two of us sat idly by to watch. She surveilled for signs of improvement; I counted time. The poultice would never work so fast as to cure Bess forthwith, but if her fever broke, I would consider it a hopeful sign.

"It has been an hour," I said, standing to remove the plaster. Barlowe sprang to her feet to clean Bess's skin.

As Barlowe began wiping the mash off our patient, we were interrupted by the determined sound of footsteps in the hall. Alarmed, I was about to ask the nursemaid who could make such noise, when a jarring knock sounded at the door. Before either of us could answer, it swung open. Dressed in a fine doublet and looking every inch the prestigious nobleman to the king, Thomas Howard commanded every square inch of the threshold. Foregoing any consideration for her modesty, he studied Lady Bess as if it was his right to do so. His stare lasted uncomfortably long, making my own licentious behaviour seem puppyish by comparison. I shared with Barlowe an immediate desire to protect our invalid lady. I stepped in front of Norfolk, blocking his view, and Margaret Barlowe pulled up the sheet.

He'd gotten an eyeful. He looked at me in irritation, then remembered why he had come. He held up my saddlebag. "Perchance this belongs to you?"

I seized the bag as if it was filled with gold and rifled through its contents, retrieving the tisane Brother Ulric used to treat ague and Mistress Holland the last time we were there.

"A horse wandered onto the grounds. No rider. Fully saddled. Yours, I suppose?"

"How fortunate," I said. I looked at our still nonsensical patient burning with fever. "However, if we tried giving her the remedy now, she would either drown or be unable to swallow it. I cannot risk wasting a single drop. We shall have to wait until she stirs enough to understand."

"I can rouse her," said Norfolk. He brushed me aside and without so much as a mote of propriety, laid his hand on Lady Bess's breast.

My mouth opened, but nothing came out. Margaret Barlowe was similarly struck. The salacious gesture left the two of us completely mortified. Both of us were stymied with inaction, unable to intervene. To have confronted him would have insulted so powerful a man. To my surprise, Lady Bess moaned quietly, which further conflicted me for I was both aroused and appalled at the same time. Besides, it should have been my hand on her breast, not the duke's. I shifted uncomfortably and cleared my throat, which managed to remind Norfolk that he was being observed. He took a step back.

"She seems to be coming around now," he said.

The door clicked shut behind him, and Margaret Barlowe and I stared after, digesting what we had just seen.

The nursemaid huffed. "She's suffered enough. Let her rest." She then sat herself down on a small stool and viciously stabbed a needle into her embroidery.

The next morning, Bess Holland opened her eyes. The nursemaid continued sleeping in her chair, snoring with unpredictable sinus whistles, completely unaware. I tamped down my excitement and quietly went to Lady Bess. My relief at seeing her stir quickened my heart for I was hopeful she would resume her life, unscathed by this terrible fever. I stood by, waiting for her to clear her head.

She turned her gaze on me…and smiled.

It was as if the sun had broken through a rain-soaked day.

"How do you feel?"

Bess turned back to address the ceiling. "What day is this?"

The nursemaid suddenly snorted awake and was at her lady's side. She took her lady's hand between hers. "My lady," said Barlowe. "You are improved?"

"Help me sit, Margaret."

"Your fever is gone," I said, laying my hand against her brow while Barlowe placed a pillow behind her back. "Do you feel well enough to eat?"

Bess closed her eyes and touched her neck. "My head throbs so. Food does not appeal to me."

"You must consider it, my lady," said Barlowe. "Think of your strength."

Bess did not think of her strength. She looked down at her chest and with a brief look of bewilderment, tied the neck strings of her smock. She settled her head upon the pillow. "I feel very… small," she said.

"It is why you must eat," insisted her maid. "You have gone without for nearly three days."

Bess sighed. "Very well, Margaret. Bring me broth and I shall try."

Margaret practically flew to the door. She was so relieved that I wondered if she realised she was leaving me alone with her beloved charge. I suppose she remembered later as her feet carried her swiftly away, but perhaps she believed her lady well enough to fend off any advances from untoward dwarfs. I doubt that she suddenly found me trustworthy.

"Mistress Holland, I have the tisane that you were given when you suffered before. I believe it might help with your aching head."

"I would take anything to be rid of this pulsing feeling."

"There is no certainty that it shall cure you, but it is worth a try."

Lady Bess drank down the preparation and daintily wiped her mouth with her fingers. When she was done arranging herself, she looked at me. "I remember you."

"I *am* somewhat memorable."

"I think that must be true."

I took no offence. I tended to make an indelible impression

in anyone's mind. First and foremost, they saw my shortness. Yet I was always astounded when people seemed to think that I had a choice in the matter. Who can control the colour of one's skin, or the hue of one's eyes? The monks believe it is God's will. God does have a peculiar wit. Every now and again, He must tire of putting out the same product over and over. Or, perhaps He was interrupted when it was my turn. Perhaps He had run out of longer shins.

"You are a novice?" she asked.

"Nay. I shall not enter the brotherhood."

"Why not?" She played with one end of her smock ties. "Remind me of your name?"

"Kronos."

Her eyebrows raised, and I expected her to tell me what an unusual name I had, but she did not.

"Kronos, why do you not choose the church? Is it not your desire? Or…" and here I could not fault her candour, "will they not have you?"

"My lady, they have asked me, but I have lived my entire life at Thetford Priory. I should like to try a different life." I relished telling her this, for here was an opportunity for her to see that I was capable of more than just worshipping God.

"And what different life do you envision?"

"I would like to perform for the king."

"Be King Henry's natural fool?"

"Mayhap not his personal fool, but I should like to entertain him…and his court."

"Ah! Then you sing?"

"Nay, my lady. Not so well."

"You strum the viol?"

"Nay, I do not."

"Turn flips and swallow fire?"

I shook my head. I felt as though I disappointed her.

"Then what do you do?"

Instead of answering, I moved the table and chair away from her bed.

"You rearrange furniture?" she asked.

I removed three lit candles from the stand, stood in the middle of the room, and began juggling them.

"Oh!" she cried, trying to sit up straighter. I could not see the look on her face but I knew she was delighted, if not a bit on edge—just as I had hoped. "I beg you. Do not drop them! I have no strength to run. You shall burn down Kenninghall!"

I started with a simple rotation to find my rhythm. Feeling comfortable was the key to not losing my wit in front of the lady. One of the candles snuffed itself and the melting wax dribbled onto my fingers, but I kept them circling, ignoring the discomfort of being burned. Unbeknownst to anyone, I had practised with candles in the priory's sanctuary, and the fear of being caught had added a layer of apprehension to my practising. Here, that fear was absent, and I felt immersed, focused. I moved on to throwing one candle up with two in my hand, alternating. My confidence now solid, I attempted a behind the back toss over my shoulder.

"You are proficient in this, doctor Kronos." Her tone was more relaxed and there was a smile in her voice. "If I should ever be installed at court, I shall let them know of your talent."

I could have kept juggling, so content and in command was I, except the door rattled.

I snatched the final air-borne candle and returned the three to their stand before Margaret Barlowe walked in, carrying a bowl of broth. I relit a candle as she encouraged Bess to drink.

"The duchess wishes to speak with you," she informed Bess. "I told her you were yet unwell, but we know she is a woman with a strong opinion."

"And her opinion is that I am feigning illness to avoid my duty?"

"I do not presume to know what is in her mind," muttered Margaret Barlowe, and, putting aside my general dislike of the nursemaid, I could see that she was perhaps Lady Bess's greatest ally.

Bess sipped the broth, her brow creasing in thought, turning to look at the window drapery as if answers were stitched in the fabric. She seemed to forget either of us were in the room. I wished I could have plumbed the depths of her introspection, for she had so bewitched me that I wanted to know all the inner workings of her mind. What did she think of her life at Kenninghall?

It would not be proper for me to talk with her about her duties in the presence of her maid. But my curiosity burned. I gathered she was feeling improved with every passing minute. The throbbing had disappeared, and I wondered about this strange malady that could set her down, then miraculously respond to Brother Ulric's tisane. Perhaps she did have ague. If that were true, then she would suffer again in the future—for there was no cure. Possibly I might see her again. For now, though, my time with Lady Bess was nearing an end.

I searched through the saddle bag looking for medicines that might help her. In my haste to quit Thetford, I'd only found the one jar, but I'd packed herbs and could leave her with instructions. I was considering giving her willow bark and peppermint for any future head throbbing when my attention was drawn to loud voices out in the hall.

The door swung open and in walked the duchess, looking stouter and more obstinate than the last time I'd seen her. A servant trailed behind—a spiritless woman whose tired expression I attributed to Elizabeth Stafford's difficult nature. The Duchess quickly scanned the room, caught sight of me, and tucked her chin in surprise.

"Where is the old monk?" she demanded.

"Brother Ulric was waylaid at the priory. I was sent in his stead."

Her eyebrow lifted, disappearing beneath her gable head-dress. "He has educated you in matters of doctoring?"

"Aye, Duchess."

She exhaled audibly. "I suppose healers come in all sizes." Her officious gaze ran down my person, then landed on Lady Bess. "You are better, I see."

"The pounding in my temples is lessening."

"Your colour looks returned. If there is no head throbbing then you may resume your duties. Mary has been asking for you. She refuses to cooperate until you return."

"Your Grace, I have witnessed Mistress Holland's malady and can attest to its severity," said Margaret Barlowe. "She was in a feverish state for nearly two days. It took all of her strength and has left her weakened. Mayhap another day of rest would assure her strength."

Brother Ulric had argued this before and had received an indifferent stare in return. I didn't expect lowly Barlowe to prove any more successful, but I respected her for trying.

"Minding children is not difficult labour," said the Duchess. "Bess, get dressed and attend them until evening. It requires little effort to sit and watch. Once the children have been put to bed, you will have the evening to rest."

I had never cared for children, but I was not so ignorant as to think it a simple endeavour. I'd seen farmers' wives and the no small amount of barking and herding required to control one's pups. Bess was not in the position to argue, though I under-stood she was the daughter of the duke's secretary and that must account for some bit of sway. Still, in matters domestic, this was Kenninghall and Bess was not its mistress.

Bess accepted Elizabeth Stafford's wishes. She lay motionless in bed, staring at a spot on the opposite wall, which caused everyone, including the Duchess, to follow her gaze and contemplate. The Duchess looked back at Bess, momentarily confused. With a pronounced *huff* she strode from the room followed by her servant who quietly closed the door behind them.

"I suppose that is settled," said Bess, to the sound of their receding footfalls. "Margaret, can you help me dress?"

While Margaret attended Bess, I excused myself to find some food. The ride back to the priory would feel longer on an empty stomach, and I needed to inquire whether my horse was rested for the return journey. I wondered again if this might be the last time I would see Bess Holland. Not wanting to leave without expressing a final wish of fare well, I determined I would seek her out once I had eaten my fill.

CHAPTER EIGHT

A LOUD CRASH ANNOUNCED my entry into the kitchen, which drew attention to the broken crock on the flagstone floor, then to the poor minion who dropped it, then to me—the cause of his fright. Since my last visit, several new staff had been employed. They gaped, caught off guard by my arrival. I suppose the established staff had either refrained from warning them of my "shortcomings," or they may have secretly delighted in watching how the newcomers would react. I ignored the clatter and addressed the cook, hoping for an end of bread or a wedge of cheese to stave off my hunger.

"Might there be leftovers? I will soon depart for Thetford and I haven't eaten," I said.

He motioned to the scullery maid, a thin girl whose shoulders were no wider than her face. She had just come up from the larder toting a basket of cheddar, turnips, and apples. "You can pick what you like. If you wish, you can eat with us a little later."

I chose an apple and some cheese and stood aside to munch on my selection and watch the bustle of the kitchen. The room was considerably bigger than the priory's kitchen and more fully appointed, with every size copper pot imaginable. Large windows let in an abundance of light which Brother Trelli would have envied. Dodging stands of candles and making do with the limited selection of cookery had always been a challenge at Thetford. Here, the only object needing to be avoided was a motley white cat that stood in the path of anyone wanting to get by.

The requisites of a meal fit for nobility were assembled, plated, then whisked to an expectant ducal patronage. My mouth watered as a platter of roast duck dressed in parsley sprigs with a black currant and watercress sauce sailed past inches from my nose. Brother Trelli's inspirations could not compare to the sumptuous renditions offered here. For cert, I could grow accustomed to this grand style of living.

With the cat kicked out the door and the midday meal delivered, the cook and kitchen staff relaxed around a long trestle table strewn with bowls and dirty pots, the vestiges of their frenetic meal preparation. They eyed me with curiosity and made room on a bench to join them.

They asked about my life at the priory and afterwards, I posed a few questions about Kenninghall. More specifically, about Thomas Howard and his wife.

I seem to have broached a sacrosanct topic.

Each of them looked around as if making sure neither person was in the kitchen, or peeping from a corner. This was a loyal kitchen crew, not prone to making trouble for themselves, but regardless of any possible misgivings, they took me into their confidence. As I would soon learn, there was trouble enough at Kenninghall to keep them firmly in each other's good graces. No one wanted to risk their employment because of pettiness.

The cook, a solid fellow with a purple complexion, took a drink of ale and set it on the board with a definitive thud. "I've known the duke since before he was so named. His first wife were a lovely maid and they had a son. I came on after the boy died and the Lady Anne was much aggrieved. She took ill and died not two years after her son."

Most of the staff had heard his story before, and they busied themselves with devouring the leftovers while the newcomers seemed as engaged as I.

"The Earl of Surrey—as was his title then—was much in favour with the king. The Lady Elizabeth had been an attendant of Queen Catherine and her father—Edward Stafford, the third Duke of Buckingham—was the richest subject in England. The Earl would marry none other than Elizabeth, and he was handsomely rewarded for their union." The cook took another swig of ale and cast a knowing eye at me.

"The Earl was given title or money?" I asked.

"A dowry at first, and the title came later." The cook picked out a piece of the duck floating in the bottom of a pan and dropped it in his mouth. "The king made the earl Lord Deputy of Ireland and sent him across the sea to subdue the Irish and make them English subjects. By then, there was Thomas and Mary, both barely walking. The entire family accompanied him to Ireland, but a war is not a place for a young family. Elizabeth and her children suffered. They often went without food, so she returned to England."

The kitchen cat, who had snuck back in after its unceremonious boot out the door, leapt on the cook's lap and began licking his plate.

"You scamp," he admonished, not completely meaning it. He stroked the cat's back, which further emboldened the little thief.

"If circumstances in Ireland had given her complaint, returning to England gave her more. Within a month of her return, the king accused Elizabeth Stafford's father of treason. He was tried—and her father-in-law presided over the trial."

A collective gasp rose from the new staff.

"The treachery of family," I said, noting that entitlement came at a cost.

"Her father was quickly condemned and beheaded." The cook ran a finger around his plate and licked it. "A botched job, so I heard."

"What was his treasonous act?" I asked.

"The Duke of Buckingham had a legitimate claim to the throne. Plus, he disliked the king's chief minister—Cardinal Wolsey." The cook leaned forward and lowered his voice. "By a noble's reckoning, a lowly butcher's boy should never rise above his station. But you see, Cardinal Wolsey did just that for he was an intelligent and cunning man." The cook sat back, a knowing smile on his face. "The Duke of Buckingham's swift conviction did much to turn the Lady Elizabeth against her father-in-law and…her husband. She believed her husband did nothing to stop this unfortunate outcome."

"He was in Ireland," added the scullery maid, obviously familiar with the story. "What could he do from there?"

"As it were," continued the cook, "the Earl's five-hundred-man army was not large enough to repress the Irish. The campaign was too costly, and he was brought home."

Again, the cook glanced around before continuing. "Elizabeth said her father-in-law and husband conspired to convict her father. Indeed, they were both handsomely rewarded for their sufferance in the matter. The king gave them six of her father's manors to divide between them."

"And she with no right to inherit them," I said. "That does make for ill will."

"It is a wound that has never healed," said the cook. He pushed his plate forward and finished his ale, planting the mug upon the table in front of him as if marking the end of his statement.

His tale of court politics gave me pause. Men's fortunes wavered with the whims of others and their influence on the king. Theirs was an unseemly game of shameless pretence. Had I the stomach for such artful deceit? The monks had impressed upon me that a man's character is only as good as his word. In court, a man's word was thin assurance. Saving one's neck was the priority.

Whatever evil these men conducted, whatever evil tainted their souls, all could be unburdened with enough money for prayers of absolution and indulgences. My stomach roiled at the deceit and favouritism at play. If man is cast in God's image, what does that say about Him?

As I sat in sullen silence, my thoughts were interrupted by a boisterous laugh from the scullery maid and one other.

The cook scowled at the two giggling women questioningly. "Share your jest. We need a laugh to end our meal."

The scullery maid flushed, but her cohort nary flinched. The girl possessed no filter for propriety. She elbowed the scullery maid and said, "She wants to know if 'is pizzle is miniature."

The cook looked at me. "We go from noblemen to little men," he said. He pushed the cat off his lap and glanced about as he dabbed his mouth with a napkin. "I daresay 'tis a question that has crossed all our minds." He looked at the scullery maid. "But a maid should not be so interested."

Heat radiated from my cheeks. To be called a 'little man' by another of similar station, my equal (not nobility), nettled my newly-found confidence. My mind may be filled with bawdy Greek poetry, but I blushed to think others were interested in my personal. The giddy girl pinched a smile in expectation.

"I am the same as any other," I said, drawing myself up in an effort to restore my pride. Then, recovering my temerity (for I was not in the company of monks), I said, "You will have to take me at my word; for this is not the place to prove it to you." I finished my ale to stifle my smile. There followed a lusty round of sniggers and back slapping.

Truth be, this banter amused me. I could have dallied longer, but if word got back to Thetford of my impertinence, I would have paid a price for my audacity. I rose from the table and excused myself to inquire after my gelding.

I found the ostler hanging tack in the stall next to my horse.

"He's rested well enough from his adventure," answered the stableman on seeing me. "I've fed him and watered him."

"I shall be leaving presently. Could you saddle him as I make my farewells?"

I refused to leave Mistress Holland without wishing her well. The connivance of her employer to enrich himself troubled me, but I assured myself that her father would protect her from any unsavoury encounters with his master. It is a father's duty to do so. Besides, Bess needed final instructions for the remedies that I was leaving.

I made my way down the hall to her room, and was within a few steps of it, when her door swung open. She exited, wearing an olive kirtle and gable headpiece which unfortunately, covered her soft dark hair.

"Mistress Holland," I said. "I wanted to instruct you about the medicines."

"Doctor Kronos, do you expect additional poor health of me?"

I bowed respectfully. "Nay, my lady, I wish only good health for you. But in the event that help is not forthcoming from Thetford Priory, I prefer that you not suffer unnecessarily while waiting."

"That is kind of you. I will afford you a moment of instruction." She turned back to her room and invited me in.

Her nursemaid, Margaret Barlowe was nowhere in sight. Nor was anyone else. I was alone with Lady Bess.

My mind flew in a hundred directions. Surely she could hear my thundering heart. Or if not, then the flush of my neck must be obvious. Brother Ulric took a long breath in and blew it out before stitching a man's torn skin. I did the same and it served me well. My speech was even. I was as smooth as a marble column.

I held up the first bottle—the tisane that would cure her throbbing head—and explained the dosage. She listened intently, her green gaze alternating between mine and the bottle. I went through the selection of remedies, what they were used for, how to make preparations with them. When I had finished, I searched my mind for more to talk about. I could have spent hours studying the curve of her lips and the shape of her nose, blathering away, nonsensical. The sun streaming through her window played on the tendrils of her hair loose at her face and the highlights were of gradient browns and reds. I was rendered speechless.

"Doctor Kronos," said Lady Bess, "I should like you to juggle for the children."

I blinked in surprise. "Now?"

"Of course. Then you may be on your way."

I followed her (or, perhaps I floated) to the other side of Kenninghall. We passed through stately rooms with colourful tapestries and wood panelling polished to gleaming. I hardly noticed them as I studied her easy stride, noting the width of her shoulders and the shape of her back disappearing into yards of cloth gathered at her waist, then flowing to the ground and tickling the floor as she walked. If I should hope to describe her self-assurance it would sound pretentious. She was not portentous. Hers was a calm demeanour that settled those around her. Even my raging impulse to pull her aside and know what her body would feel like next to mine was muted by my admiration and the desire to just be in her presence and know what peace I could.

We entered a room where an older woman stood over a girl who was in the throes of mischief, wielding a wooden doll missing its head. She flailed her brother with the little corpse and he attempted to fend her off with a wooden sword. Blunt though it was, he still had the advantage of position and size.

Mistress Holland snatched away the doll and I grabbed the blunt sword before either child realised they were missing their weapons. They looked at their empty hands, surprised, a result of their governess's swift action and the fact that she was accompanied by a queer-looking consort.

"Mary and Thomas, for shame," said Lady Bess. "This mischief is what I come back to? I had the intention of treating you to something special."

Mary, a dark-haired, lithe girl, was the first to recover. She ran to Lady Bess and embraced her governess about the thighs. "Mistress Holland, I've missed you so!" She then turned to her brother and pointed at him. "He was taunting me!"

"She called me a weasel."

"Thomas has been hateful," said Mary. "I could have called him worse."

Thomas, equal in height to Mary but not as old, launched into a list of offences perpetrated by his sister.

"Thomas, I shall hear no more complaints. If you are

interested in being entertained by Doc…Master Kronos," and here she nodded to me, and in response I bowed, "then I expect exceptional behaviour from both of you."

The servant maid in charge sighed in relief to see Lady Bess taking control. "I've done the best I could by them," she murmured. "I am glad you have returned."

"Please stay a while, Janice, I am not so recovered that I couldn't use your help."

"Of course, my lady," agreed the woman. But she would have no more to do with disciplining the children and removed herself to collecting bowls of a half-eaten meal and putting them on a tray to take away.

Lady Bess sat the two offenders down in front of her and let them know her displeasure at their lack of manners towards one another and to their substitute governess. After getting their solemn promise to behave, she looked up at me and formally made my introduction.

"Why does he look strange?" queried Thomas.

"His legs are short," commented Mary.

"He was born that way," said Lady Bess. "Just like you were born with brown eyes and dark hair."

Lady Bess's reasonable reply succeeded in multiplying my admiration for her three-fold.

"Was his mother evil?" asked Thomas.

Ah, the influence of prejudice begins at an early age. I wondered by whose example he was taught to think less of those of physical distinction.

"We have no way of knowing, but his appearance is not because of any wrong committed against God."

I was relieved to hear Lady Bess say this. The children, however, remained sceptical and continued to eye me suspiciously.

"Children, we do not understand why some people are born the way they are. We are all created in his image."

The children looked puzzled.

"Our Lord looks like him?" asked Thomas.

Lady Bess smiled. "No one knows, because no one has seen Him."

This led to more discussion about who was this God anyway, and why did we have to obey Him if no one has seen Him lately? I remained blithely happy to let the governess tackle these questions and admired her resolve to answer them.

Finally, she answered to their satisfaction and she was able to introduce the "treat" she had promised.

"If the two of you will sit quietly, over here," she said, directing them to a bench, "Kronos will perform for you."

While they settled on the bench, I looked around for objects to juggle. I found a small bladder ball and the missing head to Mary's doll. I needed one last round object, and after being confounded over the lack of suitable toys to choose from, I found an apple with a bite taken out of it on the tray of plates to be washed.

Lady Bess sat between the two siblings and modelled courteous behaviour, sitting with her chin level to the floor and her hands folded in her lap. Janice sat on a small stool near the window. With a sublime smile Lady Bess tipped her head to me, giving permission to proceed.

To start, I bowed low, exaggerating a deep, solemn greeting to great effect which encouraged the children to feel important and captured their undivided attention. I placed my feet and tossed the objects into the air, creating a circle, an easy start to becoming comfortable. I needed to feel the space around me and to command it. With each rotation I thought less about trying to impress. I concentrated on the objects hitting my hand and their weight. I relaxed into a rhythm of movement. After a minute, I reversed the circle, then flawlessly caught two in one hand and alternately tossed one object to match the height of the second object from the other hand. The effect was an up and down movement, like columns, like following the trunk of a tree.

Thomas was more excited than Mary. He laughed and yelped, barely able to sit still. Their happiness was a result of my ease and comfort in performing for them. I felt as though I held their emotions in the palm of my hand and that realisation translated into even more confidence. I thrilled at the attention I was garnering and my glee translated into waggish playfulness. I did some under leg tosses, easily catching the objects, then knelt and stood. I spun around a couple of times and ended by throwing the apple and bladder ball higher and catching them, then ended with the doll's head balancing on the crook of my elbow, staring at them.

"More, Master Kronos, more!" cried Mary, as I swept into a final bow.

My small audience applauded, and I took more delight in seeing Mistress Holland's smile than I did in having completed my juggling without a drop. Instead of feeling limited by my dwarfism and vulnerable to people's first impressions, I felt in that moment, that I was a titan. My confidence and mastery had melded into perfection. Perhaps others sensed something of this, but for cert, I had found my passion, and I excelled in it. I could have done more; however I could prolong being in the same room with Bess Holland would have been worth every effort, but Lady Bess knew how to leave a man wanting.

"Our guest has a long trip ahead of him and we should not want him on the road after dark," she said.

"Where is he going?" asked Mary. "Could he stay another night?"

"He must return to the priory. They are expecting his return.

Besides, I am not the mistress here. I cannot give him permission to stay."

"Then we shall ask mother!" chimed the two children, jumping up.

They both started for the door, and I could read in Bess's face a subtle weariness intuiting how that would likely play out. I suspected she was still tired from her illness and not embracing the thought of confrontation either from the Duchess or the children.

"You must listen to your governess," I said, stopping them short. Then, hating to have to say it, "and I must return to Thetford." I could see I had saved Lady Bess from an unpleasant conflict and I hoped that her relief wasn't from me leaving soon. "But if it pleases you and if your mother is willing, I will return and give you a proper demonstration of my juggling skills."

At this suggestion, even Lady Bess cheered. "Kronos, we should very much enjoy having you visit again."

I nearly leapt with joy, but I hid my giddy smile with a quick bow to compose myself. No monk or duty at Thetford Priory could keep me from denying Lady Bess. I would find an excuse to come. I would lie to make it happen.

I left Kenninghall knowing I would see her again. I had hope in my heart.

CHAPTER NINE

For most of my journey, I thought about Bess and
Kenninghall. The Duchess's concern for the young
governess was wholly dependent upon Bess's usefulness to
her. Bess tolerated her misuse without complaint, but I wondered
if she dreamt of being free from the conventions of a manor
house? Or did she dream of being mistress of her own manor?
Would she be charitable if given the opportunity, or was the
Duchess's strident manner how noble women behaved?

In a sense, Bess was consigned to this life because her father
was the duke's right-hand man. Just as I was beholden to the
priory, we were both prisoners of our circumstantial births. For
her, the only escape from a given path, was marriage. Marry
well or forever live in regret. Though she came from wealth, the
chances for contentment seemed far slimmer for Lady Bess than
for me.

I was aware of the social boundaries imposed on us by birth,
but I did not fully accept them. My indifference was caused, in
part, by my ignorance of the outside world and my isolation from
it. But something inside of me always made me rail against expectations. Because I was so obviously different, I came to embrace

my individuality and it began to shape my decisions. Looking back, this brazen confidence was built on inexperience—a precarious foundation and one not worthy of supporting a single toe. I was still young and had much to learn.

As I neared Thetford Priory, my thoughts turned to Brother Giles. If he had not survived, I might be held responsible. I gave him the remedy; they thought I hadn't the proper knowledge to administer it. I slowed my horse to a plodding walk. Would I be spending the next few months in penance, atoning for my sins?

By the time I neared the priory, the dark curtain of celestial wonderment ruled, and I made out the nave's silhouette against a waxing gibbous moon. Usually, the familiar smell of earth in the adjacent moss-laden woods comforted me, for I'd spent hours in those woods collecting scapes and truffles and contemplating the towering oaks. This time, the scent filled me with a sense of dread thinking what awaited me on my return. I pulled my mount to a stop and stared at the flicker of lights in the refectory windows. Soon the monks would retire for the evening, waking at night vigil for more prayers and then return for more sleep.

A choice.

I could flee. I could spur my horse on and travel. I could turn back to Kenninghall. I looked over my shoulder in the direction of Lady Bess. But there would be no place for a dwarf in a bustling manor home. If I returned to the priory, would I face punishment for Brother Giles' condition or his possible demise? They would have to decide if my action was careless or intentional. But if I returned to the priory, I could wait for the right opportunity to leave. A flick of my wrist either way, and it would be decided.

I remained motionless, imagining myself with Lady Bess, indulging in every fantastical permutation—both chivalrous and depraved. I could have sat all night at the edge of the woods, contemplating, but the call of an owl reminded me of my place. I was not ready to leave Thetford Priory. My conscience still bore the weight of religious influence, and while I did not know what awaited me there, I could not ignore my responsibility. I watched until the last flicker of candle was snuffed, then I walked my horse to the stable and slept in the straw until morning.

⁓

My dreams were interrupted by a swift boot in the arse.

"'Tis a sin to leave a tired horse bearing his saddle and bit after a long ride," said the ostler. "Then ye block 'is stall with your lazy, inept self. You be lucky he didn't stomp yer fool head."

"I was long tired," I said, squinting up at him. "I was not thinking."

"Doesn't justify 'is poor treatment none. Credit him a better horse than ye deserved."

I wished the stableman would let me be. My arms itched from sleeping in the hay and my sleep had been fitful. "I did not want to wake anyone," I said. "'Twas late and everyone had retired."

"There is no retiring here in the stables, and no excuse for treating your ride so poorly. I shall speak to Brother Ulric about you mucking stalls in recompense."

I did not argue. Indeed, I was too tired to face the long looks awaiting me in the infirmary and shovelling horse manure all day seemed preferable.

The ostler brought me an apple and cheese to assuage my appetite, and kept me working well into the afternoon. I not only cleaned my horse's stall but six others in addition. It was late to the day before I returned to the infirmary. I sheepishly poked my head into the herbarium and found Brother Ulric with his back to me, mincing willow root. A mound of dried herbs was piled on the table before him. He must have sensed my presence and looked around. Either that or the smell of horse manure preceded me.

"You've returned."

"Aye, master." I took a hesitant step into the workroom.

"You need to change your clothing," he said, stating the obvious. "And scrub yourself."

That was all he said. He did not ask after Mistress Holland or Kenninghall, but neither did I inquire after Brother Giles. I knew him well enough to sense that he was not pleased with me and he would have more to say once I returned.

The chamberlain had not yet dumped a tub of tepid water for laundering sheets.

"'Tis good enough for the likes of you," he said, upon seeing me.

I gritted my teeth against the cool water and air of the lavatorium and scrubbed the stink of stable from my skin. A dip in the murky pond at Thetford's edge would have left me cleaner. I took my time dressing, then emptied the water into a trough which carried it away with the rest of the day's used water. Rather than cross through the infirmary past Brother Giles's pallet, I walked around the exterior of the building, which gave me time to prepare myself. I entered the herbarium through the garden door.

Brother Ulric was sealing the cork on a jar of his latest concoction. The heavy drops of wax languidly fell. I tried to gauge his mood in the flickering flame, but Brother Ulric can be as even tempered as a rod of iron. He blew out the candle and laid it on the table.

"That is an improvement," he said, noting my more presentable person. He set the jar on a shelf then took a seat on a bench, motioning for me to sit opposite.

His formality set me on edge. All was not well at Thetford Priory; I could see it in his face. The quiet was unbearable and my overactive mind began imagining scenarios. Unable to wait one breath more, I said, "Brother Giles…" for wasn't the elderly monk on both our minds?

Brother Ulric studied my face before answering. "He is alive." He said this in a way that was not so decisive. I sensed the word 'however' and information being withheld.

My shoulders dropped and the air moved through my nostrils in a long exhalation.

Brother Ulric peered over the rims of his spectacles. "He requires more attention and care than before. This recent incident has robbed him of vigour."

I waited for him to explain. Perhaps if I voiced a platitude of concern, it might allay his misgivings. But why struggle to sound convincing?

"Keep away from him, Kronos."

Something unspoken lurked behind this request and made me uneasy. I waited for an explanation and I agonised whether I should inquire, *why*? Instead, I sat. Silent and uncertain.

Brother Ulric continued. "He is uncomfortable around you."

"Brother Ulric, he has always felt that way." I was not going to mention that I believed Brother Giles incapable of even the smallest amount of human compassion required to accept me as one of God's creatures. To Brother Giles I *was* a "creature", an aberration of God's image if ever there was one.

"Instead of you serving his meals, Brother Trelli's boy will serve him. You will empty his chamber pot. Nothing more."

I resisted delving into Brother Giles's reasons for despising me so. Brother Ulric would not hear about or acknowledge the old monk's prejudice. I was left to try to comprehend the old man's hate in whatever way suited me. Requiring me to empty the old monk's chamber pot told me what Brother Ulric would not.

Rather than reiterate my response to the old man in the cloister that day, I simply accepted my master's request. I would avoid the old goat and leave him gasping for breath the next time he was in trouble.

"What did you find at Kenninghall?" asked Brother Ulric, returning to other matters.

"Mistress Holland was again taken with fever and chills, debilitating headaches. I gave her your tisane and she recovered soon after."

"It sounds like the symptoms of ague," he said. "Is this her first relapse since last we visited?"

"Her nursemaid spoke of no other."

"Odd that her symptoms took so long to cycle."

"I left her with remedies for a throbbing head and the remainder of the tisane. However, I doubt it will be enough should she fall ill again."

"I will make more and send you to deliver it in a fortnight."

Brother Ulric's instructions regarding Brother Giles stopped mattering to me. Soon I would be visiting Mistress Holland, delivering more medicine, and I didn't even have to contrive an excuse for going. I could endure the worst Brother Giles could sling at me for the opportunity to see the lovely Bess one more time.

That night I helped in the infirmary kitchen preparing a thick stew for the few elderly and infirmed monks in our care. Brother

Ulric worked in the pharmacy. I was setting out a stack of bowls when Pinter Pender strode into the kitchen.

"Prior Ixworth wishes to speak with you," he said, helping himself to a carrot on the board.

"With me?"

"I see no one else standing here." He took a bite and chewed with his mouth open.

"What does he want to speak to me about?"

Pender shrugged. "I imagine there is plenty for him to say. Go to him after Terce tomorrow." He nibbled on the carrot and sauntered towards the door, stopping once as if to say something else but thinking better of it, and walked on.

I'd never spoken to Prior Ixworth before. The Prior never troubled with the lay brothers or anyone who was not a monk or novice. An intangible air of superiority, or perhaps just piety, insulated him from the common and mundane routine that characterised everyday life at Thetford. When one is singled out from a sea of fish, one can't help wondering why. Living in a monastery had taught my conscience to think in terms of sin and transgression. Was this to do with Brother Giles, or had one of the monks noticed my interest in the forbidden transcripts tucked in the dark corners of the library? Had they seen into my soul and deemed me unworthy? It was with some diffidence that I served the meal that evening in the infirmary. As I set the bowls before the aged and the infirmed, I couldn't stop wondering what the Prior wanted with me.

I had spent the day tending to my chores in the infirmary and garden and never so much as glanced at Brother Giles sitting in a chair next to his bed for what appeared to be the greater part of the afternoon. I gathered the old monk had recovered enough to be there and was probably just as tetchy as before.

That evening, the Windrow boy was not available to serve

the evening meal. Brother Ulric could not leave his latest concoction, and with a sigh he gave me leave to serve Brother Giles and the others.

"He'll just have to accept it, or else he'll have to wait for me to finish this. It might be quite a while."

I took my time preparing the tray and ladling the stew into Brother Giles's bowl. It would be the first time since the incident that I would have dealings with him. It was with some trepidation that I approached the old man sitting at a table where he had been brought to join the others. The monks watched me near, their eyes flicking from me to Brother Giles and back again. I offered no words in explanation, nor did I greet him. I placed the bowl on the table and continued serving the others.

The old monk stared at the bowl. He did not sign the cross, nor did he offer a prayer or a single word of grace. I almost wondered if his sight had worsened, but then, in a burst of petulance, he pushed the bowl away, the stew sloshing onto the table.

Perhaps I should have walked off and let the matter alone, but I still desired to appear honourable in the eyes of the other monks.

"Brother Giles, it is a beef broth thickened with barley," I said. "You've found it agreeable in the past."

When he did not respond, I sniffed the bowl, wondering if the meat had gone off, but I detected nothing foul.

He set his jaw and his head and hands began rattling from his tremors.

"Why do you refuse your food?" Not getting a response, I glanced at the other monks. None of them met my eye. "Should I call for Brother Ulric?" I asked of them.

Not a single monk gave me so much as a nod or grunt in reply.

"Do you want bread instead, Brother Giles?" I set a small manchet loaf before him. "Brother Trelli baked it this morning."

He stared at the bread, trembling.

Exasperated, I let him be and tended to the remaining brethren. The other monks accepted their portions without complaint or comment. They glanced at Brother Giles, then took up their spoons to eat.

I returned to Brother Ulric still working on his distillation.

"Shall I bring your bowl so that you may eat?" I asked.

"Save my portion for later, Kronos."

I hesitated, wondering if I should tell him of Brother Giles's behaviour. For one, I did not want to alert Brother Ulric to more conflict between the old monk and myself. It seemed obvious the old monk refused his dinner because I had served it. But I wondered if his refusal was perhaps a result of his slow recovery. Was I expected to spoon it into him?

"Brother Giles is not eating," I said.

"An old man's appetite is not the same as a young man's. Leave him be, he may partake later."

I looked at the distillation apparatus, the tarnished copper coils sloping down and ending with the steady drip of purified essence collecting in a glass vesicle. Perhaps to find the true essence of anything, it must first be placed in fire.

"Prior Ixworth has asked to speak with me," I said.

"Yes," replied Brother Ulric, without shifting his gaze.

"You are aware?"

"Yes."

I had always respected Brother Ulric and thought him the most forthcoming of any monk at Thetford Priory. Perhaps I was mistaken to think that he had seen potential in me. I had been in his tutelage long enough for him to realise my ability. For years I'd met his encouragement to become a physician with scepticism; thinking that I would fail because of my physical appearance and people's aversion, not because I lacked the wit for understanding tinctures. All of this schooling in plants and their healing qualities…was it all for naught?

I lingered, hoping Brother Ulric might tell me what to expect, offer some advice, or at least prepare me for meeting the prior. Instead, he extinguished the small fire burning under the mother receptacle and removed his apron to hang on a hook.

"Kronos, I should like to finish this and have my dinner."

It was then that I realised, whatever shame might befall me, I was to endure it alone.

That night, I listened to the rhythmic breathing of novices sleeping beside me, their souls at enviable peace. Their contemplative faces reflected the Queen Moon's generous gaze; her silver light bathing them so that they looked like a row of marble effigies. A novice must have a desire for order and subservience to become a monk. They must abandon their human passions, or at least curb them to follow their Godly path. Staring up at the beams, I concluded that I possessed no desire to stem my inclinations before I had experienced them to their full. What is the sense of living if one must be constantly denied?

While I was grateful to the monks for taking me in, for feeding and educating me, I cannot refute that I nursed a kernel of resentment. That resentment was the unspoken expectation that I was indebted to them. Because they had invested their time and effort in shaping me, in giving me a home, they expected unequivocal conformity and loyalty to their way of life. I couldn't do it. I knew that I could not conform. Perhaps they knew it, too.

The next morning, I worked in the cloister garden with an ear for the call to morning office. Brother Ulric followed the line of monks walking to the nave as I collected cranesbill for his return. When I'd finished, I left the basket on his board and headed to the cloister. On my way, I paused outside the Prior's lodgings, then hurried on.

Chants filled the open clerestory and flowed into the adjoining garth where I sat on a bench and listened. Though the stone walls amplified the song and the lilting melody enveloped me, my inner dialogue of apprehension could not be muted. Once Terce was over, I would meet with Prior Ixworth.

The last note faded and I hesitantly entered the nave to wait for the Prior as the monks exited. The monks filed past, some meeting my eyes, most averting their gazes as if I didn't exist.

The massive door was closed after the last monk, leaving me alone to ponder my predicament. I stared at the blurred edges of colour cast by the stained glass windows on the tiled floor rather than watch the Prior finish his prayers. What biblical scene created this particular patchwork of splendid hues? Following the beams of colour to their source, I found Judas reaching for his bag of silver.

"Kronos," said Prior Ixworth, interrupting my study. He gestured for me to follow him to his lodgings where he kept a separate room for conference. Inside, every window was made of stained glass even more brilliant than those in the nave, and on the wall behind his desk, a tapestry depicting Belshazzar feasting while Persian soldiers gathered outside his city's gates hung in reproachful warning. A stack of books and leatherbound portfolios sat neatly arranged on his desk. Beside them, a quill and decorative silver pot of ink. An unlit brazier took up one corner and I presumed that he kept comfortably warm during the raw winter days when the cold blew down from the north and inevitably seeped between the cracks in the window fittings. His was a comfortable existence, as affluent and easy as a nobleman's.

He invited me to sit opposite him and I climbed onto a chair. I peered across the wide expanse of desk, feeling insignificant. Rather than show him the bottom of my sandals, I scooched towards the edge so that I could bend my knees and dangle my legs. Even though my toes barely grazed the floor, at least I didn't look like a child in an adult chair. Expressionless, Prior Ixworth folded his hands and waited for me to settle.

He was as opposite a man to me as one could imagine. His height placed him a head taller than most, and though he was in his senior years he appeared spry and sharp of mind—a man not to be trifled with. His clear blue eyes considered me, stripping me of my courage and leaving me feeling exposed and vulnerable. Finally, he spoke.

"Kronos, you've been at the priory for how long?"

I was not one to keep count, but Brother Dowser reminded me this past winter how many years it had been since he scooped me out of the midden heap. "Sixteen years, abouts," I answered.

His brow flicked almost imperceptibly.

"And what is your opinion of our brotherhood?"

"Prior Ixworth, if I had not been discovered those many years ago, I would have frozen solid to the midden heap then been spread like manure upon the garden in the spring. It is a kindness that I was taken in by the priory." I smiled, but saw no softening in the Prior's face. "I have been educated and fed, I've been given shelter when I have not deserved it, and I have been spared from a life of toil and ridicule."

"It would follow that you have an obligation to the priory," he replied.

Though I yearned for the chance to experience life beyond the priory's walls, in truth, I had not devised a plan to do so. I was not prepared to leave the safety of Thetford Priory. My breath grew shallow waiting for him to continue.

"We had expectations that you would become a novice." He paused; I suppose to gauge my reaction.

I sat as stoically as I could.

He continued, "However, I have been informed that you do not wish to further your service to God."

For all of my bluster, I lacked the spine to agree. If I said yes, I could be released from Thetford immediately. I thought of Mistress Holland and my chance to see her under the auspice of the priory and Brother Ulric. Delivering the medicine to her was my only viable excuse to be allowed into Kenninghall. My mind whirled. I needed a plan.

"I admit that I do not think myself worthy of God's path." My words sounded partly true, but I was hedging and I hoped the Prior didn't notice.

He turned his head slightly as if observing me from the side of his eye, as if he couldn't decide what to think of me.

"We are all unworthy, Kronos. You would do well to remember that."

He could have interpreted my hesitancy as a form of deception. A crooked way to play for time and delay my decision. But, in truth, my inferiority was one reason why I patently did not want to become a monk. Every day I would be reminded of my pointless existence. As far as I could tell, God would never be pleased with my service to Him.

"It is time for you to make a decision." Those blue eyes bored into me, trying to read what might be sloshing about in my head.

My armpits became as wet as a baptismal font.

He continued. "Let me simplify it for you. Either become a novice, or be dismissed from Thetford Priory."

I had been cast out once before. The monks had rescued me

from a midden heap, but now it was their turn to abandon me. Who would save me this time? "If I stay, will I continue to help Brother Ulric in the infirmary?"

"Only until a suitable apprentice is found to replace you." He looked down at the portfolio on his desk and straightened it. It didn't need straightening.

I sensed there was more he could say, but that he chose not to say it. Brother Ulric had been reticent since my return. Had this meeting been discussed between them? For cert, this meeting had been prompted by the incident with Brother Giles.

For all his authority and pressing matters needing his attention, Prior Ixworth was a patient man. He understood the serious nature of this question and knew that a man must come to his decision in his own time. He seemed prepared to wait—at least for one more minute.

A rill of perspiration snaked down my spine, exploring every vertebra on its journey, then pooled at the small of my back.

There was no more delaying the inevitable.

"Prior Ixworth, I will take the cowl."

CHAPTER TEN

BROTHER PAGE CUT off the bottom half of a habit and showed me how to wield a needle to stitch a hem. I spent my first morning sewing between prayers and pricking my fingers, leaving dots of blood on the cloth. Pinter Pender (now Brother Pender) strolled by; his eyes full of snide amusement. He had long since taken his sacred vows and I expected he would use his seniority to lord over me and remind me of my place.

"You had a change of heart, I see," he said, stopping to watch me fumble with the needle.

"I am of the same heart as always, but now I know its place."

His eyebrows raised and I returned to my task rather than grow more irritated by his obvious scepticism.

"So, you are done working in the infirmary," he commented.

"More time to devote to prayer and meditation," I said.

He gave a short snort of derision. "It is because of that incident with Brother Giles. Brother Ulric won't have you anymore."

I drew the needle through the cloth and set my project in my lap. "It is because I have chosen the brotherhood and must follow the path. I did what I could to help him. Brother Ulric knows that."

"Your account differs from Brother Giles's."

"Of course it does. Brother Giles can barely remember what he had to eat an hour before." I picked up my needle and pushed it through the cloth, pricking my finger underneath. Since the time I'd first come to work in the infirmary, Brother Giles had never trusted me. I had cared for him, served him, and fed him. But with every passing month, I had seen the old monk become more distrustful and peevish. Surely, I could not have been the only one to notice his decline. Even Brother Ulric had schooled me in how to handle the old man's temper.

"Is it age that compromises his memory…or something else?" replied Pinter Pender.

I looked up. "What do you mean? What are you implying?"

"Brother Giles says you tried to poison him."

Was this widespread hearsay or was Pender goading me? "Brother Giles imagines things. Ask Brother Ulric. He knows my side of the story."

"Oh, he has been asked." Pinter Pender picked up the cross hanging around his neck and looked it over. "Brother Ulric said he was not present at the time. He said that he was unable to comment on the matter."

If what Pinter Pender said was true, the hurt drilled down to the core of my soul.

He continued, "You do not care for Brother Giles…and he does not care for you."

"Brother Giles has always been difficult," I said. "I have worked for my master long enough that he knows my ability… and my character."

"So, you hold no animus towards a man accusing you of trying to murder him?"

Here was an old, addled monk corrupting my standing in the monastery. His health was so poor, his mind so addled, how could he possibly influence others? I didn't deserve this enmity. The old monk was not long for this world, of that I was certain. I kept my mouth shut and returned to my stitching despite Pinter Pender's effective needling.

Pender headed towards the door. "Seems Brother Giles still holds sway around here."

As a novice, I got a true taste of monastic life. Until my new labour was assigned, my days consisted of prayer and meditation. I looked forward to my time in the library for reading and studying. The pretext afforded me the chance to read my favourite poems by bawdy Catullus secretly tucked inside my copy of the Benedictine Rule. I assumed that I would still be given leave to take Brother Ulric's tisane to Mistress Holland in a few days' time. By now I knew the way to Kenninghall and its inhabitants had become familiar with me. My visit was the one thing that I looked forward to in my newly restricted life, the constraints of which I found worse than being an apprentice to either Brother Trelli or Brother Ulric.

One afternoon, after I had finished my studies, I visited Brother Ulric. I wanted to remind him of my upcoming journey and be certain that the tisane would be ready. It was with some reservations that I approached the herbarium, for I had not spoken to him since choosing my new path. As I neared Brother Ulric's workplace, a young boy hurried out the door, basket in hand, no doubt off to gather ingredients. No time had been wasted in replacing me.

Brother Ulric had been nothing but kind and accepting of me up until the incident with Brother Giles, yet I couldn't help but feel betrayed that he did not come to my defence when I needed him to. He chose not to vouch for my character, and the resentment that caused was still fresh in my mind.

He was not in the herbarium, and after a search in the cloister garden I found him collecting peppermint behind the infirmary. His glasses sat on top of his head as he bent over to snip several sprigs. The sun reflected off his lenses like two small mirrors shining on me.

"Brother Ulric," I said, replacing my usual "master" with the more egalitarian address. "I wanted to remind you that I am still delivering Mistress Holland's tisane to Kenninghall."

He rose up to his full height and peered down at me. "You have sought permission from Brother Froude?"

"I have. He has agreed that I should fulfil my promise to you."

He tilted his head. "Promise?"

"My obligation," I corrected myself. Perhaps I was overly sensitive and trying to pick my words too carefully so as not to displease.

Brother Ulric set his spectacles on his nose and studied me. "The meadowsweet has dried and I will have the remedy ready for you. I have not forgotten." He tossed the stems into his basket and stepped out of the garden onto the path. "You have surprised me, Kronos. Your decision to join the brotherhood is unexpected."

"I am not ready to face the world on my own."

"Insecurity is not a reason to choose the brotherhood. I should hope there is more to your decision than the wish to avoid discomfort and uncertainty."

I was not going to lie and tell him that I wished to follow God's path. He knew me well enough to recognise my insincerity and to make me uncomfortable by questioning my motive.

"May I carry that for you?" I asked of his basket of herbs.

"If you would take them to Brother Trelli that would be appreciated."

I welcomed the chance to avoid further discussion, yet I wanted to leave by doing him a kindness; perhaps it would improve my standing in his eyes.

⚭

Brother Trelli took the basket and dumped the stems onto a wood tray. "Many of us were surprised by your decision," he said, picking out an orange beetle and flicking it away. "You've been given a second chance."

"A second chance?"

"You were nearly expelled. Brother Giles says you tried to poison him."

"He's an old dote. He and his rattlepated ideas. I cannot be the only one who has noticed his delusional claims." To my mind, Brother Giles's word had been given undeserved precedence in the sense that he once had a reputation for being a gifted scholar. I was nothing but a misshapen lump of flesh—a kitchen helper and jake changer in the infirmary. Weary of their baseless beliefs, I sought to dispel the notion of my ill-intent by being forthcoming. I would challenge their thinking.

Brother Trelli bundled a group of stems and wound them with string. "Even men of God struggle with innate misconceptions. Kronos, you must realise that you will always be subject to men's suspicions."

"Because I am a dwarf? I had no more say in the matter than you did in determining the colour of your eyes!"

"I merely point out the hypocrisies of man. The brethren are not immune. Some are more aware of their faults than others."

"But to suspect evil of me because of my physical appearance?"

"Man rejects snakes because we do not understand them."

"Man rejects snakes because they represent deceit and the original sin. It is a burden man has placed on them." I gathered a group of stems and handed them to him.

"Mayhap that is part of it, but a snake has no arms or limbs. It is unlike any other creature."

"And I am unlike any other creature?" I said, indignant. "Is that a reason to distrust me?"

"It is not," said Brother Trelli, "but you know it to be true."

Frustration boiled beneath my skin. If I was not accepted here, if I could not be trusted at Thetford Priory—a monastery full of chaste and pious men—where could I go where people judged me on my character and not on my appearance? As a wave of heat rolled up my neck, it occurred to me that perhaps Brother Trelli simply wanted me to understand my circumstance. Perhaps he did not wish to demoralise me. Perhaps he simply wished to slap me in the face with the immutable fact that I would always suffer in the eyes of others. Even here at Thetford, I would not find sanctuary.

No matter what I did, no matter how loyal or obedient, how earnest my effort, I would never be trusted. My dwarfism gave men pause. My strangeness gave men permission to distrust and to hate me. If I was physically afflicted, then surely, I was morally afflicted as well.

I could fight against this notion—I could spend my life trying to disprove people's suspicions—or I could give myself permission to do as I wanted because the outcome would be the same.

The days leading up to my visit to Kenninghall, I woke every night for Vigils, and every morning for Lauds. I said my prayers and put aside my Roman poet for Saint Benedict's rule. My ostensive sincerity could give the brothers no excuse to dismiss me before my visit to Kenninghall. In truth, I was disinterested, but I would do nothing that might interfere with me seeing Mistress Holland again. The monks continued to whisper and cast disapproving glances, which I bore with humility.

And I wished the worst for Brother Giles.

The night before my journey I could not sleep. Rather than think on my sins and mutter prayers of forgiveness, I imagined lovely Bess sitting astride my lap with my habit bunched around my waist and her kirtle hiked above her legs. We rocked like boats in a wake while I buried my face between her breasts, imagining their softness…feeling safe haven until she…until I…finished myself quietly without waking my fellow brethren.

Would I blush when next I saw her? Nay, it was my secret, but I share it with you.

Brother Ulric had prepared an ample supply of remedy, negating the need for me to travel to Kenninghall to deliver again anytime soon. He included a variety of cures for the more common complaints—healing balms for cuts and rashes, a carminative for the easing of gastric bloat, two types of sleeping draughts, and an expectorant. He gave me instructions on their use and dosage which I would relay word for word. I waited as he checked their seals then wrapped them in cloth to prevent breakage. When he was done, I packed them carefully in my pannier.

"You are accustomed to the route?" he inquired.

"I could travel it with my eyes closed."

"Do not dawdle, you invite highwaymen to take advantage of you."

"Do not concern yourself, Brother Ulric. My skills as a horseman are much improved since you and I first travelled."

He peered at me over his spectacles, giving me that familiar 'beg to differ, but deciding to leave well enough alone' look. Besides, I would walk to Kenninghall if I had to.

I was boosted on to my horse, a new mount, which I welcomed, not wishing a repeat performance from the skittish geld who made his way to Kenninghall without me. The sky threatened rain but the clouds moved with visible speed. At some point the wet would come, but I wagered it would not last and I would be left with tolerable conditions for most of my ride. In the event that I should arrive soaked through, I had a change of clothes—my old attire that I wore as Brother Ulric's apprentice. Once one becomes a novice, one usually disposes of such effects of secular life, but since there was no one to discourage me, I gladly chose practicality over devotion.

Dinbrow—for that was my horse's name—and I set out at a smart pace on the road to Kenninghall. Once free of Thetford Priory and its bordering woods, the green fields stretched before us on either side, intersecting with the occasional hedge and stands of oak. I breathed deep, as if inhaling the entirety of the expanse before me. There are times in life when such beauty and freedom can create such an unshakeable joy of spirit that even when the clouds opened and cold rain splattered down my front, I laughed and tilted my face skyward, cackling like a madman.

My journey to Kenninghall seemingly took less time because I rode with an anticipation and acceptance of myself that I had rarely experienced up until then. Call it faith in oneself, being at peace, or merely a naïve expectation that one's hope might soon be fulfilled.

I arrived at the door of Kenninghall late to the afternoon. My habit had not dried and I smelled of wet wool. A servant greeted me with surprise—from expecting someone taller? Or perhaps their astonishment was from seeing me clad in a Benedictine robe. To his credit, he quickly recovered and led me to a room off the larder where I waited for the clerk of the kitchen.

Sitting in the stark confines of that room, I listened to the kitchen staff readying for the evening meal. Priority was given to serving the family and the steward's family. Once that had been accomplished, an efficient and neatly dressed clerk greeted me.

He cleared his throat and addressed me uncertainly. "Brother Kronos," he said, questioningly. The last time I had visited, I was simply Kronos.

"Novice Kronos," I corrected.

"You are welcome to join the kitchen staff for dinner."

"Afterward I shall meet with Mistress Holland?"

"It is unnecessary," he replied. "I shall take copious notes and deliver them to the steward."

"I have instructions from Brother Ulric to question her about the course of her malady," I said. This was entirely untrue, but it sounded reasonable and of good conscience. "He wishes to understand more about her course of illness. The knowledge would benefit him in his search for a cure."

"I shall inquire with the lady," he said. "However, it is too late in the day for a return journey to Thetford, so we shall have a bed prepared for you." At this point I did not need to press the importance of a meeting, but the thought of her reluctance had me scheming an alternative excuse should I need one.

I followed him to the kitchen, where I was remembered by the staff and a place was set for me. Their conversation grew suddenly stilted, which I attributed to the habit I now wore.

"I have not taken my vows," I told them, breaking the uneasy silence. "So, I am no better than the worst of you. I have more years as a layman than as a man of God. Call me Kronos, as you did before, and do not think me pious."

A few crossed themselves, ensuring God's forgiveness,

and the servants' general spirit lifted. Interrupted stories were taken up again, and soon the room was filled with the laughs and exclamations of camaraderie, that is until the clerk of the kitchen returned.

"Mistress Holland will see you in the morning," he said, his voice cutting through the respectful silence. "She will send for you when she is ready." The clerk exited to shifting glances and a discreet cough.

Rather than ask what tattle occupied their minds, I returned to my soup and waited for someone to comment. A manor is not a priory and servants are not beholden to discretion or silence when eating.

"If she can be wrenched away from the adoring gaze of our Lord," said the gardener under his breath.

"So like the king," added the cook. "The duke has lost his wits for a woman young enough to be his daughter."

I was stunned to learn this of Bess. My heart sank. The duke was a married man. Where was his restraint? Surely this sordid attraction could not have been her doing. But neither had I heard that the king had forsaken Queen Catherine.

"The king is enamoured of another?" I asked.

"He is taken with the duke's niece! Rumoured a beauty and French-bred," said the cook, pinching a sly grin.

The servants chortled and there was some elbow-jabbing.

"And familiar with French ways," said the gardener. A string of drool stretched to his soup, and I wondered if it was from his meal or his imagination.

"Our queen will not abide such behaviour," said a servant, an older man with a ruddy complexion and thin lips.

"Indeed! She is above it. No doubt the king has tired of her."

When the staff had stopped tittering, the cook attempted to correct their wayward assumptions.

"It is not just his niece's French ways that so intrigues our king," said the cook. "He has no heir to the throne. Unfortunately, Queen Catherine is past her prime."

"Oh, there is Princess Mary," said the scullery maid. For such a low office in the hierarchy of Kenninghall, she had high aspirations for the daughter of the king.

"A girl, and of no use," said a servant.

"There is the bastard, Fitzroy," offered another.

"Also, of no use!" said the cook.

"It is not for us to opinionate. The king has his duty to England and must secure the succession. 'Elst we be ruled by foppish hidalgos and frog lickers."

The staff grew sullen as they mulled over this possibility.

"Is the duke's arrangement with Bess Holland agreeable to the Duchess?" I ventured.

"Heavens no!" said the cook.

"We hear the shrieks and collect the broken crockery as proof of her displeasure," said a chambermaid.

"But he will not hide his intrigue. Indeed, he seems to enjoy flaunting his infidelity. As if rousing the duchess to heights of hysteria is as pleasurable as docking the Lady Bess," said the cook.

I was as gutted as the carp we ate for dinner.

Troubled into silence, I excused myself for the rest of the evening and sat brooding in my room.

The next morning, I was summoned to Lady Bess's room in a new section of Kenninghall, directly above the duke's quarters. The steward rapped on her door and announced me. Her room was no longer plainly appointed, but was now more sumptuous, in keeping with her newfound importance. Gone, too, was her simple governess's kirtle.

She sat at a desk, her back to me, the drape of her skirt pooled below her waist, creating a puddle of pine green velvet.

"Master Kronos, I am nearly finished." She spoke over her shoulder while she finished her writing. I stood quietly by, taking in the elaborate bed that now dominated the room. She laid down her quill and delicately blew on her missive.

"I am told that you have brought a bag full of potions."

"Indeed. Brother Ulric asked that I deliver them."

She put down her writing and turned to face me.

It was as if I had not seen her in a year. The maturity in her face left me speechless. Her features had not changed, but her demeanour had. She carried herself like a woman now. How else can I explain it without offending?

For her part, I do not believe she expected to see me wearing the robe of my order. She regarded me a moment, her face keen with interest.

"Shall I call you Brother Kronos?"

"My lady, I shall always be Kronos to you. I am not a brother."

"Oh? Is deception not dangerous for your soul?" She stood and walked over to me. "You were never invested in taking the vow. What has changed? Why the pretence?"

"I am not ready to leave Thetford." In truth, my only reason was so that I might see her again. But I could not say so.

"Why ever not? You had a desire to know the world."

I felt like a coward. I could not admit the real reason, and I looked spineless staying in the protection of the priory in order to spare myself the vicissitudes of the greater world.

"I still wish to leave. I have not, yet, figured out a plan."

"Who among us can follow our heart's desire without correcting its course? Do you still wish to juggle for the king?"

"I should like to view life at court. Seeing women dressed as you is preferable to seeing men dressed like me."

"Ah. You want to visit court, but not be a part of it?"

"I should like whatever I might be granted."

"Then you should endeavour to find your way there, Kronos."

"Is court *your* desire, my lady?"

"You are brazen to suggest it," said Lady Bess. She took no exception to my question; I was relieved she had not changed on that count. Indeed, the spark in her eyes implied it was exactly her desire. "If I should find my way there, I shall suggest your talent for entertaining."

"Thank you, my lady." I bowed in appreciation.

"But you must leave your protected world and learn something of the one outside its walls. I say this because life is a game. You must learn to play it."

"And if I leave Thetford Priory," I replied. "How will you know where to find me?"

"I am not concerned. If a man wants to be found, he makes sure he is noticed."

CHAPTER ELEVEN

S HE WOULD NOT now, nor would she ever, be my lover.
I knew that patently; and on my ride back to Thetford,
I tried to come to terms with my wounded heart. Bess Holland, whether through coercion or her own lustful desire, was the lover of the third Duke of Norfolk. Over time, I would learn more about the man and his reputation for being cruel and calculating and it would puzzle me why Bess would attach herself to him. Did she have a choice? Her father's employment at Kenninghall may have offered no alternatives. She may have been as much a prisoner of Kenninghall as I was of Thetford Priory.

My breath hitched as I wondered if I would ever see her again. Even if I could, I wondered if I should. Unfortunately, I could no longer hope for the chance delivery of medicine in order to visit her.

Halting in the woods next to the priory, I studied its walls and the soaring *Domus Dei* exterior. The monks' faint chanting carried on the late afternoon breeze. I scanned the priory against a backdrop of a setting sun, watched the stone façade fall into sharp relief against the bruising sky. My eyes settled on the midden heap tucked in a discreet corner. 'Tis from whence I came. Others were born by natural birth, they sucked a woman's teat, but not me. My life started in a pile of turd. I am not like others. Why do I try to deny it?

I nudged my horse forward to the stables, and the ostler, having heard the clopping on cobbles, came out to meet me. He took hold of the bridle while I dismounted onto a block, then inspected his gelding with a keen eye from head to tail. After a small grunt of approval, he removed the pannier and handed it to me.

"Your ride appears to have fared better than your last mount."

"He didn't run off and abandon me like the other," I said.

I returned to the lavatorium to wash my face and scrub the grit from my feet. I had no sooner finished when Pinter Pender appeared seemingly out of nowhere.

"Kronos, you have returned," he said. "Brother Trelli wants to see you."

"Brother Trelli?"

"You are not alone in being surprised by his request."

Though Brother Trelli desired my presence, I went to the herbarium to meet with Brother Ulric first, and let him know that the medicines were delivered to Kenninghall. On my way there, I walked through the infirmary and saw Brother Giles slumped in a chair, nodding off, a blanket covering his shoulders even though the air was temperate. Knowing he'd find the sight of me irritating, I walked directly towards him. When I got within a few feet, I greeted him loudly. His head jerked from my sudden address and once he saw it was me, he turned away until I'd passed.

Why should I not take some satisfaction in causing him a little distress when he had caused me so much more?

Brother Ulric was preparing a poultice when I entered.

"I delivered the remedies to Kenninghall with instructions

on how to use them," I said. "Mistress Holland appears healthy, as if she had never suffered from an illness."

He made no comment, and the awkward silence that had divided us of late seemed more palpable. If I wanted to have any conversation with him at all, I would be reduced to speaking about the cloud cover or some other tiddle. The division saddened me to the point where I could not bear the strain between us. Perhaps Bess Holland knew better than I that we had both reached a time in our lives when it was better to lay one's cards on the table and simply deal with the consequences. Nothing was gained by inaction and maintaining the current circumstance. But certainly, much could be lost.

"Brother Ulric," I said, "I can't ignore your change in attitude towards me. Am I correct that it stems from the incident with Brother Giles?"

He continued to mix the contents of his bowl. In my impatience I persisted. "You know me and my work here in the infirmary. Do you believe that I would purposely harm Brother Giles?"

Brother Ulric stopped stirring. He pushed his eye lenses back on his nose, then resumed mixing with faster strokes, the wet glop of mash forming a paste. "You do not want me to answer that."

"Unless you tell me otherwise, what shall I believe?"

The infirmarian kept his gaze on his mixture, refusing to meet my stare.

It was the second time in as many days that I would be forsaken and the hurt flowed from the pain of abandonment that I had never truly overcome. "What has turned you against me?"

My pitiful plea did not elicit Brother Ulric's sympathy. It was as if he'd hardened himself against the possibility well before I ever asked.

Now he looked up and set down his bowl. "I have known

Brother Giles for longer than you have been alive. I remember when his mind was so facile, he could recite the entire book of Psalms from memory. He was a most fair and thoughtful man. It has pained me to watch him physically decline. He has lost the ability to control his misgivings and relies on inchoate perceptions. His instincts have always been infallible. He is not the woolly-headed old man that you believe him to be."

"He never liked me," I said. At so young an age, what lad is practised in self-restraint? I was convinced that my master was wrong. From our very first meeting, Brother Giles had disliked me. I could not explain his revulsion except to attribute it to my appearance. Here, though, Brother Ulric was implying that there was something untoward, something sinister that tainted my being.

"I cannot speak for him," said Brother Ulric. He wiped the spoon against the bowl. "If you will," he said, setting the bowl aside and placing another in front of him. "I have work to do."

My dismay weighed so heavily on my mind that I forgot about Brother Trelli's request. I felt strangely absent reciting my liturgy, as if I were an empty vessel and someone else mouthed the words. When I sought to engage others, I sensed their hesitation. Brother Giles had so tainted them against me that I was now a scourge best to be avoided. I wondered how long it would be before my presence at Thetford was completely intolerable. Who would reach that conclusion first? Prior Ixworth—or me?

It was with some gladness that Brother Trelli sought me out later.

"I've lost the Windrow lad and I need help in the kitchen. Can you come between your studies?"

The simple joy of being needed lifted my spirits.

For the moment, helping Brother Trelli dulled my inner turmoil; for I knew, without a doubt, I would never be a monk. Not only had I no interest, but my brotherhood had no desire to keep me. It was only a matter of days before a decision had to be made—either by the Prior, or by me.

But where to go? The question kept me obedient and in my place.

Then came a day of profound consequence.

Winter had depleted the priory's larder, and the supply of cheese consisted of one small round of cheddar which would not last the week. Root vegetables were rotting and what few greens poked out of the ground had been judiciously harvested to get through another few days. Brother Trelli sent for a tenant farmer to bring what stores they could spare and with no inspection, purchased the contents of a cartload brought round by the farmer's daughter.

I was summoned to help unload the rounds of cheese and produce and to take them to the cellarium near the kitchen.

The maid was about my age, a flirtatious girl, who reserved her sly looks and comments for when we were alone or outside lifting wooden crates off the back of the cart. Mayhap she was as curious and as bored as I?

She seemed undeterred by the serious clime of the monastery. I found her liveliness infectious, though I remained careful to give the appearance of propriety within earshot of the kitchen. We had finished delivering the final wheels of cheese and were arranging the crates, stacking them into neat aisles, when she unexpectedly turned and pressed her hand where no one else ever had.

I sucked in my breath.

"You 'ave a pleasing face," said she, looking into my eyes. "Does your pipe touch your knees?"

"Keep your hand there," I breathed, "and we shall see."

She smiled. She kept her hand there.

I leaned against the crates of vegetables for fear I'd fall over. Her hand reached beneath my habit. A heady mix of anticipation, disorientation, and indifference fogged my mind. I cared not if my moans reached the celibate ears of Brother Trelli for this was my destiny! My bliss!

She playfully nipped my ear then whispered, "Turnabout is fair play."

She took my hand and led me to the back corner of the cellarium where she perched atop a sack of flour. There, she hoisted her skirt and leaned back. Before me was the deep secret of woman revealed. Catallus had not sufficiently prepared me for the wonder and magic of this.

Before I could think what to do, she placed her hands on either side of my face and guided me. She told me what to do, and I did it.

Tentative at first, I was soon expert. I felt myself recover and desired more than anything to feel myself become engulfed by her warm body. A fleeting thought of Bess mixed all of my sentiments of lust and love together. Gone were my inhibitions. Gone was my sense of time. Gone was my modesty. I realised then, that we are only true to ourselves when we abandon our morality and give over to physical desire.

However, the monks of Thetford Priory did not agree.

Nor did I make the argument to Brother Trelli when he found us.

The Jongleur

CHAPTER TWELVE

Y EAR MET the road before the rest of me did.
Sometimes the only way to move on is to be pushed.
How, then, did I find my way to King Henry
VIII's court? That is where I left off so many pages ago, only to
lull you into abject tedium with tales of my youth in a monastery.
Let me, then, capsulise my more formative years, a time in my
life where I came into my own—a time more influential than the
years I spent walking the halls of Thetford Priory.

The first day had been the most difficult.

To my advantage, the days were warming with the advent of
spring. The silky heat of sunshine on my face wasn't enough to
stave off the cool nights, but they were not so cold as to make me
desperate. I learned to make do with the curving roots of fallen
trees and shelters made of collected boughs. The monks stripped
me of any evidence that I might have been associated with them.
They took my homespun robe and returned my stained and worn
clothing of days past, when I was but a humble oblate before I
sought the cowl.

First on my mind was where to go? For as long as I had wondered about life outside the monastery walls, I had not thought

of, nor settled on, what I would do should the chance present itself. I knew the road to Kenninghall, but there was not much between Thetford and there. Nor did I know what lay beyond Kenninghall, except probably a broad expanse of sheep and then the sea. I needed some means to sustain myself, which meant I needed to walk in the direction of humanity. London was in the opposite direction of Kenninghall. How far? I would find out.

Food consisted of ramson and mushrumps foraged from the forest floor and eaten raw. This could not be sustained for the combination twisted my insides so that it was impossible to stand straight at times. I needed regular fare. Anything would be preferable to this banquet that created a constant bodily gale blowing from my arse.

The first place I came upon proved to be as good a home as I deserved. For a time, I worked in a tavern in Newmarket, having arrived there via the Icknield Way, the only viable road out of the dense forests on one side of Thetford and the flooding fens on the other. I slept in a stall with a horse named Jezebel at the adjoining inn and got accustomed to smelling like hay and horse manure. They set me to work in the kitchen, cooking and washing pots—my time with Brother Trelli had taught me well.

The barbs about my appearance became less stinging with time, and my banter became more sardonic, which sometimes got me chased around town until whatever instigator, usually a sot frequenting the tavern, gave up and went back to nod off in his trencher. Observing human nature in all of its profane variations became my fascination. At the priory, men's thoughts were concealed beneath the guise of propriety. A man struggled with his conscience with only God as his witness. In the small village of Newmarket, a man's struggles were often obvious, and if God was his witness, He didn't much seem to care.

Although I was noticeable and singled out by travellers

and newcomers, I mastered folding into the background and not drawing attention to myself. If I wanted a day of relative peace, I stayed quiet and unobtrusive. Did I want to remain in Newmarket blending into the suety daub walls of The Pickled Pigeon? Decidedly not. I kept my ears and eyes open for any opportunity that could possibly benefit me.

One came a couple of years later.

On the day of the Feast of St. Benedict, the cook at The Pickled Pigeon prepared a thick porridge of barley and cabbage. The day was more of a traditional observance than it was a religious one, only I had reason to reflect on the day with more introspection than most villagers. My only regret at leaving Thetford was that I had no further opportunities with the opposite sex. I remained impressively celibate, not wishing to end any worse off than after what had happened at Thetford.

The day started cool but warmed enough to bring winter weary villagers out in the hopes of putting colour back in their ashen faces. Women washed laundry in a pasture and dried it on the grass and hedgerows, children dashed about, the blacksmith flung open his doors, the waterwheel at the grain mill turned. A general liveliness to the day only grew when a wagon of strangers arrived in town. Their wagon drew interest, not because it was any different from any other in appearance, or that the goat tethered to its rear axle had ribbons braided through its beard, but because four men and one woman rode in it, looking not at all like farmers or traders.

Most notable was their matching mustard-coloured flat caps with impressively long plumes. Each of them wore the pretentious lids, even the woman. If they had hoped to slip in and out of Newmarket unnoticed, they had failed on that count. We soon realised that anonymity was not their intent. These travellers wanted to be seen.

They pulled their wagon in front of The Pickled Pigeon, left the driver to wait, and went inside. I followed, curiosity drawing me in, but as expected I was not allowed to dawdle and listen to their stories. The tavern wench pulled me by the ear and set me to work scrubbing pots. I was reduced to kitchen blateration to keep informed. Once their order of ale and bowls of soup were served, their tongues loosened and they spoke of their travels.

Here was an opportunity I had long hoped for. I sorely wanted to meet them and to hear what they had to say.

"Let me serve the next round of ales to the travellers," I pleaded to the tavern wench. "I can relieve you and you can rest."

She gave me a sidelong look as she poured the ale and set them on a board. "Mind ye bring me the coin. 'Tis a favour to you, not a help to me."

If I should be free of The Pickled Pigeon, I would have paid her five times over.

The entire tavern fell quiet when I appeared toting the second round of ales. Rarely did I serve. I wondered if the regular patrons preferred me to keep hidden? Did they think my strange self a reflection on them? For whatever story was being told, the entire troupe stopped their animated telling. Their eyes scrutinised every inch of me as I set an ale before each of them, the thud of each mug on the table the only sound.

"Little man," said one of them, a fellow named Daegan. "From whence do you come?"

"A midden heap at Thetford Priory."

"Those kind are a sneaky lot," said a second mustard-lidded performer with unsettling grey eyes. "Are you the afterbirth of a monk's carnal relations?"

In truth, the thought had never occurred to me. "If I am," I replied, "then it gives me great pleasure thinking it."

Daegan considered this with a look of interest. "Have you any talents besides serving ale?"

"I can juggle," I said, near to bursting so eager was I to tell them.

"Forsooth!" He exchanged glances with two of his troupe. "Are you worth our time to watch?"

"Verily, I believe it so."

"Then come by after we perform this eve, and you shall have our attention."

Perhaps that traveller from long ago was right. Perhaps my curse was in fact my gift. However, for as much as I desired it, adoption into their troupe was not for certain. They didn't want just an anomaly to attract customers, they wanted one who could perform.

That night I scrubbed every pot and dish doubly fast. It would be of some luck that most of the patrons at The Pickled Pigeon were more interested in the novelty of the troupe's entertainment than they were in their routine of getting drunk and pestering the tavern wench.

I arrived at the pasture as the woman sang a sweet lament that had nearly everyone to weeping. 'Twas about a duel of honour with a brother killing his sister's lover. The final verse she crooned:

> "She kiss'd his lips, she kaim'd his hair,
>
> As aft she had dune before, O;
>
> And there wi' grief her heart did break,
>
> Upon the banks o' Yarrow."

As the last note lofted across the quiet night, a murmur of sighs arose, bespeaking an audience familiar with heartbreak. Surely, she would not leave the villagers to return to their beds sorrowful. Not a soul stirred.

She had conjured a spell. The silence was as still as the blush on an apple. She remained quiet, her hand over her heart and her eyes focused on some distant love.

I squirmed. Only one woman held my heart, and she would never have me.

The audience continued to sink into the depths of pathos when suddenly, raucous tambourines jarred us from our maudlin thoughts. Soon the ground thumped with foot stomping and folks yelped and clapped to a bawdy broadside. People smiled and sang, they whooped and laughed.

This was spellcraft. I marvelled at this woman's ability to hold people rapt—she could send them into a wretched pit, let them dip their toes in the black water there. Then, quick as a nymph, she launched them free into a starry sky of joy. How different from the chants of monks hoping to elevate their spirits beyond their earthly shackles. This was more accessible and more to my liking.

I clapped and hooted as loud as any of them.

One by one the townsfolk sauntered home but my bed of straw could wait. I lingered until the final citizen dropped their penny into a pot, then approached the singer and the storyteller.

"'Tis the little man," said the storyteller, Daegan, upon seeing me. "Your townsfolk are most generous." He shook the pot of coins.

"Then you might stay for another night?" I asked.

The storyteller tutted. "We think the whole town came out tonight. It is not our habit to overstay." He handed the pot to the woman who peered into it and fished out a coin to pocket to no one's objection. "And have you come to entertain us or is there some other reason why you tarry?"

"I shall impress you with my juggling."

"Ho, such confidence! We shall see. It takes some effort to

amuse us." He gave me a puzzled look. "Well, now. What will you juggle?"

I had been so consumed with finishing my work at The Pickled Pigeon that I had forgotten to bring the turnips I had set aside.

"A juggler with nothing to throw?" He looked at the woman, then back at me. "Well, no matter. I shall remedy that." He disappeared to the wagon and left me with the singer, whose heavy-lidded eyes studied me indifferently. I would have to work hard to impress her. The rest of the troupe came round to see what was keeping them.

"Ah, so now we shall be entertained," said the piper. He set down his drum and laid his flute on top.

"Just looking at him is entertainment enough," said the lute player, and the two snorted.

Daegan returned and handed me an apple, a goose egg, a stick, and a knife.

I stared at the offering. The varied shapes and weights would be difficult if not impossible to juggle even on my best day.

"Why the mumpish countenance? Any juggler can circle turnips. We want to be impressed."

"I must familiarise myself with them first." After a moment of feeling their weight and thinking about how I might best juggle the knife without cutting myself, I looked up at them. "It would only take me a moment to run back to The Pickled to get my turnips."

"We'll be off to bed then. We haven't time to sit and wait." Daegan waved his troupe along. "Mayhaps tomorrow you will have found your wits." They began to walk back to their makeshift camp where one of them had succeeded in building a fire and erecting a tripod with a heavy pot hung over it.

"Wait!" I cried. Another day working at The Pickled Pigeon

had become suddenly intolerable. Besides, putting off performing would only stoke my unease. I would not sleep for anticipation and my worry would multiply my dread of failing. "I shall do it."

The troupe stopped and turned. They waited for me to begin, to show proof of my claim.

I tucked the knife under my arm and tossed the three objects in a circle until they felt comfortable in my hands. First the apple, then the egg…the dark night swallowed the objects making them almost invisible. I missed after a couple of rotations, dropping the apple. It rolled away, lost in the dark.

"You dropped," said Daegan, as if I hadn't noticed.

"It is fearsome difficult to see," I said, hoping they might ask me to come back when it was light. Instead, they waited for me to continue. "You are asking me to juggle a knife in the dark."

Daegan shrugged. "How expert are you?"

I began again; this time juggling the egg, the stick, and finally, the knife. At first, I had a rhythm and the weighty handle landed firmly in my palm. In that brief moment of thought, I dared not chance any dips or turns. The troupe would have to content themselves with a simple rotating circle. Though, if I did it well enough, if I could impress, then I might earn another chance to show them my tricks. But my mind had wandered from my focus (if only for half a thought). The blade sliced my palm and I dropped the knife, cursing.

"For a monk born and bred, ye sound like a grave digger!" said Daegan.

The sting of the wound brought tears to my eyes and I pressed my thumb into my hand trying to stop the pain and bleeding.

"Well, now," said the woman. "It has been a long day."

"Come Tish," said Daegan, draping his arm over her shoulders. "You must be hungry and this is a waste of our evening." They walked on and the others followed.

"This was a poor demonstration of my abilities. I'm not so poor a juggler," I told Daegan, running after. "It is nearly impossible to do what you've asked of me. I can't see in the dark!"

Daegan stopped, letting the troupe walk ahead. "We ask no more than a king would expect," he said. "You have the look to be of good entertainment. That is to your advantage. But I regret that you sorely lack talent. 'Tis a pity," he said, walking on. "You might have benefited us."

I watched him rejoin the others, leaving me to return to the stable and to make my bed in the hay.

Disappointment pained me more than my wounded hand, though. I could not sleep for fear that I was doomed to scrub pots at The Pickled Pigeon for the remainder of my days. Wide-eyed and determined, I collected my turnips, bandaged my palm, and practised juggling a knife into the mix. Jezebel watched with interest (or perhaps with concern). After several hours of rehearsal, I reached a point that I impressed even myself. But I was sore tired. My hand throbbed and my legs dragged me to bed in the hay where I slept past dawn.

The sharp tines of a pitchfork dug into the straw next to my cheek. My eyes flew open and peering down at me was the ostler.

"You have slept longer than your wont," he said. "I don't suppose The Pickled takes kindly to such laziness."

"It cannot be so late to the day that I am needed just yet," I said, scrambling to my feet. From the look of the sun, I may have been mistaken.

I snatched up my turnips and knife, not to forget them this time, and ran into the lane. They would put me to work if I showed my face in The Pickled Pigeon, so I took care to creep beneath the tavern window. Unable to resist looking, I peered over the sill and saw a sizable crowd taking their mid-day meal.

The kitchen would expect me, but I still harboured a hope to impress the troupe of travellers. I ran to the edge of town past the grist mill with its water wheel methodically turning, and towards the pasture where they camped. A tall hedge blocked me from seeing beyond, but I found a gap and squeezed through the tangle of hazelnut. I looked out onto the field. Nothing. Not even a cow.

I spun around. They were nowhere in sight. I looked up the road one way and down the other. Neither direction gave a clue as to which way they went. Surely someone had seen them leave.

I stood in the middle of the road, dejected and alone. I had failed my one opportunity to escape a life of scrubbing pots, and had slept through a second chance. I cursed my poor luck and sat in the road, my head in my hands.

I was thinking how I'd catch a good cuffing from the cook's wife for being late when, over the knoll, came a boy herding a goose into town. I jumped up and hurried to meet him.

"Have you passed a wagon with a goat tied behind?"

The boy's brow furrowed in thought. "I did see something of the kind a ways back." He pointed over his shoulder.

"How long ago do you think?" The goose took exception to me, honking and flapping its wings in a great show of bluster.

"Quite a time, it seems," he replied, distracted and moving his goose past me.

My legs were a quarter as long as a horse's and even if the horse took a plodding gait, by now it would have put a sizable distance between us. Even if I ran, I could not make up that distance nor could I keep up such a pace.

I ran back to the stables. The ostler was engaged with taking in a newly arrived traveller so I snuck back to the stall where I usually slept to put a bridle on Jezebel. It had been a while since I'd ridden. I couldn't manage the cumbersome saddle, so I unlatched her stall, climbed up the sides and eased myself onto her bare back.

"Come on, girl. We've a ride to take." I urged her out the back of the stable and onto the street. It took some measure of self-control to keep from nudging her into a gallop. We walked to the edge of town, me smiling and nodding to onlookers who scratched their heads at the sight of me on a horse. Once we cleared the last pedestrian, I urged Jezebel into a gallop, and we took off as if demons nipped our heels.

CHAPTER THIRTEEN

J EZEBEL AND I travelled the road well beyond Newmarket into country I'd never seen before. We had the road to ourselves, and the rise of excitement spurred both of us on. No doubt I would be in trouble for having taken a horse without asking, but my focus was to find the travelling troupe and impress them with my juggling. Besides, I wasn't stealing, I told myself. I was merely borrowing Jezebel for a time. And, she, seemed keen for the adventure.

We had travelled less than an hour when we came upon the wagon lumbering up ahead. I nudged her for one last burst of speed, sending clotted mud flying up behind us. I yelled for their attention and combined with the sound of our thundering approach, Tish turned and saw us bearing down on them.

They pulled to the side of the road and slowed.

"An unexpected surprise," said the storyteller, as I pulled Jezebel to a stop. "But it isn't a surprise if it is expected."

The troupe looked at me in amazement, and I didn't let them wonder for long.

"I've come to juggle for you."

"God's nigs," said the contortionist. "Here's a man with determination."

"Determination is a form of madness," said Tish. She took off her headrail and shook out a mane of resplendent buttery yellow hair. "Why would you think we care to see more of your juggling? It is a conceit to think it so."

"I could not see properly. I am a better juggler than what you witnessed last night."

"We are not looking for a competent juggler. We want an exceptional one," said Daegan.

"I believe that I am." Their unimpressed stares made me realise how much I must overcome.

"This your horse, little man?" asked the lute player after a moment.

"I'm borrowing her." I glanced away so that they could not see the lie on my face.

"Let us think it so, 'elst I hate to imagine the trouble awaiting you on your return."

Daegan looked at the road ahead of them and for a moment I thought he would click his horse on and I would be left to return to Newmarket as a horse thief. Instead, he motioned to the lute player.

"Help him down, Robert. He has put himself in a difficult position when he returns. We might as well indulge him for a moment."

Robert reluctantly eased himself down from the wagon and stood beside Jezebel, reaching for my waist as I slid off the horse then planting me firmly next to her. I handed him Jezebel's reins, then pulled the turnips from my pockets and found an even patch of ground on the side of the road. My heart beat so rapidly that I knew I must settle myself before I started juggling, or else be doomed to repeating the previous night's disastrous performance.

"Well, little man," said Daegan. "You have our attention, but not forever. We want to make the next village before nightfall."

The press for time further rattled me, but I pushed away my worry and took a breath. I tossed the first turnip into the air.

Soon I was circling five turnips and felt comfortable enough to reverse direction twice, then I changed the pattern to where I threw two turnips at different heights in the same direction. For added flair, I spun about, dropped to my knees, then stood. This I managed without mishap and neatly caught each turnip. I swept into an indulgent bow.

"You have some talent when you can see what you are tossing," said Tish. She granted me a slight smile, and I returned a bigger one in kind.

"A gentle sport this performance," said Daegan, "but we wish for a juggler who knows how to leave an audience breathless."

"I am not done." With some show, I took out the knife and flashed it at them. "If I may be given but a moment more of your time."

"I hope you fare better than last night with that knife. We haven't the means to mend you," warned Tish.

I began juggling three turnips until the rhythm was so smooth as to be mesmerising. After a couple more rotations, I added the knife. "If you have another, toss it to me."

"Another knife?" asked Daegan.

My eyes remained on my moving objects, but I could tell the members of the troupe exchanged looks with one another. Of course they would want to see if I was just being a cock.

The contortionist produced a dagger and held it up. "I've a blade." He jumped down from the wagon and stood in front of me.

"Toss it to my left hand when the knife touches my right," I said. This was a dangerous request, one that could easily be bungled and end with me slicing my hand if his timing was off. As it were, I was still nursing the painful wound from last night and had my palm tightly bound.

The contortionist watched me juggle for a minute. I could see his head bobbing in rhythm to time his toss and knew he was in earnest and would not just throw it at me. I hoped I would anticipate his move and be ready for it.

"Come now," said Robert. "We haven't all day."

His lack of patience needled me but I forced myself to concentrate.

Luckily, the contortionist would not be harried. Perhaps he'd grown accustomed to such impatience and mostly ignored it. I kept juggling, reading him while concentrating on my rotating objects. When he was ready, he tossed the dagger into the mix.

His timing was not perfect. My heart stopped for an instant. I felt a rush of jitters as I moved towards the blade and snatched it at the bottom of the handle. After a slight wobble, I recovered enough to keep the objects spinning. I came so close to nicking myself that the blood momentarily left my head, but I managed a turn and an under leg catch. After another few rotations, I reversed direction and ended by catching each turnip and finally the knives, without dropping a single one.

The members of the troupe stared at me. I could read nothing in their stone-faced expressions.

Tish leaned over and spoke into Daegan's ear. His face remained unmoved. No one said a word. Only the sound of birdsong in a nearby tree broke the lengthening silence.

Then, Daegan spoke, "Little man, you have a place with us if you wish."

It was to be! I would become a juggler at last!

Daegan hopped off the wagon, and tied Jezebel to walk alongside their goat. I would come to know Daegan as the leader of the troupe with a flair for dramatic storytelling. Robert, the lute player with inscrutable gray eyes, lifted me into the wagon where I sat beside Bertram—a man of bendable limbs. Bertram was of small stature, though not as small as me. Later, I would see him contort himself into the most impossible of Gordian knots. An older fellow of penetrating dark eyes, Tallis, played the pipe and tabor. Tallis fancied himself a seer of men's fortunes though he kept most of his predictions to himself. And finally, there was Tish, a beauty and singer of crystalline voice.

At the next town we sold Jezebel to a stable, and with money in hand, my way to London was paid. A pang of guilt niggled me for having taken the mare, but I appeased my troubled conscience knowing that I had left faithful Jezebel in a more handsome stable with an ostler of kinder temperament. In time, my fear of punishment for horse thievery diminished and eventually became a distant memory. All was well. I was a performer.

On the way to London, we stopped at a village near Kirtling Brook to perform. Money was needed to restock some of our stores as we were running low on cheese and apples. One could only survive on goat milk for so long. This would be my first appearance juggling with the troupe, and I was eager to earn my keep.

My tattered homespun did not inspire confidence for a performer who might dazzle, but Tish wound a bright yellow sash around my waist that we hoped would distract the onlookers from noticing the ragged hem of my smock, torn condition of my hosen, and worn shoes.

"There you are," she said, adjusting the fabric to hang lower on one hip. "That looks a bit rakish." She stood back to admire her handiwork. "Appropriate, given that you will be juggling knives."

I had not thought about juggling knives at night again, not since that fateful eve when I had tried so hard to impress. My hand had just about healed, and I did not relish the thought of a repeat debacle.

"There will be torches staged so that I might see?" I inquired, trying to keep an edge of desperation out of my voice. I looked to Robert who arranged the makeshift stage and props for each performance.

"Certainly, we want you to impress the audience, not terrorise them," said Daegan. "You will be able to juggle knives if you can properly see them." His absolute confidence made it difficult for me to disagree with him and I glanced at Robert for reassurance. The lutist sat immobile on a boulder and barely acknowledged the discussion, making me wonder if he had heard, or in some manner had heard but disregarded the request.

Besides wondering if Robert would provide me with adequate lighting, I worried how I might contain my jitters since I had never even practised under the light of torches. As it were, there was no time for me to feel comfortable or to practise—the performance was that night.

"'Tis your turn to water Hazel, little man," said Robert, standing to collect brush for a fire. He seemed irritated that I had not thought of tending the goat without his mentioning it. His pale eyes followed me as I untied her from the rear of the wagon. "Take her into town to the water conduit," he said. "And interest people in our show tonight."

I expected to be an object of curiosity—what dwarf leading

a costumed goat into town wouldn't be? Plenty of townsfolk stopped in their steps to gawp. Women stared, kept a wide berth, while children laughed and pointed. Men, however…

As if my size were a challenge to their manhood. But as I thought more on it later, I believe I was a challenge to their sense of convention. Most had probably never seen a smidge of a human. I think some considered me an insult, a queeb, Satan's fart. I led Hazel to the conduit and stood by while she drank. One child was attracted to Hazel's colourful harness and approached to stroke her back.

"She likes to be scratched here," I said, showing him the spot between her shoulder blades.

"I like your goat," he said. He concentrated on rubbing Hazel, then looked at me and tilted his head. "You look strange," he said.

"I am a dwarf," I answered. "I'm not strange, I'm just built differently from you."

"Why are you here? I've never seen you before."

"I'm travelling through with a group of performers. I juggle. Come see us tonight on the edge of town. We will make you and your mother happy."

"I'm already happy."

"Then you are a blessed child," I said. "Tell others we shall put on a show an hour after nightfall."

He ran off, like children do, intent on their next adventure, and leaving me to wonder if he would remember to tell his mother or forget he'd even talked to me.

Hazel stepped away from the water trough and shook her head, the bells on her bridle jingling cheerfully. I started towards our camp, but as people stared at my retreat, I did my best to stir interest in our show that night. I swept low in numerous bows, removing my flat cap, and exaggerated the gesture enough to make a spectacle of myself. Then, in a robust voice, I announced, "A show of great and most excellent recreation, a show brimming with stories, music, and recitation. Come to the edge of town on the west road, an hour after sunset. Bring one, bring all, for you will not want to miss an event so fine only to learn of it afterward from your neighbour. For you shall sorely regret having missed such an exceptional occasion."

As I said, a dwarf and a costumed goat can stir some notice in a cheerless little village.

That night we looked on with excitement as the townsfolk gathered at our periphery. Robert had cleared an area for us to perform and had staked the edge with rushlights that would be lit a few minutes before the show. I distractedly practised my knife juggling behind the wagon in the dim light of the campfire. Every time I dropped, I chided myself for my shakiness, which only seemed to compound my jitters. Robert watched while tuning his lute.

"Let us hope you perform better than that," he said. He plucked a string several times while turning a peg. "Maybe you should omit the knives." The string came into pleasant range, and he worked on the next. "But then, Daegan expects you to be expert with your knives—it was the whole reason for your being here."

I said nothing and practised a simple cascade, but the light was not enough for me to visualise the handles in rotation. I jumped back fearing being sliced and the knives fell to the ground one after another, their clatter a strong admonishment. Robert shook his head. He turned away, and continued tuning his lute, leaving me to wallow in my worry.

My legs began trembling. If I should fail tonight, what would become of me? I envisioned the troupe of actors abandoning me, their wagon rolling out of town with Hazel tied to the rear. Her bright bells tinkling a sad farewell to my failure. Would I spend my life washing trenchers at the local boozing ken, waiting for another opportunity that might never come? I sat on a stump and put my head in my hands.

I can't say for how long I moped, but the troupe must have completed their acts without my realising, when I heard my name being yelled.

"Kronos! Come! You are next!" announced Tallis, ready to perform with his drum strapped to his waist. He saw my glum expression and took hold of my elbow, pulling me to my feet. "Do not tarry. The crowd has no patience for amateurs!"

Amateur was exactly what I was. The word filled my spine with ice. I gulped in air, panicking at the thought of performing for a multitude of judging eyes watching my every move. Tallis pulled me along, my bag of wood balls and knives spilling on the ground behind me. He dragged me past Robert, whose grey eyes followed, piercing my back as I walked past towards the row of rushlights and audience, there with their expectations.

I was the last to perform, and I should have questioned the reasoning in that, for as I stood before the gathered townsfolk emptying my bag of wooden balls, the rushlights flickered and were not as bright as earlier on. What does a storyteller or a singer need light for? But I could not complain, I could only make do. I stood, holding the spheres in my hands, feeling their weight resting easily in my palms. With a calming breath, I tossed one, then another in the air.

Soon the rhythm and the weight became comfortable and I probably *could* have juggled with my eyes closed. I worked through my usual routine, feeling my comfort and confidence return, then turned around. The circle remained steady as I lifted my arms and lowered them. The wooden balls and yellow sash mesmerised, for out of my peripheral vision, I saw faces entranced by my juggling dance. Even in the wavering light, I knew my art and worried not. The audience was with me and I held their attention, feeling the strength and satisfaction that comes with their interest. When I had snatched the last ball out of the air, a round of applause and cheers rewarded me.

I looked over at the troupe members watching. Daegan shouted, "The knives!"

I shook my head. One of the rushlights flickered wildly, about to extinguish.

The storyteller firmly nodded his head. I looked back at the audience and bowed, ignoring him. I straightened and took another bow. As I soaked up the crowd's adulation, I was unaware of him striding out to join me. I stood just as he swept my bag off the ground and pulled three knives out, holding them up for the crowd to see.

"And now, for his final act, Kronos shall juggle knives!" He swiped the air with one of the blades, the metal gleaming in the firelight. "These blades are sharp enough to cut off a finger!" He then pricked his finger and showed the first row of onlookers the blood.

A collective gasp rose from the audience, and the ice that I had felt in my spine came back to crack it apart.

Telling Daegan that it was too dark to see the knives in the flickering rushlight was useless. Feigned sudden sickness would appear suspect, it would show a lack of courage. Nothing would do but to attempt the feat, even if I left with fewer fingers. Perhaps that was the final daring act he hoped to excite the crowd into talking about. What did it matter if a dwarf lost a finger? One less digit mattered not when it came to physical attributes in one such as me.

Reluctantly, I accepted the knives from Daegan and took time to square myself. Glancing at my cohorts, I saw them watching from the side, the future of my addition to their performance troupe now hanging in the balance. They didn't want just a juggler. They wanted an exceptional one.

The longer I delayed, the less light I would have to juggle by. The rushlights had near run their course and the crowd began to murmur impatiently.

My shaky breath did not calm, but I tossed the first knife into the air, then the second. The blades caught the light, the steel flashed, reminding everyone of their weight and potential hazard. I believe the entire audience held their breath as I added a third into the mix. My concentration was as unyielding as the knives circling in front of me. The rushlights flickered, then suddenly dimmed. One, then two fizzled out, their smoke wisping skyward, and I was left juggling by the light of the moon.

After one last rotation, for I could barely see and was operating on chance and rhythm, I caught each knife, the handles landing firmly in my palms. My hands were unbloodied.

My focus remained intact and unbroken. I stood a moment, as much in astonishment as in profound relief. The audience broke into cheers and applause and my concentration faded with the resounding adulation. I swept low to increasing 'huzzahs', then looked over at my cohorts, who were also cheering and stomping. They all smiled and approved of my success…all but one. Robert.

CHAPTER FOURTEEN

M Y SUCCESS LED to further stops and shows, squeezing them in at the remaining few villages before reaching London. Daegan capitalised on my ability and filled his pockets with extra coin, so that when we did arrive in London we could acquire whatever we needed, plus enjoy some of the offerings of the city—its boozing kens, an inn with soft pallets on which to sleep (if only for one night), fine shops, and markets.

Daegan thought that my ability to juggle knives in dim light was assured, and though I felt as though I was relying more on luck than skill, I was able to avoid nicking myself or others those first performances. I had become the anticipated final act, the act of daring that would leave the audience breathless. The entire troupe relied on me to bring in those extra few coins, and they treated me with a respect that I'd not experienced since assisting Brother Ulric in surgery. However, my newfound regard was not embraced by everyone in the troupe.

We were nearly to London when, one day, the clime proved inexplicably hot. Tiny flying insects hounded us like flies on filth. We spent our ride wildly swatting and cursing them, when Bertram spied a pond not far from the road. A dunk in the water would offer relief from the swarm that plagued us and a much welcome break from the incessant jostling in the wagon.

Without hesitation, Daegan pulled the wagon to the side of the road and we hopped out. He led Tinker, our horse, to the pond's edge to drink, and I untied Hazel to do the same. Tish and Bertram hurriedly disrobed at the pond's edge and were wading knee deep by the time I got Hazel free of her tether. Only Tallis stayed behind.

"You are not weary from riding long on the road?" I asked him.

He looked at the pond, unsure. "Nay, I shall stay here."

Whenever Tallis became hesitant, it was because he had "tum rumbles" as he called them. These 'gut feelings' he valued above logic or experience.

"Ah, you fear the water?" I prompted, thinking I'd found the reason for his hesitation.

"Nay, not that," he said, shaking his head. "But *you* might do better to avoid it."

No premonition or "tum rumble" was going to put me off a cool respite from the dusty road. I pulled Hazel along and joined the others.

I stripped off my hosen and sank to my knee with the first step in the water, its coolness like a balm. The niggling flies had followed me, so I submerged my arms then splashed water around my neck, not caring that my smock got wet.

Tish and Bertram floated on their backs among the lily pads and dragonflies. Tish's smock clung to her breasts, offering a thin layer between her and my imagination. I'd been privy to seeing her naked, we all had. The others went about their way, accustomed to seeing her insouciantly exposed. She was, of course, Daegan's lover, but I was not so used to seeing a woman naked that I could blithely ignore her nipples pointed towards the sky.

After tying Tinker to drink, Daegan sat a distance off on the bank, dangling his feet, leaning back on his elbows, his head tipped back to soak in the sun. Robert was nowhere in sight and I took him to be squatting somewhere in the woods. All were enjoying our momentary pause from travelling, though the goat, for some reason, was not interested in drinking. I stood at Hazel's head, coaxing and pulling her chin forward. Bertram laughed.

"She doesn't know what is good for her," he called. "Let her chew on the tall grass."

"She must drink!" I insisted. "She's gone too long without water."

I continued to pull her lead and made some small progress, when Robert appeared out of nowhere. Before I knew it, he put his shoulder against the goat's rear and gave her a great shove. Usually there is nothing more sure-footed than a goat, but even she could not recover from his sudden brute force. I stumbled backward into the water, and she landed on top of me.

Her hooves churned, trying to find purchase. The more I struggled to get out from under her, the more my smock tangled in her hooves. The silty bottom was beyond the reach of my feet. I tried to stand, but in my desperate attempt, murky water filled my nose and began seeping into my lungs. What may have only been a moment felt hours long. I panicked and my racing heart filled my head with its deafening thuds.

My insides burned as if on fire, and I fought the urge to gasp for air. If only I could free myself of Hazel's thrashing, but my smock was twisted around her hooves. My lungs felt increasingly heavy, on the brink of rupturing, when, just as suddenly, all became light. My mouth opened; the water rushed in. The dark murk of the pond turned white before my eyes.

I cannot say how long it was before I heard my name. It sounded faint at first, then became louder.

"Little man, you were not long for this world," said Daegan, as I sputtered then vomited pond water. "We spared you from everlasting purgatory. You can thank us now."

My eyelids felt impossibly heavy, but when I finally opened them, I saw Daegan, Tish, and Tallis staring down at me.

"If a goat doesn't want to drink, drowning won't solve her reluctance," said Tish.

"Did I not warn you to stay away from the water?" said Tallis.

Never mind that Robert was the cause for the mishap. He stood back from the others with an inscrutable look on his face.

Later, when I had control of my wits, I sought him out. It was just the two of us, the others were engaged elsewhere. "Why did you not warn me that you were about to push Hazel?"

"You wanted her to drink," he said. "You should have stood aside if you didn't want to end in the water."

"You could have warned me."

"I thought that you saw me. You were pulling her, I thought I'd help."

"I cannot swim! I nearly drowned because of you!"

"But I thought that you could. Why else were you so deep in the water?"

I stared at Robert, realising I would never get an apology, nor would he ever admit his part in the incident.

Robert shrugged. "Now I know you can't swim."

He was the burr in my shoe—an annoyance. An annoyance that I felt compelled to deal with. Once you sense someone's disfavour, you become their object to loathe. And here I must remind you—I am most unlike our Lord saviour. I cannot meet malice with kindness in return. Because every act of spite deserves retaliation 'elst one's enemies never learn to stop their harassment.

Finally, we arrived at Aldgate and paid our toll for entering London. We then proceeded onto a thoroughfare that was claggy with mud and excrement of all kinds. A notable stench hung in the air that I thought impossible to become accustomed to. The day before, we had passed a steady parade of wagons and farmers, a flock of sheep being herded to market, and even noblemen on horses. The variety and liveliness of humanity excited me. My years at Thetford had isolated me so that my comfort was rooted in quiet. The abrupt change left me gaping like a doddypol.

A group of men rode past dressed in the formal livery of a nobleman, and of particular note was a man of brown skin. Bertram caught me staring and leaned over to inform me that his kind hailed from Africa; perhaps he had come to London by way of Portugal. "He's no different than you," he said, laying a hand on my knee, then shaking it as if waking me from a stupor. "Only they bake them longer on the other side of the sea."

Besides men of obvious foreign lineage, there were those of eccentric nature. Men who spoke to spectres only they could see. This disturbed me more than I dared admit, but it would become a familiar sight, especially in the vicinity of Bethlehem Hospital, also known as Bedlam. For who among us knows if one day we will end in a similar condition of mind? An evil deed might emerge from our past, transform into a prickish demon, and trouble us into madness. Beggars littered the streets almost as numerous as the piles of rubbish and kitchen scraps, and it would be in my future to accept and perhaps 'see without judgement' these societal warts so frequent in London as to become unnotable.

The strange words of other countries filled my ears and then every so often a clock chimed or a church bell tolled. Indeed, there seemed a rivalry between the parish churches as to who could clang their bells the loudest.

Then, too, I saw entertainers—minstrels strumming their mandoras or lutes for pennies tossed at their feet, a tumbler who could flip himself in the air and walk on his hands, and even a juggler who (I might add) was not as proficient as me. Here was a place wherein the sheer multitude of people assured every possible permutation of appearance, talent, and mentality. I was one in a range of humanity. Just one more oddity amongst a sea of exotical souls.

That first visit to London would not be a long one. There were certain errands that could not be done elsewhere. Tish ordered me a suit of motley. She had the tailor fashion a scalp-hugging cap of maroon wool that covered my ears and had appendages resembling three strangely long horns. Each was stuffed with bombast to give them shape so that two arced over my ears and touched my shoulders. The third curved forward like a scorpion's tail about to strike. Bells sewn on the ends jingled merrily when I moved. The cap was affixed to a collar made of alternating triangles of maroon and indigo velvet that draped over my shoulders and also ended with bells. As if this elaborate cap were not enough, Tish had the tailor stitch a simple jacket of maroon, one which allowed me to freely move and not be hindered by its bulk. My hosen consisted of one blue leg whilst the other was made of the same red as the jacket and cap. Finally, a pair of pointy shoes were crafted for my act which it would take some time for me to feel comfortable wearing. Once my costume was complete, Daegan and I traded my old homespun with a fripperer, who, with extra coin, outfitted me in hosen, shoes, a crisp smock, and a jerkin that could be easily altered by a tailor. I'd never felt so well-dressed.

A visit to London would not have been complete if I had not been able to glimpse Whitehall, the king's stately palace on the River Thames. For a penny, Bertram and I took a boat at Three Cranes in the Vintry ward.

A day of sunshine lifted my mood, and I viewed the London skyline as innocently as a country carl. The lead-paned windows of Baynard's Castle caught the sun's angle, glistening like silver plate. Church bells tolled, drowning the dissonant sounds from the street antics below. The air was filled with their sound. I thought of my life at the monastery and realised how diametric it was compared to the life I lived now.

We shared the wherry with a merchant and his wife, both attired in subdued black fashion. She must never have seen a dwarf before, because while I was busy gaping at the magnificent silhouette of London, she was busy gaping at mine.

Her husband looked at us upon boarding but seemed unaffected by my appearance. More to his pleasure was the passing skyline and bustling activity going on there.

Bertram, noticing the woman's blatant gawp, lifted his leg, cupped his heel in one hand and placed his shin behind his neck. He sat like that, comfortably, and stared back at her with a perfectly controlled indifference.

His impudent gesture roundly offended.

The woman responded with an attention-getting nudge which was initially ignored, then followed this with a more vigorous jab with her elbow. Duly roused from his contemplation, her husband looked at her with strained patience, then, following her tipped forehead, cast his gaze upon us.

His disinterest was impressive. Bertram must have been

disappointed, but the woman's discomfort grew, and her reaction further encouraged the contortionist. He stayed in that pose until we passed the stairs of Durham House where the couple disembarked, the woman hastily stepping off, followed by her less affected spouse.

"There it is," said Bertram, once we were underway and pointing with the foot that was resting on his shoulder. "Covered in scaffolding."

Ahead of us, a tall timber shell shrouded the king's palace, preventing us from seeing much of the underlying structure. Men pushed wheelbarrows of mortar and balanced hods of bricks. A great wall was being constructed facing the river. The sheer scale of the project was larger than anything I had ever experienced.

Bertram eased his foot off his shoulder and resumed a normal seated position. "Shall we get off at the next stairs and walk back?"

"That would be a long walk," I said.

"Twice as far for you," he said, patting my short thigh. "But you'll get a taste of this part of London and see it in all of its glorious and vulgar splendour."

At Whitehall stairs we leapt out and walked as far as the north gate to the palace, which was constructed of a chequered brick façade with two octagonal turrets on either side of the arch entry. Four large medallions were carved into it, one of which was the likeness of Henry VIII, I would later learn. I could not help but stare in amazement at the impressive gate. Guards prevented commoners like us from entering, and once I had my fill, we started our walk back to find the troupe.

I was grateful for Bertram's guidance. I kept close to his side, being unfamiliar and overwhelmed with the streets and sheer number of people in the city. There were districts that I would eventually come to know. In time, I would know where to find the best ale in the tamest and most accepting boozing kens. I would learn which stews received me without disdain for my person, though showing my appreciation in good coin helped.

Suffice it to say that familiarity with London would be in my future.

The monks had warned me that the secular world outside the priory could be unkind. Not just to men like me, but to anyone possessing half a heart of compassion. There is a coldness that comes with age and experience. To survive means to outwit.

Never should one take advantage of another's weakness. After all, exploitation is human nature, and it is our struggle with evil not to take advantage of those less clever, less handsome than ourselves. However, it is better to outwit oneself—to be able to suppress one's susceptibility in taking offence and feeling wounded. How well one builds his suit of armour determines his ability to endure the barbs of insult and misfortune. I would get plenty of practise.

My visit to London helped me realise that the breadth of human experience was immeasurable and I had seen only a little piece. Where would I find my corner of existence? Viewing the king's opulent palaces of Whitehall and St. James only made me more determined that I should find my way inside one of them.

But that would hinge on a bit of luck—an ingredient that had never favoured me. Or shall I say, luck never favoured me... for long.

CHAPTER FIFTEEN

OUR TROUPE LEFT London and ventured on new roads to villages unknown. That first year was a time of proving my continued worth to the performers. I juggled with bells on my cap and a foxtail sewn to my arse. They would have it no other way than for me to look a spectacle while I juggled and performed.

I continued to be the final act. Whether I had enough light to juggle by concerned no one but myself. Daegan thought the darker the better, but I argued that the audience must be able to see what I was doing. What was the use if they couldn't see three feet beyond their noses? When he overheard townsfolk complain that I could have been juggling horses for all they knew, he conceded that my argument made some sense and instructed Robert to refresh two of the rushlights before I would begin.

At first, Robert obliged. I began to relax knowing that I had sufficient light, and this comfort allowed me to become more flamboyant. I could turn around, sit, stand, leap about, stick out my tongue, and waggle my tail, confident in knowing where my objects were mid-air. As a result, my popularity translated into more money for the company. And with popularity comes adoration. Following our performances, I was often surrounded by appreciative townsfolk, whereas Robert and Tallis stood idly by.

Did I take advantage of admiring young maids, interested in a bounce behind a hedge? I was as curious as they, why should I not indulge myself? No harm came of it; I had given up any thought of becoming a monk or remaining chaste.

My confidence and success grew and I enjoyed the amenities that came with my newfound favour, but one night, in the middle of juggling knives (by now I had added another two), three of the rushlights began to flicker. The crowd thought this guttering light was part of the act and clapped appreciatively. Immediately, my comfort escaped me, and I felt as I did that first time juggling in the dark, trialling for a place with the troupe.

Having performed this stunt so many times before, there should have been a familiarity of movement that would have sustained me, but nay. I was dismayed by how much I still relied on my sight to successfully juggle. After attempting to keep the knives circling, I dropped, having missed my catch and, in the process, I severely sliced my palm. The pain shot through my body, and I jumped away as the remaining knives tumbled to the ground.

I grasped my hand to staunch the blood seeping from between my fingers to their collective gasp. The audience knew only that I had failed, and reacted to my bungle. The call of a night owl was soon drowned by deafeningly raucous boos and hisses. Daegan and Tish watched from the side in disbelief. A glance at Robert with his indifferent stare instantly raised my suspicions. I quickly gathered the fallen knives and ran for the cover of a blanket suspended from a tree limb.

Daegan hurried out to calm the jeering crowd while Tallis

and Bertram steadied me. "God's teeth that is an ugly gash," said Bertram, examining my hand.

Tish pushed past them to see. "Bertram, find a rag to wrap his palm," she said. She pressed the wound on either side. "You've managed to handily maim yourself. What happened?"

"The rushlights failed. I couldn't see."

Tish searched for Robert who was the only one in the troupe who had not come over. She saw him storing his lute in the wagon. "Robert! Come!"

While Daegan attempted to appease the grumbling crowd, a few unhappy showgoers threw acorns and rocks, demanding he return their money. Loathe was he to give back their entry coin, but after the audience dispersed, the money collected after the performance suffered because of my bungled act.

Robert walked over nonchalantly, stopping to extinguish the rushlights first.

When he was within earshot Tish addressed him. "You are tasked with assuring that Kronos has enough light for his act. Two of the rushlights failed and the other guttered terribly." She could be as fierce as a cornered badger when provoked.

"Rushlights can be unreliable," answered Robert evenly.

"We've had no issue until tonight. Why was there a problem with so many?"

Bertram returned with a long piece of linen torn from an old smock which Tish straightened then began winding around my palm. She tugged the cloth a bit too tight, jerking my hand up. "I can understand one," she said. "But three?"

Robert shrugged. He watched Tish bandage my wound, avoiding everyone's gaze.

"Were they not soaked for long enough?" she asked.

"I soaked them, aye," said Robert, stiffening. He swatted a fly that landed on his neck, then examined his fingers to see if he'd gotten it. "We've new tallow. Mayhap it is not so pure. Even a small bit of water can cause problems, making the lights sputter."

Daegan finished with the last of the dissatisfied audience members and joined the conversation. "This recent batch of tallow has worked until now. Why is it fouled all of a sudden?"

Robert offered no explanation.

"Could it have been tampered with?" asked Daegan, directing his question to Robert.

"Well, *I* didn't tamper with it, if that is what you are implying," said Robert, indignantly. "Someone else must have gotten into it to make me look at fault!" Robert's eyes landed on mine.

"No one is accusing you, Robert," said Daegan. "We shall have to acquire new tallow though. It is a cost we can ill afford. 'Tis wasteful, but we have no choice. We cannot perform without it."

Rather than defend himself, Robert stalked off and extinguished the one remaining rushlight, then yanked it out of the ground. We watched him pull the remaining lights then stomp back to the wagon and carelessly throw them in the back.

"Tallis," said Daegan, in a low voice. "Remove those lights from the wagon and make sure they are adequately doused." His eyes followed the lute player return to camp. "I should not like to lose our ride to fire."

During the time that it took for my palm to heal, I refrained from performing. I undertook tasks one-handed, but everyone understood and accepted that I could not do more. Without complaint, Tallis and Bertram often picked up the slack or took over my chores.

One day as we were collecting kindling in the woods for our

evening camp, I found several promising sticks near a hedge. On the other side, Robert approached Daegan, apparently unaware I was within earshot. Particular words of a conversation may muddle, but when your name is mentioned, its syllables sing louder than the others, and I immediately stopped foraging to give a listen.

"Why do we keep him on? He is no longer earning anything and he's taking overly long to heal."

"He brought in good coin when he juggled," said Daegan. "We can survive a few weeks without his act."

"Did he bring in so much extra that we can afford to wait? I say we leave him at the next village and if we feel he is that valuable, we can collect him on our return."

"He may find another troupe by then," said Daegan. "Besides, he draws a lot of interest. Juggling dwarves do not come oft."

"I beg to differ," said Robert. "One only needs to look to find an able replacement. Mayhap not a juggler, but someone else with desirable talents."

Robert was right. Why *should* they support me if I could not bring in coin? I wondered who else he was trying to influence against me. Daegan listened, but I could not see inside his mind. How inclined was he to side with Robert, whom he'd known for longer? Or was the added coin in his pocket when I performed worth the inconvenience of waiting for my hand to heal?

To dispel any misgivings Daegan or any of the others might entertain, I took to buffoonery. I charmed ladies and children with my antics between acts. Before the show, I welcomed women and children with sprigs of wildflowers, and afterwards, I thanked our attendants and ensured that they left in good cheer. I wove coins in and out of my fingers, produced endlessly long scarves from a sleeve, having wound them about my torso first, and kept a small mouse beneath my flat cap that I trained to run down my arm and eat nuts out of my bandaged hand. My pranks delighted, and a few extra coins landed in our jar.

I missed being the anticipated final act. The added prestige had been to my liking as it had set me apart from the others and in a sense, made me superior—a quality that I lacked when my only goal was to mildly amuse others. A buffoon does not garner respect.

Even though my reputation had suffered from my injury, Robert continued to provoke me. He objected to my antics and the attention I could still achieve with my gestures. When doling up dinner portions, he served me last and I inevitably got less than the others. If I complained, I would receive even less food the next mealtime. He vexed me in other ways, skirting the notice of anyone else in the troupe.

My privacy was never his consideration. I went to great lengths to conceal my daily "routine," often walking a distance from camp or the road to find a spot well hidden by brush or undergrowth. This did not prevent him from seeking me out at the most inopportune moment to laugh or throw rocks at me.

Those who are bored or unchallenged, those with no useful way to expend their pent-up frustrations, savour making life a misery for anyone they do not like. Left unchallenged, they see no reason to change their behaviour. One must learn to out-manoeuvre these men if one is to gain any peace.

I continued to endure Robert's harassment, thinking hard on how I might find a way to make him stop, until one night, after dinner, a sneaky idea perched on my shoulder and whispered in my ear. The troupe was sitting in the glow of a fire, telling stories and laughing, while Robert lightly stroked his beloved lute. Its soft, lilting sound was a comforting backdrop after a long day of travel.

Tish had retrieved a portion of lard from the wagon and sat next to Daegan with her skirts hitched, slathering the fat on her legs and rubbing it in to soften her skin. By now, I had grown accustomed to seeing various parts of Tish exposed, and her shapely calves were no more interesting to me than the lard she used on them.

My attention turned to Robert strumming his lute. He often had to stop and bring its strings into tune. When I thought about it, I noticed that some days he had to tune more often than others. He would turn the pegs in small increments, sometimes applying gentle pressure to get them to stay in place. This led me to wonder how the pegs might work if they were coated with lard like Tish's legs? Would they slip out of tune more often than they normally did?

And what if the neck had sticky spots under the strings? Pine resin or dots of honey might hinder Robert's ability to perform with his usual flair. I could easily manage either scenario and sit back to enjoy his reaction.

So it was that one night I chose a more subtle approach to ruining his performance. Instead of opting for slippery pegs *and* sticky strings, I chose one and waited for him to hurry off into the woods to water the grass just before his act. No one saw me dabbing tree sap on the neck of his lute—the twig nonchalantly tossed over my shoulder on his return.

"Play well," I said, as he picked up his instrument and stood at the edge of the grass, waiting for his cue.

I always told him to 'play well', preferring to be generous in my encouragement even though he never acknowledged it. To have withheld my good wishes would have invited his notice.

His annoyance made for great entertainment that night. The

strings stuck to the neck of the instrument and the twist of his mouth and scowling brow had me covering my mouth to mask my grin.

His tunes offended with strings coming unstuck at odd times to create a thoroughly dissonant sound. Instead of pleasing the audience, the effect drew puzzled faces. They shook their heads and squinted; children covered their ears. On Robert persisted, trying to tame the unwieldy lute into producing something simulating a song, but the final result sounded more like a chicken being strangled. When he finished, no one clapped. The silence and sounds of the night were infinitely more welcome than Robert's songs.

"God's nigs," said Robert, escaping their scrutiny and forgoing a final bow. He brushed past, throwing down his lute in disgust.

"Methinks they are applauding your having stopped," I said. "Are you unwell? You were not at your best tonight."

Robert picked up his lute and brought it near a burning rushlight to examine it. He held the body up to eye level and looked down its long, fretted neck. "What *is* this?" he said, touching a sticky portion and then pressing his thumb and forefinger together. They resisted coming apart.

"It appears to be a sticky substance," said Tallis, stating the obvious.

Robert looked up at the towering trees. "Pine pitch?" he said to no one in particular.

By then, Tish had walked over. "Robert, what happened?"

"Somehow pine sap got on my fingerboard," said Robert.

I kept my mouth tightly shut, not offering an explanation that it could have dripped from the tree, but hoping someone else might mention the idea.

"You shouldn't leave your instrument under trees," said Bertram.

"The pine needles are sticky sometimes," I said, perhaps a little too quickly.

Robert's gaze shifted to me and stayed on my person extra-long.

"The sticky needles sometimes drop from the trees, and if your lute is under them…"

"I've learned never to leave my drum under trees unless I cover it," said Tallis, saving me from sounding too knowledgeable. "Especially under pines."

The humiliation Robert suffered that night stayed with him for a while. If he associated me with the sticky fingerboard, he kept his suspicions to himself. He never confronted me on the matter. Perhaps the incident taught him that two could play his game. I was a worthy opponent in spite of my size.

Then again, I may have been puffing out my chest undeservedly. He could very well have attributed the sticky fingerboard to the shedding pine trees and not me.

Either way, I enjoyed some peace from Robert's constant torment, and I quietly wondered if he had grown a conscience. Had he experienced the discomfort of being rejected and realised his continued livelihood relied on his good performance?

Once my hand healed I began juggling again, quickly resuming my place as the last act of the night. I enjoyed all the attention and fawning that came with being a gifted performer. More oft' than not, an inquisitive young maid would wait for me afterwards. She and I would 'talk' somewhere well away from the camp and prying eyes. I enjoyed more 'conversations' than anyone in the troupe, including Daegan and Tish. But I digress…

All was peaceable until one night. We set up on the outskirts of a village called Soham and expected a large gathering, having stopped at their tavern to eat and tell others about our performance spectacle later that evening. Townsfolk were weary of the vacillating conditions of late spring—sometimes warm, sometimes chill—and our troupe offered a respite from their entrenched impatience waiting for the weather to improve.

Per usual, Robert placed the rushlights along the periphery and erected a blanket drape on one side to conceal us while we waited our turn to perform. The dying torches were a faint memory, and though they did waver on occasion, I did not attribute it to Robert's tampering.

I dressed myself in my motley, overly fussing with the stuffed horns on my cap. The stuffing had compacted over time and the horns flopped about, sometimes hanging in my face and obstructing my sight—never an asset when trying to juggle. I was considering slicing off the one frontward facing horn until a time when we could fix it, when I realised the lengthening quiet was because I had missed my cue. I grabbed my bag of wooden balls and knives and ran out from behind the blanket, stopping at the sight of blinking pairs of eyes. I turned tail, and shook my attached foxtail at them, exaggerating the back-and-forth waggle of my hips until I heard a few titters and then a mild insult for being late and for being a dwarf.

"Get on, you stunt-legged sprout!" someone shouted, and an acorn pelted me on the arse. I ignored the taunt, as I had often come to expect some mention of my physical condition and anyhow, I thought these insults reflected more on the jeerer than on me.

I emptied my sack on the ground and chose five wooden balls to start with. I worked through my usual routine of cascades and backcross throws, impressing the audience with my complete control. My added flourishes drew claps and gasps of delight.

My mastery amazed, allowing me to enjoy the crowd and play to their rapt attention. When, finally, it came to my final tour de force, I was so exhilarated by the crowd that I hardly took a breath before picking up my knives. To demonstrate their danger, I sliced a plum in half without effort and tossed the halves to a boy in the front row.

I started with three. Once I got them rotating and did my requisite spins and back handed throws, I bent down and snatched up a fourth knife to add to the mix. The rushlights did not fail me, there was no gusting wind to make them warble or flicker. The night was a damp, still one, all to my liking, and my juggling was flawless and confident. After several rotations, I bent down and added a fifth.

I had only done a couple of cascades when suddenly I felt a sharp stab in my palm. The sudden pain threw off my timing and I struggled to adjust. But then as the knives circled round, I felt my palm being pricked again. This time the pain was more intense and I shook my hand to free it of the offending knife. Blood bloomed on my palm. I was not so brave as to keep juggling. I jumped back from the falling knives and grabbed my bleeding hand.

How quickly can an audience turn against you? Immediately the insults started instead of sympathy. Acorns and rocks rained down. I had disappointed…once again.

Before I rushed to the protection of the hanging drape, I gathered my spheres and knives, noticing one had a headless nail driven into the handle. It was sharpened to a point.

"Let me see your hand," said Tish, finding my wrist and ignoring the blood dripping on her kirtle.

I saw no reason not to address the reason for my mishap. "A nail has been driven into the handle." Bertram examined the offending knife, holding it near some light.

"Indeed," agreed Bertram, handing it back. "It is not so obvious, but the nail is well placed to jab your skin."

"The cut is not so deep that it will prevent you from performing like before," said Tish, running her thumb over the wound. "'Tis not as bad as the last time." She sent Bertram for some cloth to wrap my palm. "That nail didn't get there on its own. Someone has designs on you."

With the audience having gone home to their hearth fires, Daegan, Tallis, and lastly Robert walked over to see what had happened.

"Who would be so malicious?" said Tish, searching their faces then looking beyond in case the culprit was an outsider. "We are a band of performers. Our survival depends on each of us supporting one another. When I find out who did this, there will come a reckoning."

Like a mother scolding her wayward children, we all felt the shame of her accusation and hung our heads. But, as much as I wished an end to our private battle (for I roundly suspected Robert), nothing more came of that particular incident. Robert dispelled any notion of guilt by publicly treating me with the same deference he showed the others.

That is not to say that he completely avoided and stopped tormenting me—he did not. It seemed he could not control his urge to stifle any happiness or contentment I might enjoy. He became more careful, more calculating. So I became even more mistrusting, and always checked my knives before juggling them.

CHAPTER SIXTEEN

AFTER TRAVELLING A large circuit in Suffolk we eventually crossed the Waveney into Norfolk. We were north of Thetford Priory when I recognised the road leading to Kenninghall. I prompted Daegan to stop and let us perform there.

"Single households, especially of noblemen of great renown, are not accepting of us," he said, urging Tinker on. "We are better suited to villages."

"You will find otherwise, I am certain of it," I said. "I know Norfolk's mistress, Bess. She will want to see me."

Tish snorted in disbelief. "Impertinence is a dangerous trait in a dwarf," she said.

"Mayhap not," said I. "I may be given greater lenience than most."

"Meaning a small man is to be taken less seriously?"

"Most think so. It is to my advantage to let them believe it."

Daegan took a drink from his wineskin. "Then we shall make the detour. We will see if this Bess holds you in as high esteem as you believe."

For the remaining travel I thought of Lady Bess and wondered how she might react to seeing me again. I no longer wore a Benedictine habit—I was dressed as a commoner, but a commoner with some prestige. I was no labourer, no servant—I was a jongleur. Certainly, a more impressive craft than mucking horse stalls or tilling fields. And had she not said that if a man wanted to be found, he makes sure he is noticed?

At the sight of Kenninghall, my heart beat faster. The red brick façade stood in handsome contrast against the lush green wood. It had been five years since I last saw Bess Holland. I wondered if she would still act kindly towards me. Being Norfolk's mistress and living under the same roof as his wife could only be tolerable if Lady Stafford made it so. But I had difficulty imagining the older woman giving leave to the younger, more beautiful Bess and I hoped the experience had not changed my lady for the worse.

We arrived in the courtyard of Kenninghall and gazed up at the magnificent estate. The years had not changed it other than an oak growing taller and several other plantings looking fuller. My excitement built with a feeling of familiarity and the anticipation at seeing Lady Bess once again.

The storyteller nudged me with his elbow. "'Tis for you to make our introduction," he said. "Mind you, we will not entertain gratis."

I climbed down from the wagon, brushed the dust from my smock and hosen, and strode up to the door, aware that the troupe watched, intent on my every move. I knocked and waited.

A greyhound appeared, dashing out from the side of Kenninghall, and ran straight for me looking like a black demon from the gates of hell. I had no time to react at the sight of it. I envisioned his teeth in my neck and me supine in the yard, the beast feasting on my torso as the inhabitants of Kenninghall gazed on in mild amusement. I braced for my inevitable take down, when, without reason, he stopped only inches away, stone cold.

We were of equal size. He sniffed the hand I'd raised to fend him off, then his tail began wagging. I nearly collapsed in relief when the heavy door opened, and a liveryman expecting a person of similar height to his own looked straight across at the wagon. His white and red jacket embroidered with a white sallet over his heart reminded me of the hierarchy of status.

"Sir," I said, watching him draw his eyes down in surprise to see me standing there, "my fellow players request the honour to perform for the duke and his household." I swept off my cap and bowed. Before he could refuse, I added, "I am familiar to Kenninghall. Lady Bess knows me. I was an oblate from the priory who attended her when she was quite ill."

The man remained impassive, methinks recovering from the surprise of a dwarf knocking on their door.

"Of course, I am no longer associated with the priory." I gestured to the waiting wagon, adding, "The duchess also knows of me, as well as the duke."

The guard looked from me to the wagon full of players. He started to close the door and I pressed my hand against it, preventing him from shutting it.

"Lady Bess sayeth that if I should ever be near Kenninghall she would wish to see me, or else she would be sorely disappointed," I added.

The liveryman hesitated. He looked from me to the wagon again. "Wait you here. I shall inquire."

"Tell Lady Bess 'tis I, Kronos, who has"—he shut the door before I could finish—"come."

I stood a moment realising that my name was likely unnecessary for, probably, he would identify me otherwise. I returned to the wagon where the rest of the troupe had made the dog's acquaintance and we were now its most welcome guests.

"By my fay, a lady of stature wants to see *you*?" said Robert, with a snicker.

"She is generous of heart. I saved her life."

"Ho, ye be gallant and virtuous besides," said Robert. "And methinks you boast too much."

"Soft you," said Tish, admiring the exterior of the grand estate. "If Kronos should get us a night on these grounds, then why do you trouble?"

Robert snuffed and shook his head.

We sat wondering the outcome. Bertram took advantage of the delay and jumped from the wagon to find peace in the woods. A few moments later, the storyteller did the same. Tish sighed, and I began to worry why the liveryman had not returned.

"She remembers you not," said Robert, finally. "You think you hold a special place in this lady's heart, but it is your fantasy that you think it so."

I ignored Robert and took a long drink from my ale skin, wiping the warm brew from my chin and studying the grounds for signs of change instead of searching for Lady Bess possibly peeking from a window. Robert bit his thumb nail and spat it at me.

Finally, the door opened. I hopped off the wagon and met the liveryman halfway.

"You shall perform this evening for the household and be given leave to stay on the grounds overnight." His message done, he turned and started back to the house.

"What of Lady Bess? Did you speak with her?" I pressed, grabbing the hem of his jerkin.

The liveryman hesitated and looked down at my hand, which

I quickly removed. He brushed off his fine uniform as if I had soiled it. "Lady Bess will see you in the 'morrow."

Robert commented on the self-satisfied look on my face when I turned back to the wagon. "It is not as though your person is so important that she would see you straight away."

"Still, she will see me. That counts for something."

"So you tell yourself, little man. It stings less when we can fool ourselves into thinking otherwise," he said.

We moved our wagon to a flat area near where we would perform that night. Time allowed us to set up camp, and we cooked a meal of oats and blackberries picked from brambles nearby, topped off by fresh milk brought to us by a lovely young maid, whom Robert took an immediate interest in. Afterwards, there was still enough sun left in the day that we could each enjoy the expansive grounds at our leisure before that night's performance.

Beyond our camp there was a depression, a pond surrounded by tall grasses and alder, and further still, white willows gave way to hawthorn and oak. Robert had continued to sneer at my thinly disguised hopes for meeting with Lady Bess.

"Don't embarrass her in front of the duke," he said. "After all, he *is* her lover. Your mere presence just standing next to her is enough to elicit awkwardness. Indeed, I know not how you can avoid a strained and inelegant meeting."

Tish and Daegan wearied of Robert's snipes and found a spot to nap beneath a spreading oak. Tallis and Bertram tended Hazel and Tinker, feeding, then taking them to the pond to drink.

Though Robert continued to sling barbs, my mind settled on that night's performance and seeing Lady Bess. I left him practising his lute and got out my costume to find a low hanging branch on which to drape it, and with a heavy stick, I beat the dirt and dried mud out of it. A cloud of debris thickened the air.

I imagined Robert's simpering face square in the centre of my jerkin and thrashed it thoroughly.

When finished, my jacket was presentable, but I was not. I returned my costume to the wagon where Bertram was rooting about for a pan to fry mushrumps and a couple of eggs.

"'Tis a clear pond," said he, recoiling from a whiff of my person. "You might benefit from a dip. In truth, I encourage you, good friend."

Tallis arrived, having tied Hazel and Tinker to feed on a patch of clover. He looked me up and down. "You look as if you've been in a dust storm."

Taking their advice, I stripped and tied my old yellow sash around my waist in modesty then followed the path down to the water's edge. Bright yellow irises lined the periphery and damsel flies hovered then darted about, their iridescent bodies glistening in the sun. The water sparkled like a sky of stars and looked clean enough to dispense with several days' worth of dusty travel and pong.

I thought myself alone, but as I took a step into the inviting deep, I caught a glimpse of Robert on the opposite bank. Unaware of my presence, he lay nestled amongst the high reeds, sleeping, almost completely hidden in the overgrowth. I did not trust that he would leave me to bathe in peace, so I removed my sash and endeavoured to remain as quiet and as stealthy as I could.

Afterwards, I returned to camp, clean and happy. Content in myself and eager to perform.

⁘

That evening a stage was prepared for us in the side yard with several benches placed for the members of the household.

Norfolk's standard hung between two trees for a backdrop and rushlights provided by Kenninghall washed the area in an amber glow. I dressed in my motley and sat to the side watching Tallis practise his pipe and tabor. Bertram stretched his legs, lifting one up to his shoulders and then the other. My mind raced with the thought of seeing Bess again. Her being Norfolk's mistress failed to change my feelings. Any way, any existence in which she would know me, was my pleasure. Just being in her orbit of acquaintances would satisfy.

"Where be Robert?" asked Daegan, lacing the stays of his jacket.

"He was napping by the pond," I said.

"If he isn't careful, he'll miss the performance."

"It wouldn't be the first time," said Bertram. "Remember he preferred a lovely doxy in Hildersham and returned long after our show?" Bertram stretched an arm around his torso as if it were made of hawser-laid hemp. "We can perform without him."

"He did seem to like the milkmaid," I offered.

"Kronos, be prepared to go first," said Daegan. "We'll reverse the order tonight and Robert can perform later in the event that he wanders back in time. Tish can end for us."

Once the moon rose above the tree line, the members of the household began filtering into the yard. Their chatter filled the air and their anticipation fuelled our own. I placed my objects on the ground in front and stood aside to wait for Lady Bess to arrive. I wanted to know where she would be sitting, I wanted to fill my eyes with her before we began.

It was not long before every bench was filled. Looking beyond the gathering, the path leading to Kenninghall was empty. No Lady Bess. I felt a pang of disappointment.

"Kronos, I know not what has become of our lute player. We cannot delay. Are you ready?" Daegan asked.

"Mayhap, wait a moment more?" I nodded towards a few latecomers finding a place to sit. I desperately wished to see Lady Bess make her way down the aisle before I started. I had waited years.

Daegan agreed to delay until the last person settled in, then stepped out from behind the flag.

"Good wives and gentle persons of Kenninghall, welcome to our humble performance. We wish to deliver you from yon cares and woes and leave you in good cheer, if only for an hour. To begin this night, allow me to introduce our most capable stage ninny. Our man in miniature…Kronos!"

I stepped out from behind the standard, juggling apples, turning and catching, my eyes upon the spinning fruit. I added apples and took them away. I gently tossed one to a lady in the front row who did not react quick enough and the apple landed in her lap, completely startling her then causing the rest of the audience to laugh at her surprise. She, in turn, laughed along then pitched the apple back at my head. I ducked then pulled a face, which got another laugh.

When finished with the apples, I graciously bowed, searching the audience for my lady. A woman of stature now, I would have thought that she'd be given a place of prominence. But perhaps I was wrong to assume it. Perhaps the duchess insisted on attending tonight as the rightful mistress of Kenninghall. Alas, I saw neither one of them. Nor had the duke come to watch. Only servants and members of the staff sat before us.

My disappointment affected my confidence. I had difficulty suppressing the thought that my presence was not important to her, however, I had no alternative but to keep performing and put it out of my mind.

While gathering my oil-soaked torches (a new trick which I had now perfected) a disruption in the rear of the seated gallery drew everyone's notice. Several people stood to let through two liverymen carrying elegant chairs. The men came forward and placed them directly in front of the first row.

To bide my time, I slowly lit the juggling torches to a rush-light, one by one, waiting to see who would make their way to the chairs. Daegan hissed at me from behind the banner to begin. Murmurs rose from the impatient servants, and I ran the risk of my torches burning out in the middle of my juggling but I milked the moment, waiting for a glimpse of what I hoped would be Lady Bess before starting. Then, everyone stood.

Norfolk appeared and, on his arm, Bess. She wore a square necked bodice of black damask, a strand of pearls looped twice around her throat, accentuating the fairness of her lady's skin. A decorous French hood covered her silky dark hair, and while I would have preferred to see it hang loose and flowing, the shape of the hood flattered her face and the jewels on its billiment shimmered in the firelight. The two made their way down a narrow aisle to the chairs placed in front of me. I bowed before them, waiting until they had settled before standing, and caught Bess's demure smile. I fancied it was for me and my soul soared. But a glance at Thomas Howard, proud and stolid as a peacock, deflated me back to my low standing.

I placed my feet and paused to gather my wits, remembering that my skills had been honed from my long experience travelling and performing with the troupe. I tossed the first torch into the air and began juggling. The rhythm and familiarity of the moves restored my confidence, and I executed several difficult tricks with an ease that I knew would impress.

Done with the lit torches, I doused them in a bucket, the steam rising and the sizzling drowning out the applause. When once I trembled juggling knives, now I performed with unfaltering assurance. The rushlights lining the periphery were still fresh, illuminating the metal as it flashed in the air over our heads. I worked through every combination of skills that I knew in order to prolong my performance. Alas, the loud coughs coming from behind the duke's banner reminded me that my fellow players were anxious to perform. I ended by catching all my knives and took my bows only for Bess.

For the rest of the time, I watched her from the side, well out of the notice of the audience or troupe. She appeared completely engaged with the performance, laughing and then hanging on every note sung by Tish. Once, her eyes found mine. I hoped she saw the loyalty and admiration that I held for her in that brief exchange. Alas, her expression was indecipherable; she looked back at Norfolk and the moment was lost.

I studied the duke on the other side of her, his profile defined by a prominent nose and lengthy forehead. He was so much older than she. Though a capable man of proven military acumen and one of the king's closest advisors, his reputation for being cruel preceded him. How could Bess, a woman who could have enchanted anyone, submit to such a man?

When the evening's performance ended, I took a final bow with the rest of the troupe, savouring another moment being within her sights. There were times that called for a gesture of playful good will, and I broke from the line to present her with a dandelion. In the grandest of manners, I offered the little flower as if it were a ruby of inestimable worth. My puckish insolence almost always invited a good-natured jibe—either a laugh or a taunting rebuke to "Be gone, fool!"

For her part, Lady Bess graciously accepted the dandelion and thanked me as if it *were* of great value. She did not break the spell—her sincerity proved true to her nature. Norfolk, preoccupied with speaking to a servant, turned to see me take Lady Bess's hand and kiss the back of it. God's tooth! Such dagger eyes and sneer of disgust for so innocent a deed! He looked about to kick me to the ground when she spoke…

"My lord, this is Kronos. He and his master saved my life with their medicines on two separate occasions."

"I know who he is. We've met. You were absent a horse on the road."

"He was an oblate at Thetford Priory."

"But, no more. Would they not have you?"

"It is not my desire to become a monk."

"There be few choices for skits such as you. Be glad you can juggle. You could be begging on the streets."

"My meagre person may appear a hindrance but there are opportunities afforded me that others can only dream of," I responded.

"Do tell," Norfolk challenged.

"It would be impolitic for me to say." I thought better than to say something insolent to a man who could have me beaten with a snap of his fingers. I quickly took my leave, skipping away like the fool he believed me to be.

The next morning, I rose with the sun before any of the others dared wink open an eye. Truth be, I could hardly sleep, my mind was crowded with possibilities and thinking about Lady Bess and how our conference might unfold. Would she be the Lady Bess I remembered from before? Guileless, interested, and accepting? Or had her adulterous ado with Norfolk made her insensitive and unkind?

I let the others sleep, hoping that their late start might delay their impatience waiting for me while I met with Bess. Daegan was the first to rise.

"Be you quick with this duke's lady," he said. "We have miles to travel and a late start is not welcome." He glanced about with a puzzled look on his face. "Where is Robert? Has he crept back to camp?"

"Nay, not that I have seen."

Daegan scowled. "I should not want to delay waiting for him. If he has taken up with some wench, then he had better realise that we will not delay on his account." He rubbed his eyes, and added, "The same in regards for you. If we have packed and you have not been received, we will leave without you."

"My meeting with her might benefit us. We might regret it if I do not speak with her."

"One cannot regret what one does not know," he said, walking off to find a tree to sprinkle.

Fortunately, we did not wait long before a guard summoned me, and I felt encouraged. I followed behind, struggling to keep up with his long-legged stride.

The day was already warm, and Lady Bess received me outside, in a side garden lined with arbor vitae. Full and flush with green, they created a natural screen, safe from the prying eyes at ground level in Kenninghall. I would not be so trusted as to be left entirely alone with her. A guard stood by, not so close as to hear, but close enough to remind me of my place.

She watched me approach, and I steadied my stride. I lifted my chin to compensate for my self-awareness in the hopes that she was not scrutinising me in a dismissive way.

"Sit beside me, Kronos," she said, patting the bench next to her.

To sit within inches of her was more than I could have hoped for in my life.

I bowed, removing my cap, then sat, keenly aware that my feet did not touch the ground while hers did.

"When last I took ill, Brother Ulric attended me. He said you had left the monastery under scandalous circumstances."

"I am sorry to hear you took ill again." The heat rose from my collar, and I hoped she did not notice what must have been a telling flushed complexion. Inside, I felt ashamed of my brazen behaviour, though up until that moment, I had no regrets.

"It was a disagreement of sorts," I replied, glancing sideways to see if she knew more than I wanted to admit.

Bess sighed. "Taking the cowl was never your desire, was it? You told me that you wanted to find your way to the king's court."

"Aye, my lady. It is still my desire."

She listened to a robin's song warbling close by, then answered. "I am to accompany the duke to Whitehall and live with him there."

"You will be leaving Kenninghall?"

"It has become…uncomfortable here. I will attend the king's lady, the Marquess de Pembroke."

"Queen Catherine has died?" Travelling like we did, I was often unaware of news from London.

"The queen is very much alive, but she is past child-bearing age. She has never given the king a son." Lady Bess looked at an emerald ring and turned it around on her finger. "It is the king's wish to annul his marriage to Catherine and marry Anne Boleyn."

'Twas a name that I did recognise. Many a tavern rawgabbit carried on about the king's great "whore." She sought to seduce the king through witchery, though I always thought beautiful women possessed a magic missing in others less blessed. Whether witchery or God-given was not for me to ponder.

"He seeks a solution in divorce," I said. Anne Boleyn was indeed leading the king down a difficult road.

Bess nodded and sighed. "The king believes it was a sin to

marry his brother's wife. They have not had a son because God has condemned her for laying with her husband's brother."

"If a man shall take his brother's wife, it is an impurity; he hath uncovered his brother's nakedness; they shall be childless," I said, quoting the Old Testament. I contemplated this. "The king must believe he is justified."

"Thomas Cromwell will convince the Pope to agree to it."

"And who is this Thomas Cromwell?"

"The chief minister. He was once Cardinal Wolsey's man."

I was aware of Wolsey's unbridled power and influence. And I had heard he had died, having been diminished by the king. "You believe Thomas Cromwell will secure the king's wish?"

"He must. For the sake of England."

I wondered, if so goes the king, so goes Thomas Howard? The king had taken a younger woman and so, too, had the duke. Was Howard pursuing a divorce from his wife as well? These were prickly topics that I dared not broach.

"Then it is my hope that the Pope grants the king's desire." To voice an opinion was not warranted, nor was it prudent to stand on one side over the other. But taking the king's side was always the safer choice. If Lady Bess hoped for a similar outcome in her own circumstance, it would behoove me to support annulment, though it pained me to see her tied to the duke. My years in the monastery surfaced in a stab of remorse. Divorce condemned one's soul. I did not care what happened to our king's soul or to Thomas Howard's, but I did care what happened to Lady Bess's.

"My lady, do you remember our last conversation?"

"Remind me. The past is but a pinch in time," she said.

"You told me that life is a game and that I must learn to play it."

"I was cynical even then," she said, surprising me.

"You also said that if you should find your way to court, you would suggest my talent for entertaining." I paused, waiting for her to recollect.

"You wish that I remain true to my word?" she asked.

"If you believe I am worthy."

She turned and studied me, her expression and thoughts enigmatic. I felt myself failing under her scrutiny, so I clarified my desire.

"My lady, I should like to play the game."

The Player

CHAPTER SEVENTEEN

Ten years later—
October 1541

How I got from the banks of the Fleet to William Brugge's is an odd remembrance. I recall the wet of mud and blood, the stench of rot full in my nostrils, the cold damp of earth against my cheek. A jumble of words accompanied the sensation of me being hoisted then toted by my arms and legs, my head dangling unsupported, and excruciating pain. I had no sense of who had rescued me or where I was going. For all I knew, or cared, they could have chucked me into the Thames without me saying a peep.

It is all as in a dream, and when I come to, I am on a simple raised pallet in a darkened room. After a moment, my eyes adjust and the first thing I see is a woman peering down at me with a worried brow. Her eyes widen and she appears pleased to see me looking at her.

A finger goes to her lips. "Shhh," she whispers as soft as a feather.

A searing pain brings tears to my eyes. I cannot speak even if I tried. The pain is so malevolent there are no words to describe it.

She bends over a bowl, wringing pink water into it, then carefully dabs my cheek with the cloth. My sharp intake of breath not only startles her, but is an uncontrollable reaction that frightens even me. When she finishes, she brings a candle near my face and turns my head to better examine my cheek.

"In a few days we might forgo a wrapping," she says. "But for now, we must cover it."

My mouth and tongue feel as though a great weight constrains their movement. I can barely open my mouth.

"Be quiet, now. I must wrap this so that you may rest." She takes a length of soft linen and winds it about my face, securing the end, then stands back to assess her handiwork. She pats my arm.

"It will take time, but you will heal and adjust."

Her reassuring sentiment has the opposite effect. What does she mean? I shake my head, imploring her to explain. I point at my mouth, and my muffled cry sounds foreign to my ears. My missing memory and my inability to comprehend the extent of my injury frightens me.

"Part of your tongue is burned along with your cheek. You must have struggled because I believe it could have been worse. I'm afraid, though, you will have significant scarring. Given how severe your injuries are, be thankful that you escaped with your life." She pulls a blanket up to my neck and gently tucks it around my body. "You need rest. Take ease. You are safe now." She turns to leave and I seize her arm.

After more insistent screaks and imploring gestures from me she explains further.

"My husband is William Brugge and I am Joan, his wife. Two nights ago, an urgent knocking stirred us from our sleep and when William answered, he found you naked outside the door. You were senseless and covered in mud and blood. Whoever left you did not want to answer questions or be seen. We know not who you are or why you have been brutalised." She steps back and my hand falls from her arm. "William is an apothecary, and I use his medicines to heal those who come to us with little or no means." She smiles. Her face transforms and lightens with her kindness. "We believe someone must have known this and left you in our care. Eventually we expect that you will manage to tell us who you are and why you were treated thus. For now, though, take your rest and do not despair."

Her mild manner does in some measure console me. If I should be mutilated and abandoned in the weeds, then surely this gentle lady has prevented my utter demise.

I lie, piecing together my memory of that horrid day. I have no reckoning of time and I wonder how long I spent in my fitful memories. My mind drifts through how I got to court and through the political currents that came with our king's appetite for wives—

No one bothered with where a king's fool went in Whitehall. The massive palace boasts fifteen hundred rooms, more than the Pope's Vatican in Rome. Who needs a Roman pope when we have one here in London? Henry is as powerful as the weaselly-nosed Clement VII. He's made himself the supreme head of our faith and keeps all of the churches' assets instead of sending them to the Pope. I do not agree with all of our king's decisions, but I defend his right to make them. He is, after all, the ruler of our isle, the one appointed by God to lead us (though even God makes foolish decisions).

Lady Bess procured for me an audience with Will Somers, Henry's revered natural fool. If I should impress Somers then I may be brought before the king, and if I so pleaseth our liege, I may have a place entertaining at court. On first meeting Will Somers, I remember thinking I must be exceptional but take care that I did not excel in voicing my wit for he alone had the king's ear for irreverent discourse. If I were to preserve my place once I got it, then I must mind my tongue.

My first engagement at court was on St. Swithin's Day, a light-hearted fête celebrating the ninth-century King Egbert's chaplain who could mend broken eggs. I knew King Henry supported the cultivation and propagation of fruit at his Great Orchard of Hampton Palace and traditionally, orchardists prayed for a good rain on this day to plump the fruit, especially apples for the upcoming harvest. I took the day to be propitious, and so I brought eggs and apples to juggle.

I had already impressed Will Somers, but I knew if our king was of peevish humour this day, I might end back on the roads plying my talent for meals and a bed to sleep. This king's whims were incalculable, so it was crucial that I perform my best.

St. Swithin's Day arrived in favourable manner, raining hard in the morning then followed in the afternoon by brilliant sun. When Will Somers prompted me to follow him to court, he warned that I should not look Harry in the eye—ever. To do so was an affront.

I would never dare a man with the height and build of this king, who stood nearly a head taller than most. By comparison I might reach his mid-thigh and so gaze upon his handsome calves, of which (I was told) he is proud, for cert a better sight than his capricious stare.

As soon as Somers and I entered, I felt the weight of interested appraisal upon my person. I had grown accustomed to derisive comments and blatant ogling, but not when it came from royalty. My heart thrummed in my chest.

"Your Majesty, I present to you—Kronos."

Immediately I removed my cap, placed one leg forward, dropped my chin to my chest, and lowered myself in a respectful bow. Here I paused, waiting.

"Has this stump an ability?" asked the king.

"He is a juggler, your Majesty," answered Somers. "A most proficient talent, a worthy distracter."

I remained bowed as he considered me and while time lengthened, I wondered if he would never permit me to straighten. I imagined myself backing out of court, crouched and rejected without having tossed a single apple.

"Rise, minion. Let us see how much talent is stuffed into your diminutive self." Every word echoed implicit boredom, and I fought against an impending verdict of disapproval. I glanced at Somers and received a nod of encouragement.

One must never turn their back on the king. I knew this. For years I'd been able to juggle through bawling babies, dark stages, raucous brawls, and rotten fruit being thrown at me. But never had I performed for royalty. Juggling for King Henry (such an imposing figure, such a mercurial man) became frighteningly real to me and rather than shake uncontrollably, I turned my back so that I might gather my courage knowing full well that I might suffer from such a saucy gesture.

Moments can feel like hours, but I emptied my sack of apples and eggs onto the floor and picked up five apples, testing their weight in my hands.

"You present to me your puny arse?" said the king. "I could have you thrashed for such insolence."

His words should have rattled me, but they had the opposite effect. Determined to show him my talent, I ignored his threat and began juggling. After a couple of rotations where I found my comfort, I turned to face the king.

My eyes focused on the circling objects, and I disappeared King Henry into the background. An innocuous background of no consequence. All that mattered was keeping the apples moving. I went through my usual juggling ritual, then switched to juggling eggs. In the end, I managed to impress Henry well enough that I was given a place to sleep, and soon I was as commonplace at Whitehall as the falcon carvings decorating its walls.

From that day forward, I had been privy to murmurings about our liege's dalliances. Anne Boleyn, that expert in coquetry, had played him like a lute, keeping Henry strung taut with desire but never yielding to his ultimate… plucking. Nay, that indulgence was withheld until she was assured of her position to replace our beloved Queen Catherine from Aragon. Anne was a tease. I remember when she was full in belly for her coronation and needed help to get to her feet after prostrating herself before the high altar. That sycophant Archbishop Cranmer placed the Crown of St. Edward upon her arrogant head and gave her a rod and sceptre—authority over our kingdom. And there was King Henry, drooling from behind the holy rood screen, watching the entire spectacle.

Anne did not last. I've been at court long enough to wonder, who does? The king grew weary of her divisiveness. He grew tired of waiting for her to birth him a male heir. She kept promising, but what woman knows with certainty the sex of the child swimming about in her womb? Does she feel his little prick poking her in the stomach?

Her final miscarriage occurred not long after the king fell from his horse during a joust. He lay unresponsive for two hours and when he woke, he was a changed man. Some blamed Anne's miscarriage on the shock of his near death, but the lines on her face and hollowed eyes spoke more to her ability to have a child than it did to experiencing a terrible fright. Anne was growing old, just like her predecessor, just like all of us. And with Edward Seymour (then of the king's Privy Chamber) pushing his meek, younger sister at the king, Harry lost patience with Anne.

In his service, I was always a careful listener and an even more careful speaker. Though I was often accused of being a talebearer, I did not spread lies indiscriminately, casting them about like a farmer sowing seeds. Nay, my goal was to earn favour with the ladies of the court with whom I had an attraction. What harm is there in that?

Had I forgotten my Bess Holland? Had I cast her aside for easier fare? Nay, I held her in esteem, above all others, but I respected the boundary between us and I knew not to toy with Thomas Howard's possessions. Norfolk was a formidable man, as violent and spiteful as the king, and I valued my neck.

My counterpart, Will Somers, was a fool in the full sense of the word. He'd earned the trust and companionship of our king, but that was always a dangerous road to tread. He was simple of mind and ignorant of the possible consequences of his unvarnished opinions. He had the impertinence to sympathise with our former queen and her daughter Mary, while calling Anne a ribald and her daughter a bastard. This was before Anne fell out of favour. The king threatened to "kill the jester with his bare hands."

I was not so reckless.

I could smell which way the wind blew. I saw how the king became silent and distant in Anne's presence. Chief minister Thomas Cromwell saw it, too. Now *there* was a man who played the game! Cromwell engineered Anne's fall, his loyalty shifting to suit the king's needs. When Anne's head finally landed in the straw, Harry celebrated by marrying Jane Seymour ten days later. And Edward Seymour, that dissembling actor, became the Earl of Hertford shortly thereafter.

I liked Jane. Blessed with a mild nature, she wanted nothing more than to please the king. For all of the previous years' tumult, I remember her reign with fondness for the general sense of calm that descended on the realm. The king doted on her. He held her small hand in his large paw and kissed it sweetly, especially when her breasts and belly swelled with child. It was his great regret that she did not live but a few days after giving him his most desired male heir, Edward VI.

Here I must pause to turn on my side. For how long I've laid upon this bed I have no inkling, but I've been here long enough for my bladder to desire a piss. A pisspot has been left beside the bed, and I ease myself onto my feet, my legs trembling with weakness. Taking extra care to aim correctly, I suppress my sigh of relief so as not to summon Joan. Dear, thoughtful Joan. I shake off the last dribble and return to my pillow.

Two marriages later, Katherine Howard is being accused of behaviour that Anne Boleyn was innocent of. However, Thomas Cromwell is no longer here to manipulate the evidence. Perhaps he had too much power, and the king did not like that. After Jane died, Henry blamed Cromwell for arranging his marriage to the "Flander's mare" with whom he was incapable of performing his husbandly duty. Be not surprised that I know this. I was privy to plenty of idle conjecture circulating at court and in this instance, I think it true. Anne of Cleves was as bland as milk-soaked bread. I would not have wanted to bed her.

Let Thomas Cromwell be a reminder of how badly the game of court can end. The man was cunning—a trait I greatly admired. He was a blacksmith's son, of low birth like me, and like his predecessor, Cardinal Wolsey. Yet he overcame the shackles of his humble beginning and grew to great influence. Oh, he had his enemies. Norfolk despised him. My guess is that the feeling was mutual. The duke capitalised on Cromwell's mistake in suggesting the Düsseldorf dowdy. He, along with other men of court (including Edward Seymour), facilitated Cromwell's downfall. After Cromwell's body was separated from his head, Norfolk immediately championed his niece for Henry's next bride—Katherine Howard.

Shh! Murmurs of conversation seep through the door and I must be soft and listen…pah, I cannot discern a single word. The blank walls of dingy plaster are my only company and not even a window to know if it is day or night. Why should I be so confined? The only object of interest is a wood beam with a cobweb fanning to the corner and a lonely spider sitting in wait.

This humble, straw-stuffed bed is a sad commentary on how far I've fallen. Once my bed was shared by some of the loveliest women in London, and now I have a spider for companionship. And then to be maimed…I have borne more than most. I surmounted my stunted condition and rose above all condemnation to entertain the king. And now this.

Though these walls keep me obedient like Thetford Priory, the walls cannot constrain my mind. I am sorry for my circumstance, but there are others for whom I should feel worse. Our current queen being one of them.

Katherine Howard's naïveté is her undoing. She simply can't control her appetite for pleasure or rather, she can't control the men who come seeking their pleasure with her.

I recall my own promiscuity at that age, but my physicality was a hindrance. Indeed, some women thought me a monster born. I had no money and never would I have position.

If I had stayed at Thetford, eventually I would have found myself, like my brethren, without a home and without purpose. Cromwell's plan to dissolve the monasteries and fill the king's coffers with proceeds from the sales of anything deemed valuable had led to the displacement of thousands of monks, nuns, and clerics who were given a small pension and sent on their way to make do with the rest of their lives. Thetford Priory was one of the last monasteries to be closed due to its significance with the Howard family and the fact that Henry's bastard son, Henry FitzRoy, was buried there, but even Norfolk couldn't save it from Henry's ultimate greed. I wonder how Pinter Pender fared after they took his cowl and booted him out the door? At least I had my juggling—a frivolous waste of time, they thought. My disport had served me well. I had travelled the country and entertained the king. At least I was not begging for pennies outside St. Paul's.

But to end this way, mutilated and left for dead, because I overheard particulars that may or may not be true? The injustice of it! I was merely the unfortunate and unwilling recipient of a vulgar communication. Why should I be so cruelly punished?

I growl at the heavens—there, I do have some voice!—and my spider friend scuttles into hiding.

I think back to the day when I was so brutally silenced. Should I blame that ruiner John Lascelles—that rascal, that troublemaker—for my fate? For taking conference with Archbishop Cranmer, that gutless man of cloth who has kissed the king's arse so oft his teeth are stained brown? Lascelles had better be telling the truth or it will be *his* head on a pike. Was he a friend to Edward Seymour? I wonder, because his secret could bring down the Howards.

No doubt Edward Seymour desires the downfall of the Howard family, especially Norfolk—that vile influencer. Seymour has benefitted from the king's marriage to his sister, Jane. He has the security of knowing that his nephew, Edward VI, will be king someday. Besides, if the Howards fall from grace, there would be no reason for King Henry to return to the conservative beliefs of the Howards. Seymour's standing and leverage would be reaffirmed. But wait! It wasn't Seymour calling for my tongue—it was Audley. Thomas Audley.

Phht. These "Thomases" make my head spin. If I should ever have a son, that is the one name he shall never be christened.

Thomas Audley was another benefactor of the king's reformed church. Audley helped bring down Anne Boleyn and Thomas Cromwell. And he encouraged my maiming.

These men of court are liars and Janus-faced dissemblers. Watch your back, for they will surely carve their initials in it with a knife.

Fie, these men of entitlement who ruin lives. It is because of them that I find myself disgraced and outcast.

CHAPTER EIGHTEEN

Enough ladies wandered through the halls of Whitehall that I indulged my fantasies on a regular basis. Leave not to the imagination what you can make real. My reputation for pleasing the fair sex filled my time when I was not juggling or making mischief to entertain. Don't think that women are easily offended. They may appear pudibund, but beneath that demurring exterior is a lioness who wants to be ravished within an inch of being caught out.

Never was I accused of violating a woman against her wishes. A woman is hard-pressed to resist absolute rapture when given the right balance of playfulness and daring. Besides, my physical deformity was a gift—no woman would openly admit to being with me. Their reticence kept me safe.

My reminiscences so consume my mind that I am not sure if I am in a dream when I feel my shoulder being rocked. It is Joan come to see me.

"I have brought you some broth," she says. "You must regain your vigour if you are to heal."

Her hand slips under my arm and she leans me forward to arrange the bolster behind my back.

"That should do." Her eyes settle on my cheek. "You've slept quite a while. If I may take a look…" She loosens the strip of cloth holding a wad of linen against my cheek and gingerly removes it. After trying to see in the dim light, she takes the candle on the table and brings it closer to examine me. Her finger cautiously touches my wound, and I flinch.

"Still tender, but I am pleased to see improvement. I shall leave off the dressing while you eat then put on fresh."

I am wondering how I will manage to eat with a tongue swollen the size of an onion, but Joan presents me with a short piece of hollow wheat stalk through which I may suck. She holds a bowl of tepid broth under my chin.

"Let us see how you fare."

The smell stimulates my appetite, and I can't control a strand of drool escaping from my mouth. I sympathise with how Brother Giles must have felt at Thetford, embarrassed and helpless to prevent the humiliating consequences of old age. But I am not old, just maimed.

After a few tries, I place the straw so that my raw lips partly close around it, and I sip in small spurts a portion of the broth. It would not seem that a simple bowl of thin liquid would satisfy me, but my stomach growls in kind. A faint smile appears on Joan's face.

"I'm encouraged," she says, setting down the bowl when I am done. She walks to the door and exits, leaving it open enough so that I can watch her in the next room.

I can see that the room is bright compared to mine. Light streams in from high windows. Rows of crockery jars line shelving at the back. In front of the shelving is a table with wooden mortar and pestles, various size bowls, and jugs. Herbs hang from nails in rafters, green and crisp. A strong scent of peppermint stings my nose, the familiarity of which reminds me of Brother Ulric's herbarium.

Apparently, Joan is alone. She focuses on mixing the contents of a bowl and carefully adding liquid from a bottle. After a moment she returns to me, closing the door behind her.

"This will help the scarring on your cheek. Alas, there is nothing I can do for your tongue. It must heal on its own." She stirs the glutinous concoction a bit more and continues, "This is one of my husband's poultices which will draw the dry humours to the surface of your skin. That is what is needed with severe burns." Joan scoops up some mash and carefully blots it on my face. After the initial dab, my skin cools, and I do not mind her touching me. I watch her concentrate.

Joan is a handsome woman, not beautiful by court standards, but her benevolent demeanour and intelligence serves her bearing, making her a woman to be appreciated and respected. If I should guess, she is past child-bearing, but only just. The skin crinkles beside her dark eyes when she smiles, and there are folds of skin in front of her ears like those of a mature woman. It is quiet here and in the herbarium; no stomping steps from the floor above. If there are children, they are well-behaved. Given Joan's nature, I would not be surprised if her children were also thoughtful and, most likely, studious in nature. However, I have not heard a child's inquiring voice, nor the patter of light feet.

Would she be old enough to have a son or daughter of middling age? I think on this as she places a clean patch of cloth over my wound and ties it in place, her thin fingers working the ends. I am deciding she is a childless woman—the kind of woman who cares for the poor and the disenfranchised and nurses them back to being human again. That is why she has compassion and patience to spare.

My curiosity gets the better of me, and, lying one hand palm up, with the other I make a gesture of writing, hoping she will bring me what I need so that I may communicate.

"You can write?" she asks in surprise.

I am gratified that I was able to convey my desire. She understands what I want, but her astonishment makes me wonder if she assumed I was not educated. Did she think this because of my nanism? I would like to tell her that being a dwarf does not mean I am also of diminished intelligence.

I nod, exaggerating that I absolutely can write and that I wish to do so.

"Let me find a piece of shale," she says, exiting and closing the door.

For the first time, I hear voices on the other side of the wall beyond the head of my bed. Had conversations been going on with regularity and I had not noticed until now? Am I regaining my wits—but how long have I been missing them? Two men talk about a remedy. They quiet and Joan is addressed in the herbarium.

A man—William?—asks about wych elm and Joan replies that there is only a small portion left. "I used it for our guest."

"I haven't enough to fill my customer's request!"

"It can be replenished. If you need it, I shall go now and fetch more," she replies.

"This is an inconvenience for our customer. Now he must return later!"

A second voice offers placation. "Master Brugge, it is not a dire imposition. I can return tomorrow. An extra day shall not be a trouble for me."

"But what will stop you from seeking another apothecary?"

"Nay, sir. I am pleased with your work. I seek no other."

"I am glad of that, but I am aggrieved that you should wait."

"Husband, I shall go. I will not be long. Sir, can you return in the afternoon? William will have your remedy ready on your return."

"Certainly," says the customer. I think the man must be squirming over the couple's exchange and obliges if only to help keep the peace. "I shall return later," he confirms. The shop door scrapes and is followed by a brief silence. The customer has left.

"You've lost us a customer," says Brugge.

"He said he shall return," replies Joan.

"So he says, but if I were him, I'd go to Bucklersbury Lane and find another apothecary ready to serve. Fool woman. Do you think we can afford to lose another customer?"

I cringe hearing him speak to her this way. I fling back the blanket, exposing my bare legs and feet, and swing them to the edge, my feet dangling off the floor. I must intervene and stop him.

My toes are turning blue from the chill in the room, when a stir of movement draws my attention. The door opens and I get my first look at William Brugge, this man of medicines. He glowers at me, taking measure of my person, a look of disgust on his face I've not seen since Brother Giles at Thetford Priory.

For every second he glares at me, I meet his disdain with mutual revulsion. His treatment of Joan appals me; I cannot tolerate such cruelty to so kind a woman. My voice is silenced, but surely my eyes can convey what my tongue cannot.

He breaks his stare then scans the room with a look of supreme displeasure. His eyes settle back on me and in an emphatic gesture, he slams the door.

I get out of bed and creep across the floor, placing my ear against the door.

"This cannot go on," Brugge hisses in a voice just loud enough for me to hear. "This…person is using our resources and is taking advantage of our circumstances. We don't even know who he is or why he was mutilated."

"Husband, it is because of your healing balms that he has come into our care. Whoever left him on our doorstep did so because of your reputation for making effective medicines. Your ability is legend and appreciated by many. It is a blessing to be so recognised."

"What are we to do with him? We know nothing about him."

"In time we shall come to understand," says Joan. "Someone will step forward, or perhaps he himself shall tell us why he was so horribly maimed."

"Something odd surrounds this situation. It troubles me that we have no inkling as to who he is or why he was left outside our door."

"Do not concern yourself," says Joan. "Perhaps there is nothing more to it than just someone hoping for us to heal him. Some people are sensitive to others' misfortunes."

There is silence. Perhaps Joan has successfully tamped her husband's ire.

"He was able to take some nourishment," she says. "He will improve, husband. Soon he shall be able to resume his previous life, and we will no longer be burdened with his care."

Again, there is no response from William Brugge the apothecary.

"Now, while our guest rests peaceably, I shall replenish your supply of wych elm which I used without asking your permission. There is bread and broth if you are hungry. Take your rest and I shall return anon."

I scuttle back to the bed and hurriedly pull the blanket to my neck and feign sleep. Being left alone with this mad man of medicine discomfits me but I have no choice. I must remain unthreatening. If I thought court politics were fraught, then I have been thrust into contentious environs once again. Without Joan's protection I am like a babe left in the woods. Shhh! Be soft! For I hear a wolf rustling through the trees.

CHAPTER NINETEEN

The King's court is rife with wolves. They wear sheep's clothing of velvet doublets with gold chains of office and jewel-encrusted rondels tucked in their belts. They prowl the halls, the banquet rooms, the lodgings, the gardens, their noses sniffing out duplicity and their tongues dripping with saliva from a well-placed deceit.

The men of court are expert in the art of manipulation, always with an eye for self-promotion at another man's expense. If you are not thinking ahead of your cohort, then you leave yourself vulnerable. You had better retire from the court than suffer the consequences of a distrusting king who would just as soon see your rictus leer displayed on a pike over Southgate than grant you leave. Guile is the currency, and a man could line his pockets and rise in stature—*if* he had the cunning and finesse to ably manage his game.

While I could have ignored every bit of chinwag, I listened and I watched. I drew my own conclusions. Look beyond to what the eyes cannot see, and listen to what the ears cannot hear. Bess Holland forewarned me. "If you should survive at court," she said, "you must remain a fool in it."

She did not mean that I should be an ass. She meant for me to be aware and act ignorant. My present circumstance is not a result of my inability to play. It is a result of happenstance. I cannot fault myself for my situation except to regret an afternoon dalliance with a laundrymaid. How should I know that the archbishop would use a random room in Whitehall, one of fifteen hundred, to hold conference with a snivelling protestant? It is my poor luck.

Outside my door, William Brugge moves about in his herbarium. Perhaps he is working on a new remedy, or perhaps he is considering what to do about me. With Joan gone, there is the distinct possibility that he will take this opportunity to at least confront me. It is disquieting lying here, watching the lantern burn, biding my time, watching the spider repair her web, waiting for Joan's return.

I slide further down between the sheets as I remember another woman whose choice of husband I deem unfortunate—Bess Holland.

Does Bess know what has befallen me? Has court gossip informed her of my fate? By now bells and ribbons have been added to embellish my story. To make it pretty. To make it sensational. But now I flatter myself. More likely my ordeal has become a rumour for the grist mill and not an important one. A tale given a cursory glance, much like the first robin of spring, then forgotten when the day becomes crowded with other, more interesting birds.

I say my tale may not be given much air, but there might be a few who will ponder why I was so cruelly treated. To think is not the same as to say and these perspicacious few will snuffle through the leavings, like pigs after truffles, rooting out their prize and devouring it full.

Because of Bess Holland, I was given an opportunity to

perform at court. My arrival followed her move to Whitehall with Thomas Howard. She was no longer his children's governess but became an attendant maid for Anne Boleyn.

As I said before, Anne Boleyn was a pot stirrer—a strong personality, with all the perils that go with it. During her debacle, I kept myself scrupulously clear of gossip; not wishing to jeopardise my appointment at court. Once Anne Boleyn had been dispatched, Bess became a maid for Jane Seymour. Such appointments, though perilous, have long been the desire of women of status, and the navigation of these dangerous waters is a skill in which Lady Bess excels.

Indeed, Thomas Howard's wife, Elizabeth Stafford, had been a lady for the former Queen Catherine. A loyal lady, Elizabeth despised the Queen's usurper, Anne Boleyn. Like our liege, Thomas Howard had also found a prettier, more nubile lover— my Bess. As expected, the duke's wife did not take kindly to the young addition.

"She called me a drab, a churl's daughter, a bawd," confided Bess. "She spat on me!"

I was stunned that a woman of Elizabeth Stafford's status could act so crass. "One might witness such behaviour in a Southwark stew," I told Bess. "But not amongst ladies!"

She shrugged her delicate shoulder. "I was living at Kenninghall when it happened. It was after your visit with the troupe. She and I commenced to shouting. Such vile words coming from her mouth. She would not be silenced. Thomas ordered her to be held down. But she would not be cowed. She kicked and fought like a netted boar. Such a temper! Thomas took hold of her hair and dragged her screaming and thrashing to her chamber. The two exchanged cruel words that I will not soon forget. He locked her in until she settled."

Norfolk's treatment of his wife troubled me. "If the duke should ever treat you thus, I will…"

Bess's eyes had glazed in thought, then she startled out of her rumination. She touched my arm and shook her head, dispelling any notion I had. "My lord has no tolerance for such noise. And, I do not growl."

Living with Norfolk at Whitehall kept Bess separated from his wife and was a necessity for Howard, for he had risen in favour with the king and was now a close advisor. To have the lovely Bess by his side must have conveyed tacit approval of the king's own circumstance. Two years would go by before Howard finally got his wife out of Kenninghall and moved to Redbourne to live out her days on a simple stipend. Another two years went by before Anne Boleyn lost her head. How easily these men dispensed with their women when expedient.

I am envisioning Bess's serene face when the sound of determined steps approaches and the door swings open. William Brugge stands on the threshold.

Brugge is composed of sharp angles. His narrow nose turns under at the tip, nearly covering his upper lip which, together with the bottom, are compressed in a thin line as if he is deciding whether or not to say what is on his mind. Sculpted cheekbones and his defined chin create a triangle, reminding me of a soldier's breastplate. There is no softness in his features, no paunch to easily push a knife into. He appears taller than most, but the low ceiling may be misleading. For the past several years, I had measured men against the expansive palace architecture I had grown accustomed to with its soaring ceilings and flying buttresses that diminished mortals to the size of ants crawling beneath them. King Henry was an exception, being tall in height—and lately, in width as well.

Though not as tall as our king, the apothecary's bearing intimidates. His eyes hold mine. I dare not move.

After a moment, his lips part and he asks, "Who are you?"

Ha! It is a question I ponder every day. But it would be impertinent to say so, even if I could speak. There was a brief time in my life when I cursed my puny self, realising how very different I really was. While it is true that my stunted build is often mocked, I remember that it is also my gift. And so far, I have been able to exploit it to fine effect.

And now I must see the advantage of a second condition—I could not speak intelligibly. I could answer William Brugge in flubbered squawks, but I will not humiliate myself. I keep my mouth shut. I remain silent.

His immobile stare does not hide what I imagine is tumbling around in his head. "You cannot communicate?" he says, incredulous. His head tilts. "Or you choose not to?"

For a moment I wonder if his science allows him to hear me thinking. A drop of perspiration snakes down the back of my neck, but I give him nothing. I know too little about this William Brugge. What would he do if he knew I had access to the king? Would he use this to further himself? How would he pursue that? I need to think. I glance at his hard eyes trained on me. For a man with a reputation for healing and helping those in need, there is no obvious compassion.

"Understand," he says, "that you will not use my wife or my residence for one day longer than you must. My home is not a haven for wounded criminals and malingerers." His eyes drift down to the jake beside my bed. "I'll not have you ruining my shop with the smells of your convalescence."

He looks angry enough to kick the pisspot but surely, he is not so imprudent. My resentment flares at being called a criminal and a malingerer. It is hardly my choice that I should end incapacitated with this scarred face. If I had hosen and shoes, I would leave without hesitation.

But where would I go?

Returning to Whitehall is riddled with risk. My only safe harbour there might be with the Lady Bess, but that is fanciful thinking. She would not be able to hide me until the matter concerning our young queen is resolved. 'Tis a matter that might take weeks, perhaps months. Then, if Thomas Howard discovered me, what would happen? It is *his* niece who is at the centre of this chaos. Imagine being the uncle of *two* disgraced queens? Methinks the rumour will not blow away like a sudden gale, upsetting the ruffles on the king's smock then settling. The scuttle of Katherine Howard's infidelity has legs and a body of likelihood. It is sound enough to run through this court and trounce everyone in it. I do not know Katherine Howard's past but I do know her present, and she is far too inexperienced to navigate the watchful eyes of courtiers.

Would my fellow performers offer refuge? Pah. Will Somers is too much of a natural fool to help my cause. He says what he thinks, and he does not think like me. His words tumble from his mouth like a gush from a tap, bold, copious, and unfiltered. I think of my musician friends but then, they are a meek and strange lot. None of them would chance sheltering me now with my face carved like a beef roast. Hiding me would implicate them. Guilty by association, as the saying goes, and none of them have the wit for me to convince them otherwise. Nay, the castle and all of its players are to be avoided.

Could I chance the streets of London? Now that is a bugbear. I've learned enough these past few years to know that our exceptional maid of a city is crawling with lice under her skirt. A man such as me should never leave a boozing ken alone past curfew. Though the few times when it couldn't be helped, I was lucky that my aggressors were drunker than me. At the sight of my little self, they would gape and assume their eyes were playing tricks on them. Just that gnat's fart of advantage would give me enough time to escape. Whether I ducked into alcoves, dropped behind barrels of rotting fish, crawled alongside a roaming pig, I used my size to advantage.

What? Would I not arm myself on such forays? There is not a single soul in all of London over the age of twelve who does not keep a dagger. I kept mine in my sheath, and did not hide it when I sat in a ken. It leaned against my padded codpiece, the two an impressive display of manhood. To be fair, such ostentation is more common than not. The dagger could deter in an establishment where men sat arse to arse, there being only a short distance from drawing it and pricking a man under the chin. However, once on the streets, my short arms would not favour me in a knife fight.

William Brugge stares, waiting for me to acknowledge that his home is not for me to abuse. I give a slight nod to appease, then my mind scuttles back to Whitehall…

Though Whitehall is my home, I did not spend all of my time pleasuring the ladies in between my duties to entertain. Across the river, the Bishop enjoys the added income of taxing establishments of ill-repute while our king coyly looks the other way. Taverns and stews are a man's playground. Men have to go somewhere, and ridding London of the worst keeps the king's city relatively decorous by comparison.

Not all of Southwark's stews are frowzy establishments filled with shopworn bawds and sticky bed linens. One learned to avoid the bordels within spitting distance of the clink and other prisons—those being the first stop for men lucky enough to be sprung. The poor doxies making a living there are as unpleasant as unsold cod fillets at the end of market. No hard piss can rid you of the burn that comes with their hot 'lips'.

My preferred house of pleasure is The Cardinal's Red, named for a particular appendage rather than for His Eminence's carmine robe. From my first step inside its doors, I was instantly surprised (and amused) by their irreverent rendition of a nunnery. A carved stoup stood by the door, but it contained ale rather than holy water. After blessing oneself under the watchful direction of the prioress (mistress of the game), you kneeled to ask forgiveness (for the sins you were about to commit).

Because the wenches mock the Pope, they are given allowance to ridicule the old religion to their and their patrons' pleasure. And while guilt did, at times, niggle my conscience, I admit I took glee in the audacity of it.

Leticia, whom I nick-named "Let us", is my favourite "nun" at The Cardinal's Red. She has a sly wit and her unapologetic role-playing would leave me exhausted in body and breathless from our ludification. Forgive me, but her religion was good for my spirit.

The first time she led me to a room in the rafters, my conscience roiled, but I followed her up the narrow stairwell, past rooms where the groans of pleasure could be heard through doors, and an unrestrained squeal told me that the nuns were not immune to enjoying their work on occasion. With all of the distractions, it was difficult to avoid tripping on her habit while I followed her through the dark hall.

A short set of steps brought us to our room and she closed the door behind me.

"Remove my veil," she directed. She sat on the bed so I could reach her head. I lifted the headpiece and reverently laid it on a table.

"Remove my habit."

"You will leave your coif and wimple?"

"If it pleases you." She smiled.

I loosened the cloth at her waist and she pointed to a stool upon which I clambered while she got to her feet. I gathered the cloth of her habit and worked it over her head. She wore nothing under her robe and I collapsed on the stool to admire her.

"You are beautiful," I told her, and I meant it.

Her face showed no sign of being moved or affected, which saddened me. Had months, perhaps years, of dispassionately servicing men so hardened her to accepting a sincerely meant compliment? I was chagrined that I had drawn attention to my appreciation. She sensed my hesitation.

"When God handed out beauty, sir, he must not have seen you."

I burst out laughing. "Nay, he neglected to look down."

We were on level footing then. She could tease and jest, and I would never take exception. She would speak truthfully, and I could never wish she would temper her taunts because there was an honesty in her that I found missing in most. That first night we did nothing more than talk and at the end of the night, I placed the requisite coins on the table by the door. She swiped them up and handed them back.

"You will visit again, Master Kronos. And then we shall see where we are."

If I had insisted, she would have been insulted.

"You must have something to give your prioress," I said, worried of the possible consequences for her. Besides, I did not want to chance being barred from The Cardinal's Red and from seeing her again.

"If you feel compelled," she said, opening the door, "make an offering to our Mother Superior on your leave." She straightened my doublet and brushed off my shoulders. "Never forget," she said, "this is a house of God."

❧

My face must have changed at the memory of Let us, because William Brugge immediately takes offence and startles me into the present with his guttural words.

"You dare to smirk?" he asks.

The mind is a curious vehicle. Look how thoughts speed past in the flit of a butterfly's wing. Brugge has voiced a warning, to which I am fixed in fear.

The uncomfortable silence lengthens into a discomfiting stalemate. My heart quickens as I imagine him throttling me but lo…we are interrupted by the sound of the shop door opening. Brugge abandons me to resume my memories of the inimitable nun. I blow out a long breath, realising how shallowly I'd been breathing. He leaves the door ajar, making me wonder if he will be back to chastise me later.

I keep still, straining to listen. It would be essential for me to know the workings of William Brugge's apothecary shop; one may never know when such information might be useful. As I lean forward to better hear, Joan's muffled words carry through the open door.

"Did you eat while I was gone?" she asks her husband.

"Nay. You can cook me a meal now that you are home."

"I found a ham hock. It will make for a good stock." There is a pause and then she says, "Here is your wych elm, husband. I was wrong to use your supply without asking."

Why does she apologise a second time only to remind him of

her transgression? Is William Brugge so unforgiving? It is wych elm, which I daresay is a readily available plant. It isn't as if she used quicksilver or gold in my poultice.

He must have accepted the wych elm without comment for I hear nothing in reply. Perhaps a cynical snort was his response. Here is a man whose every move and comment must remind his wife that he is of greater importance than she.

"His door is open," Joan says. "Have you looked in on our guest?"

"He is hardly our *guest*. Better termed a palliard, I'd say."

"Husband, once he has suitably healed, he shall be on his way." She moved from the shop into the herbarium outside my door. Unfortunately, Brugge had not left the door open wide enough for me to see into the room. A second set of steps follow the first; they are both in the herbarium now.

"And when will he be well enough?" His voice is low.

"From the looks of his wounds, I cannot say. I've never seen this sort of injury before."

The door swings open, startling me. Joan stands in the threshold before entering. She says over her shoulder (as if I cannot understand the king's tongue), "We must find him a writing implement. He indicated that he wanted one."

William Brugge joins her and the two stare at me like I am a strange bird. "He can write?" asks Brugge.

They both look at me expectantly.

If I pretend not to understand I would appear a liar, but I should not tell them why I was mutilated. As for who left me outside their door, I have no inkling. My past must be kept a secret, and there are parts I do not know. In her innocence, Joan is only wishing to help. It is my sore regret that I led her to believe that I would repay her with absolute honesty.

Joan mimes writing on her hand. She nods at me as if indicating 'yes, remember this is what you wanted'.

I have no choice. I nod.

CHAPTER TWENTY

"AH!" SAYS JOAN. "We shall soon find out who he is!" She disappears into the herbarium and moves crockery, the clatter of it sounding as if it might break from her haste. After a moment, she returns with a narrow stick of white slate and a board.

I look between them, hesitating. My preference would be to communicate exclusively with Joan and trust that she would not break our confidence but that is not a choice. William Brugge watches me take the stick from Joan, a look of keen interest on his face. How I respond might determine whether he will cast me back on the street—a fate for which I am not yet ready. In that brief exchange I decide to let him think me an imbecile. Let him think me an illiterate victim of cruelty. My wounds could be the result of a tavern tussle or I could have been robbed and left for dead. (Though not many priggers need a dwarf-sized doublet.)

I touch the stick to the board, and clutch it like a carrot. The brothers at the priory would be aggrieved to see me clumsily holding a writing implement after so conscientiously trying to tutor me in the finer art of calligraphy.

The circle I draw is purposely lop-sided; then I draw another next to it. To create the semblance of a troubadour's wagon, a rectangle must be sketched on top. What harm is there in offering a small hint of the truth? My story might be more believable. My drawing of a horse and a goat is ludicrous. The result is an egg on tenuous legs with a long neck at the front of the wagon and a smaller egg with horns at the rear. Sitting in the wagon are my former players, the Storyteller and Tish, Bertram and Tallis.

I leave out Robert.

What sense will William Brugge and Joan make of my drawing? Hopefully, this sketch of my former life will lead them astray of my present. At least that is my hope until I can decide how to communicate with Joan without her repeating our conversation to her inscrutable husband.

Finished, I hand the slate back to Joan. My attempt to smile must look like a grimace. A crease appears on Joan's forehead as she studies my drawing with Brugge peering over her shoulder, similarly beetle-browed. Are they disappointed to be caring for a lowly traveller whose only means is capitalising on his obvious physical defect? As I study their expressions, I wonder what other vocation they might have assumed for me? Surely not a monk, 'elst I would never have left my brothers and found myself in this circumstance. Do they think me an apprentice—nay, I am too old—or do they think me a master of some craft? A goldsmith? Ho, now that is rich in milly ways—I would know how to write if that were true, and word of a dwarf master of gold would have been precious tittle in London. Nay, nothing so prestigious. A tanner? A skank scraping mesentery and fur off pelts and dipping them in tubs of rancid urine. Aye! Now there is a vocation worthy of the likes of me!

"It seems to be a wagon," observes William Brugge with great sincerity. The man has no wit for the absurd 'elst he would have commented that the wagon is being pulled by an egg.

"I see a figure with a drum and a twisted person with its head between its legs," says Joan.

I want to shout "Yes, yes—a contortionist, you dullards!" but it is good that my tongue will not cooperate.

"A troupe of minstrels?" Joan asks.

I nod.

William Brugge strokes his chin. "If he travelled with the like, why would he suffer such a grievous act of violence? What could a traveller, or a player for that matter, do to be so abused?"

The couple exchange puzzled looks, then their eyes settle on me to provide an answer. This calls for another story, one that must lead them astray of the king's court and the diet of nobility which has been my fare for the past ten years. Alas, when pressured, my mind quickly recalls the circumstances surrounding my past two expulsions. Remembering my liaisons with the farmer's daughter and the Whitehall chambermaid brings a flush to my face that even a bandage cannot completely cover. True, admitting to my lascivious inclinations will not favour me with Joan. Any hopes to win her…goodwill (for I should not hope for a clandestine kiss) might be spoiled. Pah. Have I not learned anything? God forgive me, my pipe cannot be tamed.

My shoulder jerks towards my ear, my eyes dance away from their gaze. The combined gesture is enough to say what my mouth cannot, and from their stiffening necks and set jaws the meaning has not been lost on them. Alarm paints Joan's face, disgust—William Brugge's.

Let them cerebrate on this for a while. It should keep them busy.

Joan recovers enough to excuse herself with forced politeness. A stab of regret pains me as I realise I must work twice as hard to return to her good graces. She exits, leaving her husband to make his own escape.

But Brugge seems confused, as if the thought of me partaking in the most natural of inclinations is repellent if not somehow impossible. Whatever genuine shame I might have felt falls away upon seeing his reaction. Again, I am met with the realisation that others think me less than human; more devilment than man. Brugge must sense my change in manner for his face preludes his vitriol.

He lunges towards my neck, gathering up my smock there, pulling me towards his spittle-spewing mouth. "I do not know your story, drudge, but you will not continue your vulgar proclivities here. As soon as you are able, you shall be on your way. And do not even let a pip of raffish thought enter your head, for I shall sooner cut it out of you than have you think of my wife in that way."

I can do nothing more but submit to him shaking me like a terrier with a rat. He releases me, and though my survival might depend on me feigning fear, I have none within me. They burned away my worriment with part of my tongue.

My unflinching glare further incites his rage. He grabs hold of my collar again, and with a vicious show of strength, shoves me.

I fall back and my head cracks the daub wall. A fresh flow of blood begins soaking Joan's handiwork with the bandages. Brugge's ugly face swims before my eyes—where some might see stars, I see multiple Brugges. It will take a moment to shake this off, and I melt into the wall, expecting him to regroup and come at me again. I am at his mercy now, unable to escape the fuddlement his attack has inflicted. Joan's hurried steps recede farther into the shop and then Brugge is gone, the slam of the door punctuating his exit.

Plaster crumbles down the back of my neck when I finally straighten, still wavering from having my brain rattled. A divot in the wall will remind me of his threat and of my impudence. Why would he assume my inclinations would extend to his wife? Does he think me so unbridled, or do I look like a lecher? Or is it easier just to assume the worst in a man when his appearance is so unlike his own?

It shall do me no favours to try to untangle this man's thinking. I remove the bloody bandage and dab at the trickle inching down my neck. Exposure to air may clot the freshly opened wound. I toss the ruined wad of linen onto the small table. How much longer must I stay here? My weariness eclipses my care, and I sink into pondering the circumstance my Lady Bess found herself in.

I had arrived at Whitehall after the duke had separated from his wife and one day, Bess and I crossed paths in the garden. She urged her companions on, and the two of us strolled along the rows of roses, ensconced in the shades of reds and pinks, and intoxicating scent. I think this in combination with seeing my Lady Bess elevated me a foot off the ground.

Bess confided that if Elizabeth would grant Norfolk a divorce, then he would release her jointure. As it was, Elizabeth claimed she lived like a pauper at Redbourne, and so she wrote to Cromwell pleading her poor treatment at the hands of her adulterous husband and how she was entitled to the money her father had given Norfolk for her upkeep in the event that she became widowed. If only she would agree to a divorce, then she would solve her physical discomfort.

"Has Cromwell responded?" I asked, curious how the chief minister could possibly sway Norfolk.

"Nay," said Bess. Then lowering her head to say under her breath, "Why should the chief minister get involved in the domestic affairs of a court rival?"

"I see no way that doing so would serve him," I agreed.

Bess stopped to admire a butterfly on one of the blooms. "The duke's wife is a stubborn woman," she said. "She is too proud to divorce him. Her circumstance will never improve so long as she refuses."

I saw the predicament in a different light. "Her grievance could be solved if the duke released her money."

"He will never do that. He wants a divorce, and the money is his surety."

"It seems neither party will cooperate. I am sorry you find yourself in the middle of their enmity."

Bess sighed. "Kronos, be glad you can perform for the court then leave it behind to enjoy loving whoever you want. I have made my choices, and I must live with whatever good or bad comes from my decisions."

I so wanted to tell her that nay, I would never be able to love whoever I wanted. It is not a choice so much as a circumstance. Same as hers.

When next I know, I am awakened by loud arguing. At first, I am stunned to think of Brugge shouting at a customer. Such quarrels are possible if perhaps Brugge's work and time are wasted on a customer who cannot pay; or, the inevitable ignorance of a customer refusing or forgetting to follow his directions then complaining of an ineffective remedy, or a more serious accusation—that of quackery. Being a dealer in plant concoctions comes with its challenges. Even the best ingredients may not behave as intended. Care must be taken in collecting them during the right phase of the moon, or even the difference between picking a plant in the evening instead of the morning might influence the efficacy. Depending on the potency of a bloom can be as tenuous as the smile of a beautiful woman.

After a moment, Brugge's tirade subsides, and I hear a response—not the loud defence of a man, but the softer, more measured refutation of Joan. Her attempt to reason is hardly given air before I hear the word "guest" being bantered around in a most cynical and callous way. For now, I am still a "guest", but what shall I be tomorrow?

"We know nothing of this rogue," says William Brugge. "How he ended at our door remains unanswered."

Ah, so I am a rogue now.

"Joan, you are mistaken to believe that our reputation for healing outweighs some caballer's design to purposely place him here. In this king's London, in this most duplicitous and unmerciful land, who is so innocent and so blameless as to leave such a wretch here for our care?"

"Not everyone has ulterior motives, husband. There are those of good heart who see beyond a man's obvious defects. There are those who wish to lessen another man's suffering."

"I do not see why anyone would bother."

"Never mind the hearts of others. Have you forgotten your purpose? There was a time when you wished to heal all of England from its great maladies—its plagues, its dysentery, its disease. Tell me you have not forsaken your original intent?"

There is a silence that is filled with only the sound of my breathing. I slide off my bed, planting my bare feet on the floor, then lightly pad towards the door. The weight of my wounded face feels heavier than my entire body, but I ignore the raw pain from a flush of blood pooling in my mouth. I place my ear against the door.

"You are foolish to believe in such piety," says Brugge. "Men will change as the wind blows."

"It grieves me to hear you speak so despairingly. I fear for your everlasting soul."

"I fear more for our safety. And so should you. What

purgatory awaits me is only lengthened by a quick demise. My intent is to stay alive, wife."

"Our mortal time is fleeting. It is eternity to which we must aspire."

"Do not chide me on matters of the soul. You are not so virtuous."

I expect a firm negation_in response to such an accusation, but none is forthcoming. My ears strain to hear a whimper or at least a gasp. How do I interpret this silence? I want to see her face. Does it register silent rage? Perhaps her cheeks flush in shameful assent? How could he possibly question her character? I hold my breath trying to hear.

"So, instead of letting the past be buried with time," came Joan's low, careful reply. "Instead of honouring me as your wife, you withhold your forgiveness and churn my past to suit your cynical mind. And worse, you have nursed a silent grudge that you can no longer hide."

"You would better to keep your counsel, wife. Do not confront me."

"I do not seek to confront. I seek to remind."

"Then I shall help you to remember your duty."

There came such a crack I fear the lady's head has been broken like a walnut. If I should open the door, I might find Brugge noshing on her brain as if it were a sweetmeat. I move to open the door, when I hear Joan plead with her husband.

"Mercy," she pleads quietly. The woman may be bleeding out upon her husband's shoe, but her composure is the stuff of saints.

I remain beside the door, stymied by her fortitude and cowed by my despicable hesitance to intervene. Her measured plea gives me some assurance, for it does not reflect ultimate peril. For now, I wager for more time. Time to understand them as a couple, time to heal my wounds.

Hurried footsteps stir me from my thoughts like the warning of cannon fire. I scurry back to my bed and leap upon it. If Brugge should catch me eavesdropping, I might become his next nut to crack. I pull the covers over. But I judged wrongly, for the door to the shop creaks open, then resoundingly slams. Someone has left.

I wait to hear movement, and when I do not, I shrug off my trepidation and slide off the bed for a second time. I cautiously open the door to my room.

No one is in the herbarium. I stand a moment to take in Brugge's work room and the familiarity I had gained from working with Brother Ulric comes rushing back, swaddling me like a babe in a blanket. The similarity of the two spaces puts me at ease. In fact, I linger there long enough for my memories to transport me back to Thetford Priory where I prepared poultices alongside my master. The smell of rosemary and mint tweak my fond remembrance. Fresh thyme, and the mousy odour of damp earth and moss, waft past my nose. The pang of remembrance and yes—longing—hold me hostage. What could I have been if I had stayed at the priory? What if I had pursued becoming a physician? Ha! Here is a fool thinking like one. I would be a pensioned monk if I had stayed. For the king has dissolved the monasteries and sold their valuables. Besides, I'd never have been accepted as a physician. I would be no better off than I am now. Here I wallow again in times past which will do me no service; I kick myself in my arse and move on—the stymieing nature of rumination is a lesson I am doomed to never quite learn.

An arched entrance to the outer shop affords me a moderately restricted view into it. The shop appears to be a handsome space, reflecting Brugge's success. A single wide window and candles in iron stands light the interior. Care has been taken to neatly line the shelves with crocks doubtlessly filled with some of the simpler remedies, plentiful and readily accessible. But from where I stand, I cannot see the goodwife, and for one harrowing moment, I wonder if I have been mistaken. Had *she* left instead of Brugge? If that be true, then I risk another thrashing should the apothecary come striding around the corner.

I take a cautious step forward, carefully placing my foot then following with my weight. Another step changes my perspective, and I can see that the day is nearly done and the colours out the window have reduced to stealthy shades of blue and gray. The interior of the shop is cast in a wheaten glow from the candles and a lantern. Another step, not so silent as the previous, draws the attention of Joan, who sits on the floor.

I garble an attempt to say her name. Fresh blood begins filling my mouth, but I ignore this and go to her.

She appears stunned, more shocked than hurt, though I don't doubt the force of her husband's blow had not only knocked the wind out of her but had left a contusion and probably bloodied the back of her head. Obviously, she had landed on the ground and the stubborn leg of a table must have broken her fall.

She is too dazed to refuse my help, and seeing her coif darken with blood, I remove it to no objection and gently part her hair to reveal a gash.

Back in the herbarium, I find some linen once used for filtering infusions. I shake out the drying mash of what looks to be yarrow—an auspicious find as yarrow has qualities of staunching the flow of blood. Without complaint from Joan, I place it against her cut.

"I do not deserve your kindness," she says in a barely audible voice.

After a moment, I check the square of linen and dab at her cut. As I tend to her, I wonder how often she has endured her husband's violence.

"He is worried," she says. "When he feels uncertain, he is like a bear lashing out."

I have difficulty imagining Joan at a bear baiting. I have witnessed two mastiffs working in tandem to bring down George Brown—the legendary bear with a reputation for killing dogs despite his teeth being ground to nubs to prevent his injuring his handlers. With the bear defenceless and tethered to a stake in the middle of the arena, the handlers unleashed two dogs to take on the storied fighter. George Brown shredded the back thigh of one nemesis, but the dog had a strong blood lust and in spite of its mangled leg it latched onto George's hind quarters. When George turned to bite the aggressor, the other mastiff lunged for his exposed neck. The whoops and cheers filled the stands, and I watched the beast be torn apart, limb by limb.

He was a ferocious beast, horrible to look at, yet his circumstances made him vulnerable. He was taunted and abused for the pleasure of others. And, ultimately, his life was extinguished. No one saw beyond his physical appearance; the construct God chose for him. He was alone in a cruel world.

But I fail to see the similarity between a bear and William Brugge. Certainly Brugge could lash out like George Brown, but he was not at a disadvantage. William Brugge has all the opportunities afforded a man of his education and scope. He has a shop of reputation and a clientele who believe in his work. His fear and distrust over my presence are overly suspicious, and for all we know, perhaps I *was* the fortunate recipient of a compassionate passerby. And most unlike George Brown the bear, Brugge has someone who cares about him.

I help Joan to her feet. She takes an unsteady step, so I lead her to a chair and assist her into it. I dab the linen against her gash. Thankfully, the flow of blood is slowing.

"He has gone to The Crooked Cork to drown his misgivings," she says. "It is his fancy when he runs against me."

This conversation is one-sided, for I can do little more than grunt and gargle at anything she says.

"It is getting late," says Joan, looking out the window. "I am of no mind to answer a patron should they call. Close the shutters, will you? I do not wish to give the appearance of being open."

Luckily, I can reach the wooden shutters and the room darkens with them closed. Joan is coming round, returning to her even, equable self. I am alone with her and would be so for a while. My frustration churns inside me. If I had a full tongue, I would inquire. I would lure her opinions out into the open, but I am a prisoner of my mutilation and of her reticence. Joan is not the sort to divulge her sentiments freely. They would have to be cajoled out of her.

Though the shutters are closed and the day is nearly passed, a knock comes at the door. I look to Joan for what to do. She waves me off.

"Go to your room and shut the door. I will take care of this."

CHAPTER TWENTY-ONE

I AM TORN LEAVING Joan, for I am not sure if she has her legs under her, but I retreat into the herbarium and keep out of sight. Surely it is too soon for William Brugge to return and ask for forgiveness—if he even would.

The latch falls away and the door scrapes open.

A woman speaks. "Joan, I am on my way home, but I stopped at market and bought more shank than I need. Would you and Uncle care for some?" She has entered the shop and the door is closed against a gust of cold that makes it all the way to where I stand. "I wasn't sure you were home. The shutters have been closed."

The light smock that I wear is piddling armour against the draft, as evidenced by my blue-tinged feet. I return to my room where I linger near the door to listen.

Before Joan can answer, the woman detects something is amiss. "Joan what has happened? You look unwell."

"'Tis no worry. I am a bit less than my usual," said Joan. "Now let me see what you've brought."

"Aunt Joan, you look as if you will topple. Come, sit here. Let me get you a drink."

"Nay, I do not need it. Like I said, I am feeling a bit puny and will retire to my bed when you leave."

"Where is Uncle? Does he know that you are not feeling well?"

"He is at The Crooked Cork."

"Then I must go and find him!"

"You will not!" Joan's cry is an outburst. Her voice immediately softens, "Leave him to his pleasure."

"It is a pleasure that does not agree with your marriage."

"Dear Meg, when a woman marries, she marries the man, flaws and all. The illusion of a compatible union is fiction. Life changes and so do marriages."

"I am no innocent in that matter. But you are not telling me why there is blood on your collar."

I imagine Joan lifting a hand to her smock in response. Before she is able to think what to say, her niece continues.

"Oh, there is blood in your hair. Has he struck you?"

No reply is forthcoming unless it is a shake or a nod. A husband can do as he wishes to his wife; she is his property, his ward, his indentured servant. And to be fair, I've known women to counter their inequitable standing in wily ways. What woman has lain in the marriage bed and never resisted her mate's quotidian desires?

"If mother were alive, she would be much aggrieved. Uncle is a fool not to realise the gift he has in you. I will stay and confront him!"

"No, you shall not! It is nearly dark, and you must be on your way. The streets are not safe for a woman alone without an escort. You must go."

"You worry unnecessarily. I am well able to fend for myself."

"I do not doubt you could scream louder than the bawds on Bankside. But don't be foolish. Why chance your safety? Go, for you are tiring me. I want nothing more than to be abed."

In my effort to hear every word and even peek to see this dauntless young woman, I brush against the door to my room, and it closes with a pronounced click. The sound horrifies me because it is like a monkey escaped from its cage—what can you do to get it back without it first causing all manner of mischief?

Where can I disappear myself if she should come looking? Ultimately there is nowhere for me to go but beneath my bed covers. I retreat to their refuge and wait. Hopefully, Joan can explain well enough to placate her inquisitive niece.

Their words are muffled, and the sound of their footfall grows outside my door in the herbarium. My hair stands on end. I am about to be caught out.

What would this Meg do upon discovering me? Would she trade this information as if I was a commodity at Cheapside? I never thought myself to be of any value to anyone beyond the pleasure that I could give them, but why was I saved and who, exactly, deposited me with this distrustful apothecary and his subservient wife? Am I to be kept a secret? But for how long and to what purpose?

"It is nothing but a draft that we have been unable to staunch," says Joan. "If I leave the door open, it will inevitably slam shut. It happens at the strangest times. A gust of wind, whether from outside or from within, will set the door to swinging. It's as tetchy as a weather cock."

"There is no window in there that I recall," says Meg.

"The wall is as leaky as a sieve. The mice have chewed through in places." Joan sounds recovered enough from the earlier incident to steer Meg out of the herbarium.

"Well…" A pause as if considering. "Aunt, if you are sure that I can be of no further use, and if you are feeling well enough, then I shall be on my way. But I will leave you with some of this meat." They are back in the herbarium again, and Joan must be finding a pan and a knife for they talk about where they should cut for a good roast and stew.

I hold my breath, daring not to move a muscle for fear of giving myself away. It was not so long ago that I hid behind the tapestry in Whitehall. If I should be found out here, my punishment might only be a boot to my arse, and I'd be back on the street again.

"That is more than we need," says Joan. The women chitter on about what makes for a hearty stew, the addition of parsnips sweetens the broth, their conversation carries on into the outer shop. I breathe a sigh and close my eyes. Meg is nearly out the door. Be gone, meddlesome Meg. You are overstaying your welcome. Finally, when the outer door scrapes open, then closes, I throw back my sheets and will my beating heart to slow.

After such an eventful afternoon, I imagine Goodwife Joan must desire the comfort of her bed, when I am surprised by her visit. I draw myself up as she enters, the glow of a candle accentuating the hollows beneath her eyes. As if an explanation were needed, she tells me that her niece, Meg, is the daughter of her deceased sister who died when Meg was not yet twelve. She and William took her in as their own, and after eight years they saw her married to a ranking member of the Butcher's Guild. A man with a fine reputation and a shiny array of knives. Though to my mind, I've always found men of the cleaver a bit coarse.

"The girl still frequents the market for cuts of meat as though she mistrusts what her husband can secure. I suppose it is best that a woman finds her own victuals." She glances sideways in a private chuckle. "We've always looked out for one another. Meg seems to think I need looking after more than she." Her eyes meet mine. "Perhaps she is wiser than I allow her."

She looks around the room. There is not much to see. "I have some broth I can give you."

Her unfailing care takes precedence over her own needs. I am not the worthy recipient she thinks I am. I shake my head, preferring her to escape to what little peace she might find before her husband returns. But I cannot say this. I can only play obstinate and show my indifference. Perhaps she will come to realise that she need not invest such effort in me.

"Well, then I shall place it on your bedside. I believe you are able to manage if I leave a straw like before." She disappears and soon returns with a cup of warm liquid smelling of beef. "I believe you are well enough to manage. You know better than I how much your wound can withstand."

She leaves me, taking her candle with her.

These women with men of status. Bess Holland and Norfolk, Joan Brugge and her apothecary husband. Katherine Howard and the King. Were I to be a woman, would I be better kept? Methinks not. I should revel in my person though it be inferior in height, but at least I have a pipe. That counts for something in this backwater realm.

But a wife…is forever beholden to her husband.

Tether me to no one! The Brothers asked for my service, but I could not give it. My troupe demanded my loyalty, but I saw an opportunity. Certainly, I was an attraction and I earned my keep. People paid to gape at me and laugh at my antics. But how could I have resisted a chance at court? To see beautiful women sumptuously costumed? To make the king smile? To have a queen tease me and give me a sprig of rosemary from her garden? I would have kept to the halls of these stately palaces if I had not been kicked out of them, for they suited me. I was not bored, nor was I a bother.

Is Will Somers glad to see me gone? He probably sits next to the king and avoids mentioning my name. Better forgotten, thinks he. But if my name is spoken, is it to ask where I have gone?

If Archbishop Cranmer is nearby waiting for the king's signature, does he pretend not to hear? Courtiers and entertainment are not his concern. Perhaps a barb of disparagement is inserted for good measure—a little seed of distrust planted.

Somers, that privileged fool, is well-served by his affected wit. He has that advantage over me. He lacks the introspection that has allowed me to play and weave my intrigues. Somers's childlike innocence, his lack of guile, gives him credence in Henry's eyes. For how can a witless ninny contrive? He is only able to parrot the truth. The tallow burning on my nightstand is nearly spent so I use what light I have left to sip some broth. When I am finished, I lie back in my bed and listen to the house settle—the creaks and sighs of a sedentary building giving way to the contemplative night. I should like to lock my door against a squidgy William Brugge returning home from The Crooked Cork. Nothing good can come of a resentful man after hours spent pouring ale down his throat.

But I remain at his mercy. At *their* mercy; and rather than ruminate on the unpredictable quality of our association, I think on the unflagging faith I have in myself. How I've always managed to survive. From dung heap to dungeon room in an apothecary's shop, my journey is not over. It continues…and so I sleep.

CHAPTER TWENTY-TWO

THE NEXT DAY I am woken by William and Joan's conversation. They are in the shop but I can hear them clearly. They must think me capable of sleeping like the dead, for their attempts to keep me from overhearing are woefully remiss. William Brugge returned in the middle of the night, stumbling and belching, waking me enough to set me on edge. I didn't fall back to sleep until after the stairs stopped creaking from his plodding footfall, and he had stopped rustling about with his blankets. He talks of his time at The Crooked Cork and what he learned. I water the pisspot in the corner then sidle up to the door for a better listen.

"The guard said they had caught him spying on Archbishop Cranmer who had taken private conference."

"Spying!" Joan is impressed. Methinks they both are.

"He is not as he appears," says Brugge. "This business of him travelling with minstrels is a fabrication."

"You don't know. There may be some truth in it," says Joan.

"I think it is not his most recent venture. Not if he was caught spying!"

"Then he must have connections, but with whom? Who placed him there?"

"I do not know. Archbishop Cranmer took advisement on the matter. The decision was made to prevent him from speaking."

"Without a tongue he cannot tell," says Joan. "But what does he know that they must keep secret?"

Silence follows as no doubt they are thinking on this. As do I.

"Eventually he will be able to speak again," says Joan.

"If they had wanted to completely prevent him from talking, they could have done so," says Brugge. "They could have clipped his tongue, damaged it more seriously." He snorts then says, "Why not club him over the head and be done with it?"

"Perhaps his injury was only meant to waylay him. Someone may have believed him useful."

"A possibility." There is another pause before William Brugge continues.

"The guard said they stripped him of his clothing and tossed him in the overgrowth next to the Fleet. He was senseless and nearly dead. On their return to Whitehall, they were approached by one of Edward Seymour's men."

"Related to our late Queen Jane?" asks Joan.

"Aye. The Earl of Hertford. A member of the king's privy council and the eldest brother of Jane Seymour. Apparently whilst the king was on progress in the north, Seymour managed the affairs of state."

"Alone?"

"Nay, that would be irresponsible to place so much power in the hands of one man other than the king. In truth, I do not know the inner workings of the privy chamber, but there must be several who confer. Certainly, Archbishop Cranmer is among them."

It occurs to me that their conversation has not been disrupted by Brugge insulting his wife or lashing out at her in some way. The two are remarkably civil.

"What did Seymour's man say to the guards?" asks Joan.

"They were told to find the mutilated dwarf and leave him at an apothecary's shop near the Fleet."

"Here?" Joan sounds astonished. "Your reputation for healing has indeed been noticed at Whitehall."

William Brugge must be puffing out his chest like a proud cockerel.

"Did you make yourself known to the guard at The Crooked Cork?" she asks.

"Nay! Do you think I want every man there to gawk or follow me home? 'Tis fortunate that I sat in the corner unbeknownst to the guard and his coterie of sotted retainers. They know not that I am the recipient apothecary of whom they spoke."

"But what does this mean?" asks Joan. "Why did the Earl want him saved?"

"I do not know. However, I worry for our safety. There are men in positions of power who know of us. And I wonder if the earl will be paying us a visit."

"That should not be a concern. We are here to help others. Our gift brings glory to God. Regardless of anyone's opinion or religious preference, whether they love our king or not, we do God's work by healing the sick and the infirmed. It is a sin to turn away someone in need of our help."

"The king is an impulsive man. We can't take in just anyone. Helping someone with a political stance counter to the king's is dangerous. They would associate us with his treacherous beliefs. We can't possibly keep him here."

"We know nothing about what he believes. They call him a spy, an eavesdropper, but we know nothing of his intent. To cast him out without a full understanding would be wrong."

"Wife, if they should throw us in Newgate, would you moralise that our incarceration is God's will? You would condemn us to the rack for heresy. I've seen men hanged for lesser crimes."

"You must trust in God. If it is His will that we are wrongly accused then you must believe that we are ultimately serving His greater purpose."

"What greater purpose is served by being naïve? I doubt God would approve of abject stupidity. Do you think God cares for fools any more than he cares for a maggot? Abominations of his great design—the both of them. There is no advantage in treating individuals as worthy equals. If that were God's plan, then He would have made us all kings!"

Ha! A topic I once brought up to Brother Trelli, who had stopped chopping fennel and said, "We are only like God in that we can reason, love, and be self-aware. Physical appearance is variable and encompasses all of what God has created. No one has seen God; He might be beautiful or hideous, incorporating every physical anomaly known to man." He pointed the tip of his knife at me. "For all we know, God may be as you. But status and social division—that is a construct of man, not God."

Brother Trelli had a more generous view of mankind than I did. Physical appearance has as much to do with status as money does. There is nowhere in this king's realm where dwarves are held in high esteem.

Joan's voice becomes tremulous. "What would you do with our guest, husband? Someone has entrusted us with his care. To expel him may be a decision we regret. It may end worse for us."

"We must find out what he knows."

"The knowledge of which may further incriminate us. Besides, we may never know," says Joan.

"You said that his speech will recover."

"Truly, I cannot judge if and when that will be," says

Joan. "I told him he shall recover his speech, but as a means of encouragement. And why should he entrust us with any valuable information?"

"We needn't secure his trust to learn what he knows," says William Brugge.

The familiar scrape of the shop door opening startles me out of my eavesdropping. It is morning and with it comes the flurry of retail. The Brugges' conversation comes to an abrupt halt, and the apothecary greets his first client of the day. Joan excuses herself to the herbarium as I swiftly make for my bed and hop onto it.

A moment later, a preemptive rap at the door precedes Joan's appearance. She glances my way, avoiding my gaze, and casts her eyes on the bowl of broth left the night before.

"You've been able to eat I see." She looks over at the pisspot in the corner. She'll have to remove it because certainly her husband won't. He'd let the smell overtake that of his sage and mint before he'd touch my filth.

What is called for is niceties. 'How do you fare today, Goodwife?' 'Has the sun decided to show herself today?' Or, 'Must we endure yet another day of dreary drizzle?' But all I can muster is a gorp and a gargle, and I shall not embarrass myself a second time.

How can I allay her suspicions? She should know that I was not punished for any malice. I was punished as a precaution—and an unnecessary one at that. True, I knew the queen's licentious secret, but they assumed I would spread the scandalous tale all over court. Why would I risk the king's wrath? Doing so has always caused devastating results for all involved, especially if the jaw jangle was found to be false. But even in those cases when the talk is true, you take a risk in spreading it. Trading secrets that are not your own is always ill-advised. And the men in charge at

Whitehall would not chance this secret being exposed. Not by an unnatural fool. Not when there is a hot poker handy.

Joan regards my soiled bandage and picks up the bowl. "I'll tend to your wound once I take care of my other tasks," she says.

I am not so infirmed that I cannot take care of my own leavings. I slide out of bed and take up the jake so that when she returns, she will understand that I refuse to be an unnecessary burden. At first, she is startled by my absence and then when she sees me holding the pot, her surprise is two-fold.

I gesture for her to show me the way for its removal and after confirming her husband is busy with a customer, she does so willingly. I shall win her favour in small ways.

We walk through the herbarium to a rear entrance where a door, secured by a heavy padlock, opens to a back alley. She removes a key from a ledge beyond my reach and springs the lock. "The ditch latrine is around the corner."

This is my first glimpse of sky since I was brought here. Ashen from a dense damp, the relative brightness makes me squint. The cold, spongy ground gnaws at my bare feet, sending chills up my shins. Though I'd like to linger in the fresh air of freedom, my gauzy smock ensures that I don't dawdle. But I take a moment to get my bearings. Opposite is the back side of a row of buildings, each with a rain barrel near to overflowing. The buildings are but three stories in height, if that. A few scrap piles of wood planks and other heaps of rubbish are scattered about. A scrawny dog wanders between the piles looking for food.

I know this area of London. My first clue is the stench of a low-skulking miasma of the Fleet. William Brugge's shop is not on the storied Bucklersbury Street, competing with every calibre of apothecary. I see the steeple of St. Sepulchre rising above this infernal stink; we are in the vicinity of Christ Church—a hospital taken over by the crown. With Henry and Cromwell's ruination of the monasteries, there has been little effort made to care for the sick. St. Bartholomew used to tend to the lame, the aged, and the blind. Now the building lies in disrepair, its plate and stained glass windows confiscated for the king's coffers.

Rather than carry me to Bucklersbury Road, a decidedly greater distance, they brought me here. They must have rowed me down the river from the king's palace, dragged me up the stairs beyond Bridewell, and dumped me along the stinking Fleet. At some point I must have been carried through Blackfriars. Imagine my brethren seeing me paraded through a Dominican enclave and the site of Henry's divorce hearing against our first queen.

Brugge's shop must be on Turnagain Lane. I once knew a bone rattler here. She wore a crown of rat tails and shook a box of desiccated goose bones. I had gone to her after I'd believed Will Somers wished ill for me. Obviously, her alarming ululations and frantic box shaking didn't work to protect me.

I round the corner and confront the ditch latrine boldly perfuming the air. A wobbly plank runs parallel to the trench but my gait is not so wide that I can avoid the squish of dribbled sewage between my toes. After depositing my contribution, I hurry back to the open door of William Brugge's shop where Joan wordlessly hands me a bowl of water to wash my feet.

When I return to my room Joan changes my bandages. She motions for me to sit and covers my legs with a blanket. "Let us hope for some improvement," she says, unwinding the roll of linen.

Her face shows no sign of satisfaction or displeasure—she would be a formidable card player. She leaves the room to find a washbowl, and I reach a tentative finger to my cheek. Oh, for a plate of silver to hold before my sorry likeness. How hideous am I? The pain of my own touch makes me wince just as she returns.

With impressive efficiency she anoints my cheek with a healing balm and rewraps my face, winding the fresh cloth under my chin and around my head. William Brugge speaks to a client in the shop, explaining the need to pick a plant during a full moon.

"Rest," says Joan, taking up the bowl of water and dirty wrapping. "I'll be back later with some softened bread. You might be able to manage that."

There is nothing in her expression. No distrust in her eyes. Disturbingly, no compassion, either. Just the look of a woman considering what to do, hard efficiency masking the windmill of thoughts turning in her head. Does she think me corrupt, traitorous? Or does she think I might be a victim, wrongly condemned? I have no voice to assure her that it is the latter.

CHAPTER TWENTY-THREE

I AM ALONE FOR hours, left with only my thoughts for company. The isolation gives me time to think about what Brugge has learned.

I have no clear recollection of being delivered to the door of William Brugge's apothecary shop. They could easily have disposed of me with a knife in my back, my throat opened from ear to ear in a macabre bloody grin. Being insensible, I would have been none the wiser.

If the Earl of Hertford, Edward Seymour, saw value in saving me, then I wonder, what use could I be to him? Am I to be retrieved? Did the earl hope to have me healed well enough to talk?

Seymour and his family at Wolf Hall have been supportive of the king's reformed church. After all, it has benefitted them. The very day Anne was executed, Henry could not wait to see his demure, little beauty, Seymour's younger sister—Jane. I had no stomach for watching Anne lose her head, and instead of taking in that spectacle at the Tower Green, I remained at Whitehall where there was much ado made about readying the king's barge for a trip down the Thames to see Jane. It is not my place to comment on the king's indifference towards a woman he once fanatically loved. What went through his mind as he approached the Tower in his well-appointed vessel on that fateful day? Methinks it isn't hard to imagine him popping a grape in his mouth as he passed.

Now, with Jane dead and two wives later, our king is aged and petulant with a weeping leg wound. No amount of wrapping can mask the smell of his rotting flesh, and the physicians shy away from suggesting amputation, for he'd surely die from it. Then where would *they* be? Accused of treason for conspiring to kill the king, that is where. Nay, Henry believed his new bride, Katherine Howard, was chaste—a virgin ripe for his taking. His ego required such thinking. A second male heir would dispel murmurings of his waning virulence. King Henry is a proud man.

Katherine is whimsical in that her head is filled with more puff than thoughts. But as I ponder this, I realise that she is simply a vulnerable young woman and prone to being manipulated. She never learned how to play at court. And it *is* a game. Where Anne was shrewd and could dispense with anyone who might so much as think an ungenerous thought about her, Katherine lacks the forethought to keep erstwhile, possibly dangerous acquaintances away. Why else would she appoint her former paramour—Frances Dereham—as her private secretary? Anne and Katherine, these two Howard women are the antithesis of one another, but they did have one important commonality. They were both brought to court by their uncle, that odious lech and schemer, Thomas Howard, the Duke of Norfolk.

Bess Holland's lover.

Court twaddle must be carefully dealt with. I rely on what I can infer is true, otherwise, I take it under consideration. Norfolk has always viewed politics and religion conservatively.

Even though Cromwell's machinations benefited the duke, and added to his land holdings, Norfolk still squirmed at some of the religious reforms that came with Anne's marriage. But when Henry deemed Anne was a nuisance and she was charged with adultery and incest, Norfolk couldn't distance himself from her fast enough. He even presided over her trial.

As a result of Anne's debacle, the Howards were consigned to lesser roles at court. I saw the duke pretend importance, but his eyes betrayed him. He studied others for far too long with a clenched jaw and the vein in his temple throbbing, jumping like a poked worm, especially when he considered Edward Seymour, and Thomas Cromwell. Though he retained his titles and his land, when the king turned his attention to Jane Seymour and her family, Thomas Howard watched as Thomas Cromwell—that low-born lawyer—and the Seymours, that conniving, churlish clan, parvenus the whole lot of them, replaced him and his family in favour and in power.

The fickleness of this king's court is incomparable. Fortunes can reverse.

How does one win favour? You give the king what he wants. Cromwell and Norfolk knew how to serve their king. Methinks Seymour may not be as proficient as either those two. Ultimately, Norfolk affected Cromwell's downfall. No son of a low-born smithie should possess such power and wealth as to rival the king's. Norfolk took hold of the king's ear and spewed his nasty lies, convincing him of Cromwell's heresy and treason. Condemned by Bill of Attainder, Norfolk sought for the disgraced Cromwell to be turned into a human torch. Luckily he was thwarted in that effort, but he privately arranged for a novice executioner to perform Cromwell's punishment. How did I know? My Lady Bess's conscience could not carry the burden of her lover's intense hatred for the man.

But it troubles me to see Lady Bess attached to such a conniving man. How does she bear it?

Now with hopes that Katherine would provide a much desired second male heir, the Seymours worried that even though little Prince Edward was of quick wit and Seymour blood, he had not inherited his father's robust health. As much as the Seymours hoped to retain their favoured status, now with Cromwell gone, and Katherine queen, Norfolk and his family were on the rise once again.

Is this latest scandal an attempt by the Seymours to challenge the Howards' standing? Is John Lascelles an agent for their side, encouraged to share his news, or did he undertake this meeting with the archbishop merely to alleviate his troubled conscience? He said it was the latter, but I've seen enough in Henry's court to know that no one puts themself at risk out of the goodness of his heart.

It must be getting late to the day. The light seeping under the door and through its cracks is subdued, muted to a gauzy gray. No conversations come from the shop, the door has ceased opening and closing. Someone works outside my room in the herbarium. I hear chopping and water being poured. My stomach complains, roiling in juices with nothing to digest. Subsisting on little more than clear broth is not enough to satisfy me or my stomach.

Cuds me! I am thinking about food!

The pain in my mouth is subsiding, and until now, I only thought of my discomfort and the constant misery of my injury instead of my hunger. A sign of improvement! But before we celebrate, I remember that I am not so far along that chewing wouldn't unleash considerable agony. My tongue would scream, my mouth wounds would open. So, for now I must abide the continued anguish of starvation while knowing that I cannot completely appease my hunger pangs.

As if to further my torment, the smell of roast pork sneaks into my room. The smell is like a concubine coming to sit on my bed—just to look at me. I grow desirous and conflicted. Unable to resist its seduction, I dive under my pillow and throw the covers up over my head. Be gone, demon roast, I beseech you!

My anguish dissolves into tears, and I am moaning in frustration when the latch on my door rattles.

"Show me his wounds," says the apothecary, ordering Joan into the room. I peep out from under my bolster.

Joan does not argue. The bandages must come off again, her earlier labour undone.

I do not move quick enough to please William Brugge. He stalks over and throws back the blankets, exposing my naked bum. I am like a fish tossed into the hull of a boat. The shock of it, me squirming not for breath, but for modesty. The shame flushes my hairy arse as red as my face.

He grabs my arm and hauls me up. My body stiffens, readying for violence. His professional manner falls away, replaced by his erratic outrage, and my hands go up to protect my face. I can't abide a jab to my cheek.

Saintly Joan intercedes. He is not so intractable that she cannot have some influence over him. She touches her husband's arm, and like a well-trained dog he considers, then releases me. His restraint is as sudden as his outburst, further confusing me. He wavers like a two-man sawyer—one moment violent, the next tolerant. Unpredictable either way. Brugge steps back, barely containing his desire to thrash me.

Without a word, Joan unwinds the bandage. She avoids meeting my eyes while mine bore into hers. The last bit sticks to my still weeping wound, and it is then that her gaze drops to mine. In that brief exchange I understand that she is still uncertain what to make of me. All is not lost. I may still win her alliance. With a gentle tug, the last of the bandage comes off.

Brugge examines my cheek. His brow furrows, he scowls, his nose twitches. Without pardon, he elbows Joan aside to snatch the candle off the table for a better look. The flame wavers in front of my eyes; his sour breath washes my face as he hovers. Then, without warning, he grabs hold of my chin.

"Open your mouth," he demands.

I am not certain that he won't finish the work that Cranmer's minions had started. I resist, for who in the same situation would lie there like an obedient dog? He pushes me back on the bed and thrusts the candle at Joan. "Hold this," he says.

He proceeds to hold me down while trying to wrench open my mouth. I buck and swing out my leg to push him off, but he is nearer my head and my short leg cannot reach. The sheer horror of his brutality spurs my every instinct to survive. The memory of a glowing hot poker about to be jammed in my mouth looms in my head.

"Stop!" cries Joan. "He is not so healed that you can treat him thus. I will provide the light, but you must not force open his mouth. You will undo what progress we have made."

Reluctantly, Brugge accepts the sense in this. He releases my chin.

"He only wants to see the state of your tongue," assures Joan, pushing aside her husband.

Am I to be coddled like a child? I stare at the two of them. To resist will do me no good. I lean back and watch Brugge with a wary eye for any hints of sudden aggression.

As his hands approach my face, I clutch the sheets on either side to keep myself from pushing him off. There is some measure of trust (or inexperience) in that they have not tied down my arms. Kneeing Brugge in the balls would provide much satisfaction, and indeed I distract myself from his examination by considering how easily I could draw my knee up into his baubles.

"It will be easier for everyone if you simply open your mouth," says Joan.

I cannot see her expression for the bright flame of the candle blinding me. With some reservation, I close my eyes and open as wide as I am able.

"He appears to have lost the front portion of his tongue," says Brugge, sounding suddenly like a physician. "He is fortunate. He may have some problems speaking at first, but in time he should learn to make do."

I open my eyes, and he steps back.

"Keep applying the poultice once a day. I believe it is helping."

Without further word, he turns on his heel and leaves.

Joan replaces the candle on the night stand. "I need for you to sit up."

I oblige. She replaces the bandage then steps back to examine her handiwork. "My husband becomes easily troubled when he is uncertain." She confides in a low voice. "But he would never purposely harm you."

I stare at her in disbelief. What did she think he did to me once before? He had definitely lashed out at her, creating a gash on her head. Had she conveniently forgotten? Certainly her niece had noticed it.

But I have no tongue with which to speak. Nor do I think I should ask for a slate and stick. All I can do is accept her explanation in silence.

CHAPTER TWENTY-FOUR

J OAN TRUSTS ME to dump my jake into the ditch latrine and
return to my room. She stands beside the door, and I skirt
past into the cold London dank. These brief excursions of
freedom allow me to linger long enough to inhale something
other than my weaky room. Smelling mouldering leaves and
smoke is preferable to a stinking chamber pot of one's own
making.

I return dutifully, inconspicuously taking in the herbarium
and noticing what I can without being obvious. William Brugge
has arranged his shelves using a method of organisation named
for Albertus Magnus, a Dominican friar from Germany. Brother
Ulric had read his works with great interest and thought there
was much wisdom to be found in his writings. Magnus believed
the science of medicines could be conducted in a manner com-
plementing religion. Brother Ulric found some comfort in that
reassurance, reasoning that if someone questioned him, he could
quote the famous friar. He was always concerned someone might
misconstrue his methods for alchemy or conjuration.

In accordance with Albertus Magnus, minerals, ground
stones, and other inert, passionless substances are kept separate

from plants and herbs. Desiccated mortal bits such as ground bone from rodents and birds are in another section. Brugge organises plants according to their planetary ruler. Chamomile and rosemary are ruled by the Sun. *Filius Ante Patrum* for sore throats, feverfew for reducing sweats, and yarrow for healing wounds are kept with other Venus ruled herbs. His method is simple and one with which I am familiar.

However, my small journey to the ditch latrine is not enough to satisfy my curiosity. Every day I grow stronger, and I am able to take more food. When William Brugge leaves, I venture out of my isolation and watch Joan in the herbarium. Her face has brightened of late seeing me interested in watching her make poultices for ailing clients. When the shop door opens, I scurry back to my pallet and close the door behind me.

One day Joan is making a mash for a neighbour with a complaint of gout, a painful condition one of the brothers at Thetford had. Brother Ulric would make Brother Tenbull nettle tea to thin his blood and then follow that with a poultice of comfrey and burdock for his swollen joints. Joan is making her poultice using comfrey and oats, a gentle approach to healing the man's suffering. She is about to dump it into a bowl and be done with it when I see burdock dangling from the hanging herbs. I rise from the table where she works and point to it.

"That is burdock," says Joan.

I shake my head in agreement then gesture that she should add it to her poultice. "Add," I say. My voice sounds odd, a strange croakish quality to it.

She looks at me encouragingly. "Add burdock to a poultice for gout?"

I do not chance a verbal explanation, but mime how burdock can draw out the evil swelling and shrink the painful joints. My enthusiasm convinces her, and I know she wonders how I know this. The fact that she takes my advice is a small victory for me in gaining her trust.

Out in the shop, the entry door opens, and I hurry back to my room.

"Joan, are you there?" calls a voice.

Joan replies brightly. "Meg, what brings you this day? Have you another find from the butchers at Newmarket?"

"Nay, I'm sorry to disappoint you, Aunt. I was nearby and I wanted to see how you fared. Is Uncle here?"

"He has left on an errand."

"The last time I visited, I found you with a gash in your head, and he had gone to The Crooked Cork."

"I am better now. He struggles with his worry."

"What could he be unsettled about? He has a respected practice."

"He has lost some clients to other apothecaries. I am not sure why. He takes his patients' well-being to heart. It troubles him when he can't find a solution to their maladies. And it troubles him more when he learns they have gone to a different shop for their remedies."

"I understand that he could feel some disappointment, but it is no excuse for him to lash out at you. His ire is misplaced."

"Meg, he is not so young as when we raised you. Instead of developing more tolerance in old age, he grows more irritable."

"All shops go through good years and poor."

I hear no answer, so I lean in closer to the door hoping to catch any morsel of speech. So intent am I on listening that I fail to notice a visitor in my room. Between the opening and closing of doors to the back alley and my time spent observing Joan in the herbarium, neither of us knew that an intruder was lying in wait.

It isn't the threat of harm that so alarms, but the sudden

assault on one's peace and concentration that makes one lose self-control. The sensation of sharp claws and fur across my bare foot, the glimpse of something running for cover…I slam against the door, thumping it loudly, which startles me into lurching sideways. Unable to catch myself, I stumble towards my chamber pot and my foot lands in excrement, squishing between my toes. My repulsion upsets the pot. I trip on its rim and land on the floor in a puddle of waste.

Mortified by the clamour and chaos, I then hear footsteps outside the door.

Hiding beneath the sheets will not exonerate me from the calamity or the mess I have made. I remain on the floor, contrite, sitting next to the spilled chamber pot.

The door opens, and I see Joan looking over the shoulder of a young woman who gapes at the sight of me.

Unquestioningly, Meg is related to Joan. Her neat appearance, the clean hem of her ochre brown kirtle, denotes a woman who keeps to the wooden planks of London's more muddy lanes. Her tidy appearance conveys a focused and purposeful manner— just like her aunt's. Meg's startled brow and dropped jaw lengthen her oval face, but her surprise is soon replaced with a scrunching of her nose and mouth.

"God's blood! What pray tell?" she exclaims. "Who is this?" she asks Joan.

Joan edges past and gingerly steps over the spillage to offer me a hand up.

"He was left outside our door. They tried to burn out his tongue. We are overseeing his care."

"Who? Who tried to burn out his tongue?"

"We do not know."

"And then someone brought him here?"

"It seems so." Joan assesses the mess on the floor and me. "Stand there. Do not move."

I do as she requests, and she leaves. I am alone with Meg, who looks me up and down in bewilderment, then follows Joan into the herbarium. They scrounge about then return with rags and a trowel.

Joan hands a rag to Meg. "Wipe him down. I'll take care of the floor."

"But he's a dwarf!" exclaims Meg.

"He's a man like any other."

Meg thinks on this.

Joan looks up from scooping waste. "For God's sake, Meg. Just give him the rag, and he can clean himself."

Unsure, Meg hands over the rag. She watches me unabashed, as if I were not a man, but a farm animal. Perhaps she thinks if she touched me, she would turn into a dwarf. After a minute, she fetches a bucket of water. I wring out the rag and finish wiping my feet. Poor Joan is busy with the trowel so I sop up the spilled urine and finish cleaning the floor for her.

Meg pelts her aunt with questions the entire time. "Why do you think they did that to him? Do you think they purposely left him in the lane outside your door, or was it an accident? Does he have any tongue left? Will he ever be able to talk again? Where will he go after he is healed?"

Joan continues to offer brief, evasive answers. I sense I am not alone in wishing the young woman would leave. Joan allows me to take the pot to the ditch latrine, and as I follow her to the back-alley door, Meg trails after, interested in every aspect of Joan's humanitarian undertaking. Either that, or she is just meddlesome.

This time I do not dawdle. I do not wish to leave Joan alone with Meg for fear that the young woman might instil Joan with serious doubts. As I near the two of them in the herbarium, Joan hands me a clean smock.

"Are those uncle's smocks?"

"He was stripped and left for dead when we found him," says Joan. "I have no other resource."

"I doubt uncle wants his shirts ruined."

Joan doesn't reply. She is accomplished at letting comments sit in the air like a stinking fart. I decide that I have had my fill of the young woman and gently close the door for privacy to change out of the soiled smock, but also to remove myself from their conversation.

Of late I welcome William Brugge's absence whenever it occurs. However, when I hear his voice in the shop, I am glad that maybe I won't be the topic of conversation anymore. I doubt he wants Meg to know about me, and I hear Joan tell her to play ignorant, but I am no longer Joan and William Brugge's secret. Instead of skulking near my door to listen in on their conversation, I retreat to my bed. I miss parts of their discussion but I have had enough excitement for one day. Meg leaves soon after, having dispensed with niceties and saying very little to her uncle.

"What did she want?" he asks after the door clicks closed behind her.

"Only to visit. She was nearby."

"Does she know about…?"

My ears hear no answer. What, if anything, did she tell him? If Joan blatantly lied, would it surprise me? Thinking on this, I suspect she is a woman who would rather add additional penance in purgatory for lying if it meant keeping a peaceful home.

"Watch the shop while I work in the herbarium," says Brugge. Whatever she told him, he seems accepting of it.

It is quiet except for the clatter of crockery and liquid being poured. Brugge exits through the back-alley door and returns a few moments later. I nestle against my bolster and close my eyes, the lull of pots rattling on a stove, the scrape of a stool, the rhythmic chopping, reminding me of my time at Thetford. Despite my uncertain future, the chores of an apothecary still calm me. Underneath the diligent work of creation is the virtuous desire to help others.

My mind drifts off to the golden glow of Thetford Priory's herb garden, alive with the sounds of bees and the flutter of butterflies and finch. Then, just as lovely, I see Bess approaching me at Whitehall, a rare coincidence in the labyrinthine palace. Of all the ladies at court I believe she is one of the finest dressed, with a richly dyed kirtle of russet damask and marmot-trimmed sleeves. Jewels adorn her neck and fingers; she wants for nothing. Norfolk has seen to elevating her status with finery since marriage is not possible.

I bowed low upon her approach and my expression of joy in seeing her must have been obvious.

"Dear Kronos, you need not indulge me with such a grand gesture. I do not deserve your decorous greeting."

"My lady, I think otherwise."

A faint smile lightened her otherwise sombre countenance. I ventured to inquire after her subdued mood.

With a wistful air, she replied, "I sometimes wonder what could have been."

"Ah," said I. "What could have been if the duke had not chosen you?" I knew I was boring into the crux of her thinking, but I did not fear that I would offend or overstep, such were the tethers of our connection. And, after all, I am a fool.

She did not answer, but the rise of her eyebrows told me that, yes, this weighted her condition.

"My lady, it will serve no purpose for you to muse on such narratives. We are all bound by circumstance—which is a tangle of choices—some of our own making, and some imposed upon us."

"'Tis very well to recommend such advice, but I cannot always distract myself from thinking about it. Torturing myself with regrets."

"There is prayer," I offered, the Benedictine in me asserting itself. "I am not sure what comfort there is beyond believing that a higher power hears our supplications." I could see that my words did not appease her. I saw little change in her expression and so I sought to assure her that at least one person on this great planet commiserated with her contemplations. "One is not alone."

At this, Bess took hold of my hand between hers and faced me full on. "Dear Kronos, you are ever my champion and friend." She patted my hand. "We are both constrained by what has come before. Perhaps you understand that more than most."

My ardent wish for Bess's happiness is interrupted by the boisterous greeting of a customer entering the shop.

"Sir Howard," answers William Brugge in an equally loud exchange. "What brings you? It has been a time since last we spoke."

I perk upon hearing the man's surname—Howard. Be he nobleman or citizen merchant?

"It is my usual complaint, good fellow. I can't take a piss without bracing myself. The pain is so fearsome that I must place a hand on a wall or other sturdy structure, 'elst I would topple. And if I should wankle in a pot, it be cloudy and as pink as my lady's blush. I've come for your healing tincture."

"I believe I have enough ingredients on hand. If you will wait while I put it together."

William Brugge enters the herbarium and is soon chopping and mincing, but the finer points of his remedy are a mystery. Brother Ulric used the dried leaves and berries of black currant and would steep them into a strong tea to drink three times a day. I'm certain every apothecary has his own recipe for bladder maladies, and whatever herbs Brugge uses, they must work well enough.

Joan remains in the shop to keep the man occupied in light conversation while her husband works.

"Here you are," says Brugge, on his return. "Bring an ale to a strong boil for several minutes, then steep an amount the width and length of your thumb. You must drink this as a tea five times a day, but do not continue for longer than one week. Return if you do not find relief."

"What can be done if I don't find relief?"

"There are other methods to try."

"As long as they do not involve painful intervention."

"I assure you, no more painful than your current condition."

"My uncle suffers from the same trouble on occasion."

"The Duke of Norfolk?" inquires Brugge.

I sit bolt upright in bed.

"Would you make a second portion for him?"

"I am sorry, sir. I used all of my remaining ingredients to make yours."

"Could I give him a portion of this?"

"I discourage it. You will need the entire amount to cure your ailment."

"Then I shall see how this suits me. If I am improved then I will return. I should like to keep on the good side of my uncle, and your draught might help me in that."

"Of course," says Brugge. The two men devolve into idle pleasantries. "Do I remember correctly that you were importing wine from Gascon? How does your business fare?"

And now I know for sure that this is Thomas Howard's nephew. When the Howards rose in favour with the king's marriage to his fifth wife, Katherine, Henry granted a wine licence to Norfolk's nephews, George and Charles, Katherine's brothers.

"Merchants and nobility demand as much wine with their meals as commoners do ale."

"Then you should never want for clients," says Brugge.

"I think not. Charles is not as involved in this venture. He has earned the king's ire, unfortunately."

Ah! So this is brother George.

"Pray tell, why? I thought all the Howards were kept in the king's good grace."

George Howard scoffs. "Charles dared to love Henry's niece, and for that indiscretion he must not now overstep his bounds. Charles stays well away from matters of court. Better for King Henry not to be reminded." Footsteps tread across the shop floor and the door whinges open. "Good morrow, apothecary Brugge."

I would not have suspected that this man's sister was accused of dangerous flirtations with other men. He gave no hint of her underlying court imbroglio, or the possible disgrace awaiting his family in regards to her indiscretion. But then, how wise would it be for the brother of the queen to voice his concerns with a neighbourhood apothecary?

Being removed from court and separated from anyone in it, I cannot gauge what thorny dilemma might be going on there. I am not even sure how many days I have been gone or whether Archbishop Cranmer has acted on John Lascelles' tawdry tidbit. If he has, the king would be sorely hurt, for he fancies that Katherine truly loves him.

'Tis a pity that George Howard did not see me. Would he have heard of the abuse I suffered at the hands of Archbishop Cranmer and Thomas Audley, and would he have been stunned to see me alive? I could have burst into the shop, barefoot and wearing only this smock, but then what? It isn't as if I could tell him that I had information he might find useful. He might not even recognise me as Kronos, the king's ninny, so changed am I.

But if I had shown myself, and once he recovered from his astonishment, perhaps he would realise how valuable I might be to the Howard family. If they could find out the ruinous bruit before the king learned of it, perhaps they could mitigate the damage. They could dispatch the weaselly John Lascelles, through bribe or…some other means. People who desired office with courtiers had a habit of disappearing, until someone through sudden remembrance might mention the poor dissembler, and then eyebrows lift and sideways glances ensue. How valuable could I be to the Howards?

I was not the only one wondering.

CHAPTER TWENTY-FIVE

A s is our routine, Joan enters my room to bring me sodden bread to eat. She examines my wounds, makes sounds of approval. My tongue no longer bleeds from eating, but every meal is a lesson in patience. I gingerly chew the lumps, moving them carefully from the good side of my mouth to the other. I no longer wince in pain or spit the masticated mess onto the plate in frustration.

Joan prepares a poultice and dabs it onto my cheek before replacing the bandage with a fresh one.

"You might be able to forgo the wrapping soon," she says, tucking in the end of the bandage. She takes up the empty plate and cup of ale.

William Brugge has left to find more ingredients for a second batch of medicine for George Howard. Apparently, he is confident the courtier will return for more.

On my foray to the ditch latrine, I venture a bit further since only Joan is home. She must keep an eye on the shop, and since I have always completed the task without incident, she trusts me. How easy it would be to just leave. To skip down Turnagain Lane to Seacoal, cross the Holborn Bridge to Saffron Hill and beyond to the stretch of open road leading me to new and unexplored horizons. But a barefoot dwarf wearing only a smock is suspect at best.

Besides, something else keeps me willingly confined—my curiosity.

Upon my return, I lock the padlock, and as I cross the herbarium, I hear William Brugge and Joan talking in the empty shop. For now, he doesn't mind me emptying my own pisspot. Brugge continues to associate my stature with stupidity and does not think that I might overhear them speaking. "There is news that the young Queen may not be as virtuous as once thought. Those who presented her to the king either did not know this, or they tried to keep it secret."

"Who told you? Where did you learn of this?"

"At St. Paul's."

"Paul's Walk—where all manner of flibberjib and hearsay gets air?" The cathedral has long been a venue of exchange. Not just for the sale of broadsides, trinkets and wares, but for the jargle of political rumours that passes between lips. "What proof is there?"

"Accusations have been made against her. There are rumblings coming from Whitehall. It is said that she is not of strong morals. That she took lovers before marrying the king."

"Husband, infidelity before marriage is not a reason to end matrimony. Even nobility, and I daresay, royalty, are not so naïve, or innocent."

"Aye, but she was presented falsely to the king. Her virtue is suspect. Mayhap there was a precontract. It might have happened and then been conveniently forgotten. A queen of thin morals and, by association, those who presented her falsely, cannot be trusted. The king cannot and will not be made a fool."

"But from every church, in every parish, bells pealed in celebration at their union. Remember the excitement? Every

Londoner smiled at the king's happiness. He had finally found a queen who pleased him."

I take a step back to consider this news. If the morals of the queen are now in question, could the original accusation that I overheard be the seed of her downfall? The king may have been told about John Lascelles' claim, or mayhap other criticisms have surfaced instead.

"Our guest might know something about this."

A jolt of alarm unsettles me.

"You cannot assume that. There is no way to know," says Joan. "He cannot speak. Nor can he write."

"He can't speak or he *won't* speak?"

My heart pounds at the thought of Brugge interrogating me. His methods may put King Henry's to shame.

"You expect him to tell us what he knows? Our only task is to care for him and to heal his wounds. If he knows information about the queen's private affairs, then whoever left him at our door will surely return for him. But we must remove ourselves from the affairs of court and this king. Let us remain ignorant. I am glad not to know more, for we are safer that way."

"Wife, this may be an opportunity. I am not one to sit and wait for a knock on our door. I plan to tell Sir Howard that we have someone of great import to the queen and her family."

"William! You do not know that! His reason for being here may have nothing to do with her."

"Sir Howard's reaction should tell us a great deal. If he is interested and if he recognises him, then it is possible that our guest knows something valuable. Why should we not profit?"

"Are you mad?"

"We should be recompensed for his care. For keeping him safe."

"They shall laugh in your face."

Joan is right. I've never known any courtier, especially the Howards, the family most in favour with our king, to bow to the demands of a mere merchant, much less an apothecary. If Norfolk got ear of this, he would simply send his men to pull me out of here and burn the place down. Just for the peevish fun of it.

"We should move him."

"Move him? How should I be able to care for him? Why? What necessity does that serve?"

"What if someone comes for him before I've had a chance to speak with Sir George."

"Are you thinking of securing a ransom?" Her voice rises in distress. "I am not sure that I recognise the man I call husband."

"Apparently I have made a mistake telling you this."

Not at all! I want to shout. For now I know the depth of his mendacity.

"Bother yourself with your household chores and to his care, but leave me to matters of consequence."

Joan says nothing in reply or defence. Instead, she lets the shop door slam in answer to her husband's mischief. Joan is gone. I am alone with William Brugge.

Sitting and worrying about Brugge questioning me is too unsettling. Even wandering the alleys of London barefoot and in a thin smock is preferable to being beaten. And now to be used as a pawn to wrest money from the powerful Howards. A memory of the red-hot poker coming for my mouth stirs me to action. Let Brugge make the excuse for why I am gone should anyone come asking for me.

Without a second thought, I slip out my door and make for

the back alley. My bare feet tramp across the herbarium floor but what I lose in stealth I hope to make up for in speed. I am within sight of the alley door when William Brugge comes roaring after me.

"Stop, drudge!" he shouts, as if I would do exactly that.

At the door, the formidable iron padlock hangs in place. I stand on my toes and reach overhead, feeling for the key to unlock it.

"You cannot leave!" says Brugge, hastening through the herbarium.

My hand trembles and in my panic, I accidently sweep it off the ledge and it clatters to the floor. The light is so dim, I can barely see my hand much less locate the metal piece at my feet.

"You think to escape?"

Desperately scrabbling on the floor, I find the key.

"You'll not get far."

I shove the key into the padlock hole and the wards resist turning. Frantic, I roughly wiggle the shank. There is a click and the shackle falls away.

William Brugge reaches the back entry just as I push open the door.

The bright outdoors blinds, but I pitch myself forward into the slop of the wet alley. Mud splatters up my calves as I run towards the corner. Close behind, I hear the glop of the apothecary in pursuit. My short legs are no match for his long. I am about to turn the corner when he grabs hold of my smock, throwing me off balance. I slip, and Brugge seizes my arm in a painful grip. I only partway fall. But I am caught.

He drags me back through the muck towards the shop, cursing and tightening his hold on me.

"I am not done with you," says Brugge, throwing me across the threshold.

I stumble to the floor as the door slams and the lock is secured. Struggling to my knees, I look around to see his foot meet my ribs with a savage kick.

"Until we know why you were left outside our door, you will remain here. Leaving is not for you to decide."

He takes me up under my armpit and pulls me to my feet. Pain radiates from my side as he pushes me ahead of him into the herbarium. Beside my room he shoves me up against the wall, and I fear what will surely come next.

I expect his clenched fist, a punch to my face or gut. I brace myself against his rage, but instead I feel the force of his hand across my face. The sting of it burns my cheek, and his fingernails rake across my skin. A second slap lands on the other cheek—the side that is injured, and I begin to bleed.

I am stunned. I am at his mercy. I haven't the muscles to stop him.

But it is the voice of his niece that gives him pause. She has entered the shop without him hearing.

"Uncle! God's blood, what are you doing?"

Brugge releases me and I slump to the floor.

"Meg!"

She enters the herbarium and bends down to me. The heat of her body is a reassuring gesture of humanity. "Help me get him to his feet."

Her sudden show of compassion is enough to jar William Brugge into some semblance of humility, perhaps even regret. For him to feel outright shame would be expecting too much.

"He was trying to escape."

They lift me to my feet and walk me to the bed. Meg helps me into it while Brugge watches. Never mind that I am spattered in mud and the smock is torn and I cannot sit. It is a relief to be horizontal on a relatively soft pallet with a woman nearby. But this woman is not the angel her aunt is. She limits her involvement and makes no attempt to assess my injuries. That will be left to Joan. The two of them leave me to my misery. The door shuts behind them.

"I don't know why there is a dwarf in your shop or why you were thrashing him. I don't expect an explanation, but neither should I have to remind you that murder is an offence against the king."

"He isn't so hurt."

"So says the man doing the beating."

"Keep free of this concern, Meg. The less you know the safer you will be." Perhaps he did listen to Joan. But he applies her words to others, not to himself. "This has been foisted upon us."

"I cannot unsee what I've just witnessed. If you wish to be unburdened, Uncle, why not let him leave?"

"Because we have been tasked with his care."

"By whom?"

Brugge does not answer.

"Uncle, how long has he been in your care?"

"The number of days is irrelevant."

"But during this time, has anyone come forward to communicate with you?"

"Nay."

"No one has inquired after him. Have you received money for his care?"

"Nay. Not a penny."

"Yet you believe you have been tasked with healing and keeping him. Based only on your reputation for offering succour to the ill and dispossessed?"

"Joan is known for her thoughtful care to those in need."

"Granted. But it seems to me that a man capable of running

away is no longer in need of care. Fit him out with proper clothing and let him be on his way."

"It is not that simple."

"How can that be difficult?"

"Keeping him here may have import to the king."

"Uncle, I've always known you to be a pragmatic man of measured thinking. You've always devoted your care and diligence to practising your medicine above all else. But of late I have seen a side of you that troubles me. Your treatment of Aunt, and now this. What proof is there that this person is important to our king? And if that be true, then why are you abusing him?"

Brugge hesitates. His answer comes reluctantly. "I overheard men talking at The Crooked Cork."

"Ha! Men spouting on, after how many pottlepots of ale? And you believe this over your own common sense?"

"Enough, Meg. I'll not listen to your chiding. Kindly go and leave me in peace. This is not your concern."

I wait for Meg to continue scolding him. Her spirited redress surprises me in a woman raised by such an arrogant and patronising man. Where once I found Meg condescending, now I find her brave.

But her continued argument is interrupted. Joan has returned.

Joan must be surmising her husband's dishevelled appearance; his jerkin soiled with mud, his black hair clumped with perspiration, the boot prints of alley filth still wet on the floor. She must be noticing her niece's flushed cheeks, the sudden silence between the two when she walks through the door.

"Good day, niece."

I want to think that Joan barely glanced at her husband in cordial recognition, that she understood there was no longer a secret to hide. Their private cabal had just grown by one. His actions have broken the parameters of exclusion, their wall has been breached.

"Aunt," says a now subdued Meg.

Instead of asking what has happened, Joan crosses the shop into the herbarium and arrives at my door. One look at me and her face freezes in grim acknowledgement. She is then by my side, turning my cheek to examine my wound. Without a word she exits for a bowl of water to clean me.

While she is in the herbarium, Meg tails her like a dog. It isn't long before the shop door opens and William Brugge is forced to be an apothecary again.

"I found him brutalising the dwarf," says Meg in a low voice as Joan sets down the bowl of water on the small table and brings it closer to the bed. "What is all of this about? Uncle feels compelled to keep him here based on hearsay?"

Joan busies herself with my care. First, she removes the soiled bandage and cleans the mud off my face, dabbing at the wound. The sting of it makes me wince. "He has reopened part of your injury," she tells me.

Meg persists. "Uncle believes that this runt is important to the king but he won't tell me why."

Joan sighs as she cleans the sweat from my neck. She answers after she's wrung out the cloth. "He overheard men at The Crooked Cork. They said they were instructed to burn out his tongue. Then he was carried across town and deposited at our door."

"Carried from where?"

"Whitehall."

"Whitehall! God's blood! The king's palace?" Meg's eyes reflect wonderment and dare I think, an inkling of respect? "But, why your door? There are physicians all over London. Why you?"

Joan shrugs. "I suppose whoever left him here did so based on our virtue." She pushes a loose strand of hair out of her eyes.

Meg's chin and lower lip twitch. "Unless there is some underlying reason Uncle may be hiding."

"Nay, Meg. He is just as bewildered. If you are implying there is a political motivation in all of this, there very well may be. We could have been chosen because we support the king in all ways, but we are as uninformed as you."

Meg appraises me as if she might learn the truth just by close inspection. The water sloshes in Joan's bowl. William Brugge walks into the herbarium and gathers the ingredients for a remedy. The two women speak in whispers.

"William says there are rumours circulating about our queen."

"When are there not rumours?" says Meg. "Falsehoods are an Englishman's amusement."

"It is believed that she may have misled King Henry. That she may be of light character."

Meg looks askance at me, perhaps hoping to read in my reaction whether this is true. But I am careful to appear detached.

"Is it so important? Why must a woman be held more accountable? Men gallivant around without consideration yet for a woman to cuckold her husband…"

"Meg! Shush! Speak no more of this."

Meg's eyebrow jumps with impertinence, but she will not be put off by her aunt's admonishment. She fixes me with a coy smile. "Tell me, dwarf, is the queen naughty?"

I admit it is difficult to appear indifferent. I look away, and I am glad for Joan lifting the torn smock over my head. It gives me a moment to compose myself.

My hairy chest is exposed, and I give Meg a look that I hope appals her enough to forget her question.

It works.

Meg harumphs and stalks from the room. A faint smile appears on Joan's lips.

"I don't care a worm's squirm what you know about all that. It is not for me to know one way or the other." She cleans off my back and pats me dry. "We all have our secrets."

Meanwhile, Brugge's muted conversation with his customer drifts to my ears and the freedom we'd earned from Meg is regrettably short-lived. I situate a sheet over my more exclusive parts as Joan begins washing my legs when Meg returns carrying a basket.

She sets the hamper on the bed beside me. I do not know what to make of this when from beneath a small blanket she pulls out a pair of hosen, a smock, and a child's jerkin, all neatly folded. She offers the set of clothing to the both of us, not knowing which of us should accept it.

"What is this?" asks Joan, moving the small table back against the wall, then taking the clothing from Meg and going through it, holding each item up to inspect.

"You can't expect Uncle to give up his smocks when he doesn't even like the fellow. Eventually the runt will be on his way. He has to wear something."

"It is thoughtful of you," says Joan, clearly surprised.

"I found them at a frippery near Cheapside. They aren't tailored for a dwarf, more like a young boy, but they will do."

Not nearly as fine as my crimson velvet doublet with slashed sleeves of inlaid cream coloured silk, or my woollen hosen with beaded codpiece I wore at Whitehall. Meg forgot a coif, but digs out a black flat cap and places it on my head, adjusting it to suit her.

"There," she says, stepping back to admire the effect. "He looks almost human."

CHAPTER TWENTY-SIX

MY CONFRONTATION WITH William Brugge has exhausted me. When I finally pull on the hosen Meg brought, I am surprised by how well they fit. She even included a pair of shoes, a bit worn and the worse for wear, overly large, but acceptable. I no longer have to walk barefoot to the ditch latrine.

Joan collects my food bowl and shortly thereafter leaves the shop for market. William Brugge works in the herbarium, his nearness filling me with apprehension. What little content I enjoy from wearing something other than Brugge's thin smocks is dashed at the sound of him outside my door. He's had nearly a day to contemplate his outburst and nearly a day to plan against my escape.

Is escape on my mind? Having had a taste of it only whets my appetite. Now I am clothed and could more easily assimilate into a crowded street or market. I can never avoid drawing notice for obvious reasons, but at least I wouldn't be half naked trying to skirt attention.

Never a knock to forewarn (because in his mind, I am not quite human), he barges into my room carrying a chain and dragging a block of iron. I am stunned—horrified. He closes the door behind him, preventing my sudden bolt from the room.

"You cannot be trusted," he says. "We almost believed you would never leave, but now we know that you would—if given the chance."

I shake my head no as he nears.

I have seen prisoners brought to their executions from Newgate, their skin worn to the bone from the heavy iron manacles. Even more grisly than their impending hanging, I watched as they were made to walk up the steps to the scaffold, beaten when they didn't move fast enough, their ankles bleeding, the manacles having dug into their flesh, rubbing against bone.

I am shirking from his advance when suddenly Brugge lunges for my leg. A surge of defiance steels my resolve. With all my strength, I roll towards him, surprising him as I fall off the bed and on to the floor. I keep rolling hoping to knock him over, but he is quick. Before I can get to my feet, he grabs hold of my left ankle and pins my foot to the floor. Just as quick, I force my opposite knee into his chest. He shall not easily shackle me.

We struggle for control of my leg when, from deep inside of me, I let loose a guttural scream. A fierce, savage scream. The force of it, the utter desperation and vehemence of my cry, surprises him. He leans his weight into me, crushing the air from my chest so that I can only whimper.

"So, you do have voice," he says. "Scream your displeasure, no one will hear you." And with that, he clamps the shackle around my ankle and locks the pin in place.

I screech and howl my indignation. I make sounds I never thought myself capable of. Their inventiveness inspires me. Let him find a hot poker and try to stop me, I shall not be subdued.

"Wail on, you pathetic spy! Such fruitless squawking." He relishes my performance, urging me on. "Think on your complicity.

Someday those yelps will be your penitent confession, you wicked soul. God has no mercy for miching spies!"

Like an uncorked barrel, my shrieks flow long and hard, spilling out, filling every silent corner of the room. My spider friend retreats into her hidden corner as my eyes fill with hatred. I glare at William Brugge with as much disdain as I can possibly evoke.

William Brugge checks the link connecting the chain to the leaden weight. Satisfied, he exits the room, leaving me to contemplate my fate.

Breathless, I ponder my predicament. I will my breath to slow and for my shoulders to drop. At least I have a voice. And my voice is capable of ferocity. When next a customer enters William Brugge's shop, I shall be ready to scream the devil out of hell.

Unfortunately, Brugge realises this, too. He returns with two lengths of cloth. One to tie my hands, the other for me to chew on.

"This is to ensure your silence while the shop is open and I conduct business."

I do not sit like an injured bird and wait for him to bind me. He must inflict more threats and jabs in his effort to restrain me. His advantage is that I cannot move far. My hands are made useless except for managing a piss in the pot and my tongue is held silent with a cloth wrapped around my head. From here on, my days will be spent gagged and restrained.

Did Joan know of her husband's intentions? Did she excuse herself from this unpleasantness, or will she return from market and be appalled to see me trussed like a peacock ready to bake?

The tedium of my immobility tires me even more than trying to manoeuvre around an impossibly heavy weight. William Brugge means to profit off my imposition of his time and effort, and there is nothing I can do to thwart his design. Indignation is common for a king's fool, and I am not unused to being belittled and taunted. I have crafted an armour of indifference to deflect the verbal abuse slung at me. However, I have never been shackled and gagged. People naturally think that a man of my diminutive stature couldn't possibly be a threat. Perhaps I rely on this assumption too much. My black thoughts are interrupted when a customer enters the shop.

"Sir Howard," says the apothecary. "You have returned. Do tell. How did you find my remedy?"

"Goodfellow, I have come to sing your praise. No more discomfort. My piss is as clear as boiled water. I should like more of your fine medicine."

"For yourself or for your uncle?"

"I am healed. I should like it for my uncle."

"Ah! I am honoured to help the duke. Unfortunately, I have used my entire supply of some of the ingredients, and they are difficult to find this time of year. I have a possible source, but I may have to scout for them. You will have to give me some time."

"Very well," says Sir George Howard. "I understand and I will wait for your quality remedy."

"But before you leave," says William Brugge, his footsteps ranging across the shop. The definitive click of the front door lock is secured, preventing customers from entering. "I have something to discuss with you." He pauses. "It is a matter better explained by my showing you."

The men enter the herbarium, and their footfall ends outside my door.

"I am taking care of someone involved in an…incident… which may be of significance to you and your family. The specifics concerning this mishap are unknown to me. We found him outside our door. He was senseless, nearly dead. My wife and I take it as our Christian duty to care for anyone in need, regardless of their faith or political inclination.

"No one has contacted me. Of course, I may be wrong to think this incident might pertain to matters of the king's court. But because you are a loyal customer, and because I am supportive and aligned with all political and religious values held by the Howard family, I feel compelled to show you the burden that has been thrust upon us."

"Are you implying that my family is involved?"

"Nay, sir. I am not. I am merely offering you an opportunity that your family might find useful."

"Pray leave off with your presumptions and show me."

The latch lifts and the door is pushed open.

Could I have affected an even more remarkable pose than the one I now present? Tell me how I could have looked more pathetic, more unsettling, more baleful. Who could look on me and not think me sinister? A man shackled and bound is a man not to be trusted. William Brugge's effective use of grotesque props has already condemned me.

Sir George Howard's jaw slackens at the sight of me. His eyes round in astonishment. If I had looked away, I would have missed his baffled reaction, no doubt a mirror of my own disbelief and humiliation. All I have to do is sit. I cannot add or subtract from this first, intractable impression.

"Explain why he is gagged and bound. Why the shackles?" Sir George Howard sets aside an impulsive verdict of my guilt.

"He tried to escape," says Brugge.

"Then he is well enough to do so?" Sir George studies me. His eyes carefully avoid mine.

Brugge tries to explain. "I would be remiss to let him leave without an understanding of why he was brutalised in the first place."

"How would that be remiss? Do you believe you are owed an explanation?" Sir George needed to remind Brugge that the apothecary was a humble merchant, not nobility.

"I mean no disrespect," says Brugge, tucking his chin in deference. "You must forgive my interest."

"I understand that you have invested some time and labour into this man's recovery. Men of monstrous birth do hold a certain fascination with nobility. But it is not for me to say, nor is it for you to know the inner workings of this king's court."

"Sir Howard, I operate on instinct. I know nothing of the king's matters and it is true, I have no authority to know. But surely you must agree, a dwarf who has had his tongue burned out is notable. He has admitted to being a minstrel. I am aware that his kind are often employed by the court for entertainment. Would he have been so permanently maimed if he were a common street performer?"

Sir Howard does not reply, but I take his silence for accord. I do not recognise him as the duke's nephew, but because I know his name, I know of him. It is far more likely that he remembers me. I am that anomaly who gets noticed, who gets stared at, who gets slotted into a category of low-born oddities, a spectacle, there for the amusement of others.

Brugge must tread carefully. To insinuate that George Howard knows more than he is admitting never sits well with nobility.

"I believe he is capable of speaking," ventures Brugge. "If not clearly formed words, then perhaps decipherable ones at least. His speech is improving."

Sir Howard scrutinises me. His hand goes to his chin and strokes his shortly-cropped beard. His hair is trimmed to a knuckle's length, the entire effect being that of a tidy man, given to detail. He is playing for time, waiting to hear what William Brugge offers. What else is on Brugge's mind? But I see recognition in Howard's eyes. He is putting together the buzz of court hearsay, connecting my possible role in it. Oh yes, this man knows of me.

William Brugge continues, "Let me be clear with you, Sir. If he may be of value to your family, pay me for the care we've rendered and for keeping this secret."

Sir George's neck straightens and he casts a sharp look at Brugge. "Are you proposing a bribe?" His tone is smooth. He is educated in court subterfuge.

"Call it recompense," says Brugge with an equally cool edge to his voice.

George Howard's eyebrow lifts. "How much are you asking?"

The apothecary is quick with a number, for he has given this some thought. "Two hundred pounds."

"Ho!" replies Sir George, incredulous. If my mouth wasn't stuffed with linen, I would laugh along with him. "That is nearly a lifetime of wages for one such as you."

"I grow no younger. My best years of earning are behind me. Besides, it is a small price to pay…for saving your family."

"Saving my family? You dare to think our survival is in your hands? You are assuming more than you pretend to know."

"I know that the favour your family enjoys is due to the king's affection for your sister. If the king were to change his mind, where would you be? Is it not better to safeguard against the possibility? Think of it as money wisely spent to ensure your future—the Howards' future."

George Howard considers this and after a last glance at me, exits my room. Brugge follows, shutting the door behind.

The wood cannot prevent their words seeping past and finding their way to my ears.

"I am not fond of being played, Master Brugge. You've shown a side that I haven't seen before. I am going to leave. If it weren't for your good remedy, I would have nothing more to do with you. As it is, I must secure my uncle's continued generosity. Find the ingredients and make the medicine for my uncle. When I return, I shall have an answer for you."

Norfolk requires pandering even from close family members to stay in his good graces. Like the king, these patriarchs of powerful families demand obsequious family members. I suppose the Howards are no different than the Seymours, or the Cliffords, or the Brandons. They all shuffle their alliances, deny their associations, and play mute when necessary. Don't look to noblemen for their honesty. Their duty is one of self-preservation above all else.

The conversation does not end with the familiar scrape of the shop door, for just as George Howard makes to leave, Joan hampers his hasty departure.

"Sir George," she says. I can hear the surprise in her voice.

"Goodwife. God keep you."

She can't let him pass with only a polite greeting. She attempts to prolong his stay, if just for the chance to measure his mood. "Has my husband's remedy been helpful?"

"Indeed, it has. Now if I may take my leave."

I can imagine Joan looking between Sir George and her husband. I hear the door close after he leaves.

Joan speaks brightly. "He returned. The remedy must have pleased him. Are you making more for the duke?"

"Aye, he has asked it of me."

The silences between married couples are an enigma. I've come to realise that the most destructive wars are the ones waged between husbands and wives. Joan asks no more of him because…he has put up a wall of noncommunication? Or is he busy with the shop ledger, counting orders and adding numbers and pretending normalcy? He might have turned his back to dust down the shelves and arrange his medicines. Quiet can be filled with any number of seemingly menial tasks, but this silence has significance.

Joan is perceptive enough to not insist on conversation. Whatever she has secured at market is brought past my closed door and into the kitchen. For the moment, household chores take precedence over my care, and I am content with that. She won't ignore me forever.

Common tasks such as fetching water from the rain barrel are completed more boisterously, the door slams, the bucket is set upon a table with extra vigour. Such is the war that is waged when words are repressed. Next, I expect William Brugge to leave. Avoidance is a man's mainstay, his shield against dangerous barbs that will surely be launched at him. But he does not leave.

We all succumb to curiosity, and Joan is no exception. She completes her tasks and soon the door to my room edges open.

She sucks in her breath at the sight of me. "What has he done?"

Instead of confronting her husband, Joan's first thought is to remove the stifling gag that is soaked in saliva. She recognises that the cloth is squeezing my cheeks, and she runs a finger lightly over my skin, tutting about the red imprint left behind.

Her gaze drops down to my bound wrists and shackled ankle. "What is he thinking?" Her voice is so soft that only I can hear. She works to release my hands when the apothecary appears at the door.

His eyes flare with anger. "What are you doing?"

Without so much as a glance, Joan replies, "I am not about to see you undo all the good healing that has happened. You treat him like a criminal."

"Which he very well may be!"

"You told Sir George about him."

"Wife, you are involving yourself in matters better left to

men. If I should secure a better future for us in our old age, why should you bemoan my efforts?"

"Because it is ill-gotten. Why do you insist on trying to outwit men of higher stature? No good can come of it."

"When should a man not be compensated for his services?"

"When it is a matter concerning noblemen. An accusation of treason falls as easily from their lips as sour milk."

"How could ridding ourselves of a traitor be called treason?"

"Firstly, we do not know if he is, indeed, a traitor. So, say you, based on chinwag you heard at a boozing ken and at Paul's Walk. True, I do not know if attempting to extort money from noblemen could be construed as treason, but I have seen lesser offences end on the scaffold."

"Wife, you worry overly much. We shall end better than we started."

Joan does not reply but continues to work at the knot binding my wrists, further incensing William Brugge by ignoring him.

He seizes her elbow. "Stop! He is no longer your concern."

Joan yanks her arm out of her husband's grasp and resumes untying my wrists.

Brugge's neck turns red with rage. "Are you deaf? Do not cross me!"

But when Joan dismisses his warning, Brugge reacts to her obstinance as blatant provocation. He pushes himself between me and Joan and firmly grasps her wrist, resisting her attempts to pull away. He then wrenches her arm up at an awkward angle. She steels herself against the pain but I cannot sit idly by and watch him treat her so.

I slide off the bed and with my unrestrained leg, I kick him in the shin. If I cannot wield the brute force to stop him, then let me be the irritating fly that dives at his face. He stumbles backwards, pulling Joan along with him. For an instant I think he may fall, and then I shall stomp him, but he shoves Joan aside and regains his balance. Before I know it, he rushes forward to push me, but I evade him well enough to land a second, more artfully landed kick.

A man takes issue when his bollocks are bruised.

The apothecary lets loose with a string of expletives that would keep Archbishop Cranmer busy granting dispensations for the next year.

But never underestimate a wounded bull.

He manages one well-placed punch to render me unconscious. A swift blow to my temple, a curtain of bleary black, and I am falling. My face cracks against the floor, my body follows, a searing pain rolls down my spine like a crashing wave, then nothing.

CHAPTER TWENTY-SEVEN

A SNEEZE ROUSES ME. Darkness robs me of sight. A wall presses against my back; I am confined to a small area with my ankles free and my wrists bound. My feet touch an opposite wall, and I lift a leg to run the sole of my foot against the hard surface. Pocky daub crumbles beneath my toes, exposing wood lathing. No gag stifles my mouth but thick dust clogs my nose.

I haven't the temerity to yell, nor the strength. My head is as thick as the fog on the river Thames on St. Stephen's Day. Is it night, or day? As my eyes adjust, a faint sliver of light runs the length of the wall that I sit against. Whether caused by the sun or a candle, I do not know, but my wooziness pulls me back under. My head nods to one side and my mind roams.

❧

When was the last time I saw Lady Bess? Was it during Twelfth Night celebrations? I was verily caught up in my antics and in juggling that I scarce stood still. The great hall was crowded with velvet-clad women with their inviting glances and coy smiles, so I was easily distracted. As the night wore on, my attention settled on a particular noble lady who fancied giving me a try in a dim alcove away from the festivities. Discretion was paramount for I did not want to be run through by a testy nobleman disinclined to give allowance to his wife when he himself was guilty of carnal relations a hundred-fold over.

My cuckoldress and I celebrated the holiday with great merriment. We had just finished tidying ourselves to return to the banquet hall when we heard the unmistakable sound of a hurried approach. We retreated deeper into the alcove and held our breath until the interloper had passed.

I barely restrained a gasp as I watched my Lady Bess hasten by, her sobs stifled by her hands as she brought them to her face. As much as I wanted to follow after and ask her the cause of her great sorrow, I remained silent, fraught with concern that I could not express. To go to her would have embarrassed this proud lady. I know her well enough that she would rile at my show of empathy, for she knew her place and circumstance and kept her regrets quiet, asking no one for pity.

But as she disappeared down the hall and my paramour returned to the celebration, I lingered, torn between wishing to comfort Bess as my friend, but also wishing to respect her dignity. Alas, I left my Bess to her melancholy and, feeling reflective and dejected myself, sauntered back to the banquet, taking my time, and thinking of retiring to my quarters after one more drink.

I entered the hall, keeping to the periphery, looking for an abandoned cup of ale or sack, when I saw Norfolk in all of his nasty splendour. He shamelessly laughed and danced with a woman even younger than Bess. A woman ornamented with jewels and blessed with bright blue eyes that shone with glee. A man in his sixties must exercise some restraint and maturity, surely, but nay, Norfolk thinks himself as entitled as our king.

Indeed, given half a chance, methinks he would readily usurp our liege if given a path to do so.

When next I am stirred, I can't say whether I've slept or have just been drifting in a drowsy state of insensibility. My head throbs, reminding me of the blow inflicted by the apothecary.

The pounding does not soften, and I am pondering my circumstances when I am distracted by footsteps. Something hefty and cumbersome slides in short spurts, bumping the wall against my back. I topple backwards as a thin, plank door falls open. A waft of fresh air revives me, and I look up to see Joan holding a bowl, and the smell of carrot and cabbage finds my nose. Joan helps me to sit and the herbarium stretches behind her. I am being held in a space behind Brugge's shelving.

Joan appears weary, with noticeable hollows under her eyes. Her right eye is swollen and surrounded by purpled skin; the whites coloured red from a broken blood vessel.

Alarmed, I manage to garble a semblance of words. "Did he?" I point to my own eye while looking at hers.

My words sound coarse and strained. In time, will they round out, grow fat and have sharper, more defined edges?

She looks at me kindly. "I can understand you."

Perhaps in light of her suffering, she raises a finger to her lips. "We shall keep this a secret." Our eyes lock in understanding—a pact has been made between us.

"You can't possibly eat with your wrists tied." She works to untie my wrists and stuffs the rope in a pocket. "You are capable of feeding yourself."

She offers me the bowl, and I eagerly take it. I tip the broth into my mouth, unsure how long it has been since last I ate. Joan studies the small space and realises I have no jake. She leaves me, crosses the herbarium to my old room and returns, setting the pot beside me.

"Your confinement is temporary." After I finish, she takes my empty bowl and sets it on a table. "Before long, you will be on your way back to the king's court." She says this with more cheer, as if I must be looking forward to returning to that den of dissemblers and cut throats.

Joan removes the rope from her pocket, and without hesitation, I present my wrists for her to bind. I want her to know that I trust her.

"It is imperative that you not create a commotion. Patience will serve you best." Joan removes a cloth from her pocket and studies me with sad eyes. "You understand that we must prevent your making a pother."

And so I sit with cloth on my tongue and my wrists bound in a cramped, dank, odorous hole in a wall, waiting to be released. I am not the stuff of fanciful tales where a beautiful maiden is rescued by a gallant man of genteel breeding. I am the hideous afterbirth of a mother who refused me. I am the lascivious oblate who could not be chastened. I am the tregetour who was caught.

I am a fool.

My mind pesters me. Thoughts niggle like mayflies, nipping me for attention, refusing to leave. I think of beautiful Bess Holland living with Norfolk at Whitehall—a man as mutable as the king but unflaggingly vindictive—his only steadfast trait. I remember how he dragged his wife by her hair and locked her in her chamber, though some said she deserved his ire. Men who abuse their wives know a steady diet of dispensing cruelty. They seem unable to stop themselves. It is true of Thomas Howard. It is true of William Brugge. It is true of our king.

Is Bess Holland happy? Can she quell Norfolk's savage

inclinations, or does she suffer the same outbursts as her predecessor, Elizabeth Stafford? Has she learned to suffer in silence? Instead of ruminating over his ill treatment of herself and others, does she delight in loops of pearls and buy gowns of damask instead? Does she prefer being the wife to one of the most powerful man in England, or does she regret a more mundane existence where she could have had children and the pleasure of family? I suppose I shall never understand the mind of a woman.

Then, a more pathetic thought enters my mind—does she ever think of me?

In some ways, women fare no better than I. We are both underappreciated and underutilised. Men think us of wooden wit. They believe our emotions are as changeable as the moon. Given so many faults, it is no surprise that we are treated thus. We expect nothing and often are given just that.

Though I long to see Bess Holland again, I do not relish the thought of confronting Norfolk or any of the Howards to accomplish it. If Brugge succeeds in ransoming me, the end game would be a less pleasing result with the Howards. If they see me as a threat to their continuance of power, then I shall be dispensed forthwith—my tongue clipped to its root, or worse. Perhaps I will be stabbed and fed to the wild boars in Ashdown Forest for King Henry to hunt later. I might end up on King Henry VIII's plate for him to devour, then shat out later in his garderobe. My fate depends on whether Archbishop Cranmer has informed him of John Lascelles' claim and whether the king believes him. The clock is ticking, and I cannot see its face.

I am skittish from worry and a lack of sleep when I am woken by the shelves being moved. I slide to the opposite wall, unsure who might be waiting for me on the other side, when I hear the heavy breath of William Brugge. There is a tang of fermented ale on his breath and damp soil on his boots. Another evening at The Crooked Cork. He must have wanted to assure himself that I was still his captive. A lantern swings before him, illuminating his liverish face.

"Who are you?" he inquires. Ale prevents him from standing stock still, and he lingers there, staring, trying to make sense of me. But there is no sense in a dwarf confined to a hole in a wall. "I know you can speak," he says, taking sinister pleasure at this discovery. His nose twitches; he catches a whiff of my jake and grimaces. A belch turns into a convulsive retch, and he turns away, sets the lantern on a table, then nearly falls against the shelving as he hastens to slide it back in place.

I assume it is morning when Joan brings a meal of barley and chopped apples and leaves the small door open. The smell of the porridge paired with the odour of my chamber pot nauseates me, but I eat anyway. The day must have only begun because Joan sweeps the herbarium, and I've not heard Brugge stir. Her sweeping calms me the same as listening to the lapping of the Thames against wood pilings. I am sorry to add to the chamber pot when I hear the heavy thud of the apothecary descending the stairs.

He looks in on me while I squat and grimaces.

"Why isn't he bound?"

The sweeping stops. "He had to eat," answers Joan.

"He looks to be done. Tie and gag him."

The broom resumes sweeping.

"I do not mean later."

Joan leans the broom against the wall. She takes out the length of rope, and I raise my arms over my head. It would not do for her to tie them loosely; we both know that, and I accept the over and under looping and wrapping. When she is done, she places the cloth in my mouth and winds it about my head. She averts her eyes. She removes the empty dish and slides the shelving back in place.

Joan returns to sweeping while Brugge works in the herbarium. His steps are unwieldy, plodding. His evening at The Crooked Cork did not sit well with him. A jar falls off the table and shatters.

"Joan! Clean this up."

I hear the careful sound of shards of pottery being collected and disposed of.

More time passes and then he says, "I must see about a shipment. You will have to attend the shop while I am gone."

My spirits lighten at the thought of his leaving. Mayhap Joan will let me empty my chamber pot. He is nearly out the door when he is waylaid by customers.

"William Brugge, apothecary?"

"'Tis I."

"We've been sent by the Earl of Hertford."

I push my ear against the wall and hold my breath.

"You are attending someone. A dwarf."

William Brugge must be dumbfounded. As am I, but with it comes a feeling of relief. Finally, Brugge receives the confirmation he had long suspected, and I will be released.

"He was left at our door. My wife's reputation as a healer is well-known."

"As is your reputation for creating medicines."

"We did not actively seek this responsibility," reminds Brugge. He must be uncertain if he shall stand accused of wrong-doing.

"He arrived one morning, unannounced. He would have died if we had not taken him in. It is our Christian duty to care for the sick and injured regardless of their history and beliefs."

"You were chosen for your charity and for your loyalty to the king."

"We have had no communication from anyone asking after his welfare or seeking his return."

"You must understand," said one of the men. "This was a precaution."

"Where will you take him?" asks Joan.

"The king's court, Goodwife."

"Caring for him has been a burden," says Brugge, returning to making his case for hardship.

"We came prepared to compensate you for your efforts." Coins jingle and I imagine Brugge is being offered a bag of money for his troubles.

"I appreciate this recompense," says Brugge. "But I am sorry to inform you that he is not here."

I sit, stunned at his lie. Why refuse to take the coins? The offering must have insulted him.

There is a pause, then a retainer asks, "What say you?"

Brugge says, "Truly I should like to oblige and give you his charge, but he…is no longer here."

"Where is he? What have you done with him?"

"I haven't done anything with him. Indeed, I tried to keep him here until he was fully healed." He says this with such coolness as to send a chill down my short spine.

"You have to understand, we must return with Kronos!"

"Ah! Kronos—so that is his name?" Brugge chuckles, but I miss the joke. "Neither of us knew." He is stalling, hoping to diffuse the moment and think of an excuse. But men who carry out the wishes of courtiers are not known for their lightness of spirit. No doubt, the apothecary is being met with unsmiling faces.

"Master Brugge, tell us where he is."

"In truth, I do not know. He escaped."

If it weren't for the gag in my mouth, I would have called him a liar.

Silence follows. The retainers are stymied. I wait for Joan to speak, but she says not a word, and though I slump in disappointment, she has made a prudent decision, for she already has one black eye and does not need a second. Let William Brugge contrive his own mischief.

"Master Brugge, this is unacceptable."

"Gentlemen," says Brugge, "This is indeed unfortunate. But we were unaware that he should have been waylaid until retrieved. We would have taken extra assurances had we known."

There follows more silence. I strain to hear if they accept Brugge's word and leave without recourse. But retainers have the vitriol of a nobleman to face should he be disappointed. And that vitriol is poignant motivation to never fail.

All I hear is the beating of my heart. I prefer leaving with the Seymours, but without seeing the retainers' livery I cannot know if they are truly Seymour's men. If I could choose, I would go with neither noble family, for what predicament awaits me on my return to Whitehall?

"Search the premises," says a retainer. There is a rustle of movement and the determined sound of heavy plodding boots in the herbarium. A table scrapes, a chair is pushed. A man ascends the stairs and the floor boards over my head bow from his weight as he moves across the room. The back area, where Joan cooks, is searched, as is the back entrance with the alley door. Chests and cabinets are unlocked and lids dropped shut; doors are opened and closed. "You understand that we must verify he is not here," comes the cool explanation for violating the couple's privacy. Private citizens may not object.

§

Finally, the footfall collects with Brugge and Joan in the herbarium. If they should not find me, will Brugge throw me to the wolves? Not the wolves of Wolf Hall, but to the wolves of Kenninghall? What then? Will the Howards send me on to hell, first clipping my tongue so that I can't even tell the devil why I'm there? I drive my shoulder against the wall repeatedly, hoping the thumps will gain their attention. But my effort is for nought; they begin talking, unaware of the wild paroxysm of effort only feet away, behind the shelving.

"There is no sign of him," says one of the men.

I bang my head against the wall as much in refute as frustration.

"'Tis unfortunate, aye," says Brugge.

My desperation weighs like a millstone upon my chest.

One of Seymour's men is the last to join the others. He calls from the room off the herbarium. "Look here!"

Footsteps move away from me. They are gathering in my old room.

"A block and chain shackle," says one.

"Sir, you said that you assumed it unnecessary to restrain him or you would have taken extra measures. Yet it appears that you did just that."

I imagine William Brugge's face flushing purple having been disproved. How shall he dismiss this discovery? How shall he help himself out of this incrimination? More like, he shall dig a grave and sit in it. He shall play in the dirt.

"Ah, you see," says he, "'tis evidence of the dwarf's slippery nature. We did try to curb his ability to leave, but we were conflicted. His injury made us wonder. Was he treated harshly for his miscreant nature? For his poor conduct? Perhaps he was brutalised in a dispute at a boozing ken? Or was this a punishment to silence him? We did not know. Nor did we know who exacted his punishment.

"We did attempt to question this—Kronos. But as you can imagine, he was unable to speak. Nor could he write. There was no cooperation. I felt that we should shackle him.

"But you see, my wife is a charitable soul. She convinced me to unlock his fetters, arguing that he was of no threat to us personally. And by shackling him, we would give him reason to retaliate. I admit, I saw some sense in this."

"When did you discover him missing?"

"Only this morning, sir. He may not have got far. And certainly, he is conspicuous enough for people to take notice."

Seymour's men waste not a moment more discussing the matter. They exit without issuing a threat or pricking the apothecary's chin in churlish frustration—for they had been operating at a disadvantage and until now, did not know it. Had it been bantered about whether to send Brugge a message and then been decided against? Or was someone supposed to deliver Brugge a message and had failed to do so? Either way, Seymour's retainers depart the shop posthaste, and whether they would ever discover the apothecary's deceit and act on it remained to be seen.

"What are you thinking?" asks Joan, the moment they are gone. "Lying to these men? They will ruin us at the very least."

"If Sir George does not pay, then I will send word to the earl and his men can take him, none the wiser for a slight inconvenience."

"And if Sir George takes him? What then do we say to the earl's men when the earl learns of our deceit?"

"These families do not discuss specifics. They despise one another. But, if the Seymours ask, we shall tell them that, unfortunately, the Howards must have found him."

"I would sooner leave home than lie to either party."

"A wife's duty is to her husband," says the apothecary. "But I will not stop you."

"You play a dangerous game," warns Joan. "You have gone against my wishes and better judgement. You have put everything you have ever worked for at risk."

"You shall see that it will be to our benefit."

Joan leaves her husband, passes through the herbarium, and ends in the kitchen. Pots rattle, something is chopped. It is not long before the smell of cooked apples seeps into my space again, and my stomach churns in hunger. Soon I may be freed from the simple menu of a merchant's home. I long for the scraps of Henry's feasts, the duck rillettes and roasted beef, dripping with rich, oily fat that slides down the back of my throat. I could finish my entertainment and repair to the kitchen to the platters of leftover food free to pick through. I could dance between the servers and cooks, goad the young boys, their faces red and smudged with smoke from turning boars on spits in front of cavernous fireboxes.

Once sated, I would dally with the women of Whitehall, the ladies-in-waiting dressed in their taffeta and damask kirtles swooshing as they walk past, their jewelled girdles bouncing seductively with every step, their stomachers embroidered with fanciful curlicues and flower designs, their chins lifted ever so slightly, their delicate fingers interlaced in prim decorum. If I went with the Seymours, would I be allowed to resume my antics once I'd served my purpose? Or did a more odious fate await me?

I refuse to think on that.

If I should be banished from the world of courtiers, then let me think about the chamber and scullery maids who are just as lovely. I shall bask in those memories to while away my remaining imprisonment with the apothecary and his dutiful wife.

CHAPTER TWENTY-EIGHT

THERE ARE PEOPLE in your life who you wish the worst for. Perhaps their poor treatment of you or someone you care about is enough to wish them ill. You keep two lists in your life—those whom you love on one, those you despise on the other. Mostly, you ask God to forgive your spiteful thoughts. You leave it to Him to pass final judgement and dispense punishment befitting the transgression so that you do not have to do it. You know it is wrong to hate, but who among us can resist dwelling on that second list a little too long?

I have been gone from the priory for sixteen years, and my faith in God has waned. Understandable, is it not? The king pronounced that he is the Defender of the Faith in England, the only intermediary between God and his people. The pope disagrees and methinks that Henry is on *his* second list. The pope must give the appearance of tolerance; he will say novenas for our king, but he misses the flow of money from England that is being circumvented to Henry.

People come and go on my second list, and since my mutilation the number has grown. I keep shuffling around the top placeholder; it gives me something to think about when I am not imagining more carnal pleasures.

Having narrowly avoided my discovery by the Seymours, Brugge leaves for the waterfront—I assume to secure the final ingredient for Norfolk's remedy.

Joan brings me a bowl of stewed apples with oats. She removes the cloth gag and works at the knots binding my hands. I am sore from sitting immobile and vigorously rub the skin of my wrists, and she comments that the rope has chafed my skin.

"I have a salve that will help." She searches her husband's shelves and finds an ointment of bees' wax, comfrey, and calendula. The comforting mélange of herbs permeates my space as she dabs the salve onto my reddened skin and gently rubs it in.

Joan glances at my pisspot. It is near to overflowing, and her procrastination has made the unpleasant chore even more onerous. With painful, almost unintelligible words I ask her to let me take it out to dump.

She looks long at me, deciding. Should she trust a man who has tried to escape?

I shake my head, addressing her probable fear. Again I try to tell her that I will not run. The pain and embarrassment from forming mostly unintelligible words upsets me, but I push aside those feelings and try to convince her. I manage to let her know that I realise he would hurt her if I ran, and that I do not want her to suffer the back of her husband's hand because of me.

"As you will, Kronos." My name sounds odd on her tongue, its familiarity uncomfortable, but she agrees to let me undertake the chore.

My legs shake from unuse as I follow her to the back-alley

door. When I am outside, the cool, moist air of February is a balm to my spirit. Like the first primrose spotted beside a woodland path, I am reminded of the inevitable renewal that comes with the passage of time. Though the alley is laden with thick mud and a bone-thin dog growls as I pass him guarding his rancid kitchen scraps, there is much to appreciate outside the walls of William Brugge's shop.

The planks are laid end to end. I pick my way down them, careful to keep my balance. At the corner I take the final few steps to the ditch latrine where a maid is on the opposite side dumping out an urn. Her eyes are wide with curiosity at my arrival so I blow her a kiss. My gesture seems to neither dissuade her from staring, nor does it prompt her to speak to me. Such is the response I have grown accustomed to, but I wonder how much of the staring is because of my scarred face? I have no means by which to measure its wretched appearance.

On my return, Joan stands at the alley door watching me. She holds it open, then secures the lock, replacing the key on the ledge in its usual place. Is it a matter of trust that she does not keep it in her pocket or place it well beyond my reach? Or is its placement a habit, and her thoughts distract her from taking a precaution?

We are crossing the herbarium when a woman's voice calls out in greeting upon entering the shop. Joan tips her head that I should return to my space behind the shelving. I take a few steps in that direction and Joan, satisfied that I will comply, leaves the herbarium, but as she speaks in greeting, I stop and listen. Neither woman can see me. I am out of sight.

I set the jake next to the table where Brugge mixes his medicines. Crocks and bowls are neatly stacked—the man is orderly in his art; his work surface has been wiped clean of crumbled herbs and spills. A row of bottles awaits the apothecary's customers.

One bowl, from the smell of its contents, contains currant leaves. Underneath it is a piece of parchment labelled "Howard". The combination of herbs gives off a strange, unpleasant smell that includes garlic and mint.

"My little Anna has a frightful cough and is spitting up phlegm," says the woman.

"William should be back this afternoon if you want to return later."

"Oh, I can't wait so long. Haven't you got a remedy you could give me?"

"Coltsfoot tea can dry up mucous," suggests Joan.

Brother Ulric often used the same for ailing brothers, especially in the winter.

"That should do," says the woman. "I need something now."

As Joan measures out coltsfoot from the supply in the outer shop, the door opens and a second patron enters. I step back from the table to avoid being seen and peruse the shelves of herbs divided by their ruling planet.

The symbol for Mars is scribed above a shelf where jars of ginger root, mustard seed, euphorbium, and pepper from the East Indies are stashed. All are bitter plants and hot poisons, instrumental in balancing phlegmatic humours. Venus with her sanguine disposition rules bowls of thyme, rose petal, and vervain. I pause at a jar of teasel root, whose powder can cause morbid evacuation of the bowels.

The shop door opens, leaving Joan with the new customer.

"Goodwife Tillin," says Joan, "it's been weeks since you were here."

My interest is drawn to Saturn's symbol and I gaze at its row of ingredients. Brother Ulric taught me that these plants are of narcotic virtue, but they possess a crass nature to be dispensed with thoughtfully. Rue wards off witches. Truth be, I've never seen a witch (even at the dunking chair I had my doubts). I have seen enough eccentric characters to know that lunacy need not favour one sex over the other. Hellebore treats intestinal worms, purple beardtonge…

"I can't think what to do," says Goodwife Tillin, whose voice is whispery thin from age. "I have exhausted my abilities. I must rely on your good knowledge to help me."

"What brings you today?"

"A month ago, I started gettin' pains in me head. Me scalp burns as if a hot poker were laid on it."

An involuntary shudder runs through my body.

"Then, clumps of me hair fall out."

"And your good sister, does she still live with you?"

"Oh aye, she does. Her and her dirty goose."

"And you both still spin wool?"

"Oh aye. 'Tis our livelihood."

Joan asks if she might inspect her scalp, which requires the woman to remove her coif and perhaps her hair tapes. This will keep Joan occupied for a bit.

Upon William Brugge's Saturn-ruled shelf is a respectable assortment of the most odious of herbs, enough to tweak a mixture and augment its effects. Sometimes all that is needed is a small measure more…

"Goodwife Tillin," says Joan. "Methinks it is the ring worms. Sometimes shepherds are affected."

"What? Worms from me wool? God's blood!"

"I have something which will work."

"I've got worms?"

"I have a tincture that will help. It is made of wormwood and oregano oil. Mix ten drops with vinegar and rub it into your scalp twice a day. For good measure, have your sister apply it to her scalp as well."

There is an exchange of coin and I hear Goodwife Tillin say, "Well, it is my hope that my condition will clear with your good remedy."

I hear the shop door opening, thinking Joan is seeing her customer out, when unexpectedly, she walks into the herbarium. She stops, and our eyes meet.

I replace the bowl on its parchment and shrug as I hurry to pick up my jake and return to the hole in the wall.

"You were to return to your hole forthwith."

I try to croak that I was merely curious, but my spirits sag. I cannot argue. She will bind my wrists and shut me away. I would have done the same if I had been so disregarded.

"Give me your wrists," she says. Her lips press together, turning white as she winds the rope around my wrists. For good measure, she tightens the knots, pinching my skin.

Joan bends over to finish and starts to place the cloth in my mouth.

"'eave him," I say before she can secure it.

She straightens and looks at me. "Leave…William?"

I nod, yes, yes, I gesture emphatically. I remove the cloth in my mouth. Again, I struggle to form the words but the message is worth the effort and the strangeness of their sound. I tell her that his misdeeds are not hers. Do not make them so. I look at her face to read whether she understands my garbled warning.

"My husband is determined to profit from your misfortune. What I say matters not. Unlike our king, I haven't the privilege of divorce." She snuffs as if comparing the inequities of King Henry's life with those of her own. "Besides," she says. "I have nowhere to go."

"Meg's," I spout, her name sounding clear like a crystal chime.

She blinks, and I wonder if the idea had never occurred to her? Has she so little consideration for her own well-being?

Alas, dear Joan returns the cloth to my mouth and secures it. The shelving is slid back in place.

CHAPTER TWENTY-NINE

THE SLAMMING SHOP door rouses me from my thoughts and heralds the return of the apothecary.

"Finally!" he says, "the ship is moored, and I have my couchgrass and betulina." He is a king among herbs, lording over his newly acquired stash of pungent leaves. "I can finish the duke's remedy."

With a flurry of activity, bowls clack, a stool is dragged across the floor, the clack of a pestle grinds the herb against the stone mortar. His determined steps mark his movement around the herbarium. I imagine the order in which he works to finish the expected cure.

Outside, the wind blows, and a driving rain finds a leak in the exterior wall. A puddle collects on the floor next to me and runs in a stream towards the herbarium, making me lift my legs and brace them against the wall to keep dry. From inside the workspace, the smell of mangled leaves rides the steam through a crack in the door to where I sit. The smell of chemistry masks the mouldering dank and offers some reassurance that another world exists outside this tiny hole in the wall.

Despite the foul weather, a scattering of needy clientele,

needy enough to brave the soaking rain, arrive recounting their stories of woe. Joan attends them while Brugge concentrates on his task at hand, occasionally stopping to answer questions or to make a quick concoction for a customer. He must be thinking he need only accommodate the sick for one more day. Soon he shall have two hundred pounds in hand, and the imaginings of a life spent without the tedium of shop hours or client demands.

With the arrival of every subsequent customer, I strain to hear if it is George Howard coming to collect me. With no news or court rabble-rousing to inform, I am lost. I don't even know the fate of our imprudent queen—Henry's 'Rose without a Thorn.' Methinks she has sprouted lots of little prickles since my first day in the apothecary's care.

What is left for me to think on inside my dark confinement? Shall I pray for God to save me? But would He sense my festering scepticism beneath those words? Or would I be less disappointed if I attributed my outcome to His wisdom and grace and just accept it? Was my mutilation His plan to teach me a lesson, to test me? I am no Job who accepts all manner of suffering because his faith is unshakeable.

And what of the men who ordered and carried out this cruelty—are they God's pawns in the matter? Have they no conscience, and are they forgiven for doing His will?

I see no sense in asking Him for help or forgiveness. My brethren would be displeased with me, if not offended. But my fate matters not to my creator. If I think I am abandoned now, then fool I am not to have recognised the estrangement from the beginning.

My time avoiding the coursing stream of water and listening to the stirrings of Brugge in his herbarium are interrupted when Joan calls for her husband. He abandons his work for the shop.

"Sir George," he says. "You've returned."

"Indeed, Master Brugge. I have come for my uncle's medicine."

"Of course. I have just added the final ingredient." William Brugge enters the herbarium, collects the finished remedy, then leaves. "The ship encountered rough weather coming to port and was delayed. But the medicine is done, and I believe the duke will be pleased."

The silence that follows makes me think perhaps there is an exchange of coin and medicine.

When next Brugge speaks, the apothecary dares to broach the topic of additional monies. "We have been the king's loyal servants. We have undertaken the care of someone familiar to the king's court. By now you might have confirmed that he is witness to a matter concerning your family."

"Master Brugge, the fool does have some worth. However, I have not been able to communicate with my uncle. He was due last evening, having travelled from Kenninghall when he undoubtably met with the harsh weather. He has yet to arrive."

"So, we are delayed in settling this." Brugge sounds deflated. Certainly he is wondering how much longer he can keep me hidden before his deception is uncovered.

"I expect to speak with him tonight," says George Howard.

"I am hoping the duke is aligned with our request for recompense. It is a fair price considering the value of his testimony." William Brugge's belief that the Howards would waste no time in securing me is roundly dashed. Weather has proven to be the unreliable player in this game. "I have no knowledge of court dealings," he continues. "But time does not wait for matters of consequence. Tomorrow may be too late."

"Sir, my uncle is a man of inestimable power and influence. I shall not be pressed."

William Brugge must be bristling, but he knows to appear obsequious. At least until the money is jangling in his purse.

"Very well, Sir George," he says, sounding cordial. "I will await your return."

The shop door opens. The shop door closes.

"Fool," says Brugge. "His family will suffer from his delay."

❧

Brugge could have encouraged Sir George to action by telling him that he'd had a visit from the Seymours. However, the nobleman might have then accused the apothecary of pitting the two families against one another. Better to keep quiet if one wants to keep from ending in Newgate.

Joan voices her concern for their predicament. "I worry the Seymours will learn that you have put them off in favour of the Howards."

"How would they come to know? I've told you, if that should happen we simply say that Kronos escaped—but we found him."

"You believe these families do not speak to one another, but they have retainers whose chins can wag."

"The matter will be resolved before that happens."

"This is lunacy," says Joan.

I want to shout my agreement.

"I must move him to Meg's," adds Brugge without prompt. His words hang in the air like the pestilential miasma of the Fleet.

"This is madness! Keep Meg away from your scheming. She has no part in this so do not give her one."

"Her home is not far, and I do not trust Sir George. Once he confers with Norfolk, I fear he will arrive with the duke's men and take Kronos by force. This will stymie them. We'll then give Kronos over to the Seymours if they do not pay what I ask."

"We mustn't involve Meg in this," says Joan. "I will not allow it!"

"If it means keeping us safe, she will certainly agree," says Brugge.

"I will never forgive you if she is deemed an accomplice. You must let whatever happens, be. Besides, the Howards could just as easily kill you. They do not need to pay a single pence. They will accuse you of demanding money for a duty expected of any loyal citizen."

"They won't kill me. They need Kronos."

"These men of rank will not be commanded. They will not be told, by anyone. And for cert not by an apothecary of inferior standing."

Brugge rounds on her. "Inferior standing?" he says. "In rank only. Not in wit. You would do well to remember that…wife." The final word reeks of his seething disdain for Joan like a turd on a nobleman's rug.

CHAPTER THIRTY

I N THE SMALLEST hours of the night, we meet the silence of time but relive in vivid detail the moments of its passage. Sometimes we are met with monstrous recreations of uncomfortable memories. Sometimes our mind embellishes the soft tufts of dandelions and turns them into sensations of profound contentment. In what I believe to be my final night in Brugge's apothecary, I waver distractedly between the two.

For who among us can rest when our fate is in the hands of another? If our master be of rare generous heart, then yay, we may be at ease in the direction we are led. But lo, it is a rare man who considers the needs of another and indulges him. I cannot hope for the latter.

I have lived a life confined by this strange body that God gave me. I have worked within its confines, its physical limitations, to survive better than most. But allowing a man such as William Brugge to enrich himself from my misfortune riles my blood to boil. If I can prevent him from using me thus, and I choose not to stop him, who is the greater fool?

Rather than spend the night with Joan and her roiling discontent, the apothecary is gone for most of the night and returning, he takes his puny self up the stairs to sleep away the remaining dark. He is there, overhead, suffused in ale and snoring, dreaming of riches beyond anything he has ever known. I remain propped against the door of my space, nodding off, then waking to keep from toppling into my pisspot. A night spent in fitful slumber leaves me full of spleen by morning.

The first peeps of light seep under the crack, and I wait with impending dread Brugge's arrival. For where shall I end?

Alas, the apothecary begins to stir. I hear his lumbering descent and Joan's skittery steps following after. Their combined footfall crosses the herbarium and ends next to the bookshelves.

"You must let him eat," Joan insists. "I'll not have Meg troubled any more than necessary."

"Don't be daft, he can survive for a few more hours without food." Brugge's voice sounds rough from too much drink. "I will not move him on crowded streets with hundreds of eyes watching. I must move him now."

Without Joan's care I would not have survived. Although the apothecary is also partly responsible for my survival, I cannot afford him even the slightest praise for his efforts. He made no contribution to my convalescence except to provide shelter. Instead, he complained about the responsibility foisted upon him—that is, until he found a way to make money from the inconvenience.

The cumbersome bookshelves are haltingly moved aside and the narrow plank door swings open, revealing the pair. Brugge appears uncharacteristically dishevelled, but he seems to have his legs under him and his ugly wit about him.

"I shall not miss his foul leavings," he says, wincing at a waft from my chamber pot. "We will soon part ways, and we shall both be better for it."

He grips me under my armpit and pulls me to my feet. My

legs ache from sitting and I feel unsteady but Brugge holds my arm to prevent my falling.

"Get his shoes, Joan." As Joan hurries off to fetch them, Brugge lets go of my arm, pinching his mouth in disgust as if I am a leper. I waver on my legs, still unused to standing. "He's nearly chewed through his gag," he says, yanking off the cloth then tossing it on the table, and I am glad for the release of tension on my cheek and jaw.

Joan returns and I lean against the table as she helps me into my shoes.

Brugge observes my wrist bindings. "We must replace that rope; it looks as if he's been trying to wear them through."

He finds several lengths of hemp rope and stuffs them in a small satchel, saving one for Joan. "We'll need these at Meg's," he says.

Without protest, Joan takes the rope and stands directly in front of me, blocking her husband's view. She looks me in the eye, and without a word, places a small wood wedge between my wrists, and begins binding me. I glance at the apothecary, but he is wrestling the shelving back into place.

"Shall I replace his gag?" asks Joan.

Brugge removes a dagger from his sheath and flashes the shiny blade in front of my face. "I don't believe he will squawk with a knife at his side." He nods in the direction of the alley exit. "Let us be away."

Joan leads us through the herbarium to the back-alley door while the apothecary brings up the rear, his tetchy blade pricking my back when I don't move fast enough. Soon I shall see the streets of London beyond the ditch latrine. Will I be led over Holborn Bridge past Ely's Place in the area of St. Andrews? I know that its gardens are praised for the plump, rubied strawberries that are grown there.

Or is Meg's lodging in the vicinity of Christ Church whose convenience to Newgate market pleases her butcher husband? Either way, I shall know my familiar, for I have traipsed every square foot of this king's cosmopolis and have called it home.

At the door, Joan feels along the ledge for the key. I feel myself growing anxious as she places it in the padlock. The wards give way with a discernible click, and she pulls the lock off the hasp. As she steps aside to let Brugge push open the door, we are interrupted by an unexpected knocking from the front of the shop. Joan exchanges an alarmed look with her husband.

"Answer it," he says.

Joan shakes her head. "No. I will not."

"It may only be an early customer," says Brugge. "Delay them, and I shall return forthwith."

"Nay," says Joan, clearly agitated. "You must answer the door. I will have no part in this."

"God's blood, woman! Why must you defy me?" Brugge points his dagger at her nose, stopping within an eyelash of piercing it. "Answer the door!"

Joan does not relent. She squares her shoulders and closes her eyes, waiting for her punishment.

A second, more insistent knock rattles the door.

William Brugge hesitates. He lowers his voice, "I will only give them Kronos if they accept my terms." The apothecary points his knife at my left eye. "Not a single sound from you," he warns. He hands me off to Joan, thrusting my arm forward for her to grip. "Stay here until I call for you. If they conduct a search instead of paying me, you will be able to hear them. In which case, take Kronos to Meg's. Wait for me there."

We watch Brugge cross the herbarium on his way to the shop door, the knocking growing more insistent. Joan cranes her neck to better see and hear. Her grip loosens on my arm.

I glance over my shoulder at the alley door, ajar, outlined in the soft morning light. With Joan so distracted, I might be able to break free. True, my hands are bound, but I do not need them to run.

Brugge unlocks the front door but before a single word is uttered, a clamour from men rushing in upsets the balance of quiet.

Joan pulls me towards the commotion, stopping when they speak.

"William Brugge, you will come with us."

"Ah! To speak with the duke of Norfolk? Yes, we have business."

"Indeed, sir."

Apparently, a retainer seizes hold of him.

"There is no need for your rough handling. I am well capable of following on my own."

"We think otherwise," says one of the men. "Take his knife."

"Here, now. What is all this about?"

My mind thinks of what will become of me once the Howards have custody. They would not want me voicing the damaging account in court or anywhere else. These men could make another man 'disappear' and never suffer a single consequence for their actions. No one ever crossed a nobleman about a man of lesser station. Certainly, no one would blink an eye if a court fool such as me suddenly vanished.

"There has been a murder."

"What has that to do with me?" says Brugge.

"Your remedy killed a man."

"What? Impossible! 'Twas a simple concoction."

"A tester lies dead from it."

"Hold! I am a man of reputation! I would never create something to harm another person. Certainly not Thomas Howard."

"He thinks otherwise."

"I have nothing to do with this! The tester must have died from natural cause."

The men start for the door, and Brugge resists, upsetting a stool.

"What cause would I have to do such a vile deed?" We can hear him struggling. "There must be another explanation," he cries. "Why…perhaps a dissembler works amongst the duke's staff. One of false pretence! Mayhaps his nephew, George!"

The unlocked door calls to me.

Joan's mouth falls open as she looks towards the shop, then back at me, her eyes wide with fear.

I meet her eyes and in that brief moment, she understands the depth of my deceit.

I have only a second.

I yank my arm from her grasp and push open the door.

The alley is dank and fulsome with the smell of raw earth—akin to the smell of the open road…and…my freedom.

EPILOGUE

THEY CALL ME fool, but I ask, who is the greater?

Because of me, an innocent man will be charged with murder. True, it is unfortunate that a lowly servant—a man I never knew—has lost his life. On that count, I regret that the remedy did not land in the hands of my intended victim. Instead of only freeing one woman of her cruel and pompous husband, I could have freed two. Ah, Bess, forgive me. I did try.

How oft, though, are the innocent wrongly punished? I was blameless and brutally maimed. Let Brugge be accused and suffer. So are the rewards for lower born men. At least his sentencing and demise will be swift. But I suffer the greater pain. My punishment lingers.

Surely Joan realises that I saved her. She is released from her husband's odious influence. Does William Brugge wonder if it is me who designed his fall? When he gnashes his teeth and shakes his fist, is the name on his tongue—mine? Will Joan visit him one last time and confirm his notion? 'Tis mere conjecture, and I shall be long gone before any action can be undertaken.

For now, I am staying with the 'nuns' in Southwark in the Bishop's district. Though Leticia was stunned to see me dressed in hosen and a commoner's smock, my cheek red with lumpy weals, she and the skilful ladies of The Cardinal's Red give me succour until the nasty business of court politics settles. For Archbishop Cranmer, the Duke of Suffolk, and his miching cabal have succeeded in dashing the king's hopes. Queen Katherine will go the way of her cousin—the king shall have her head. She is guilty of what Anne was so wrongly accused. Norfolk has sacrificed two nieces in the cause of bettering and saving himself. He is not so kind an uncle. And he escapes his day of reckoning yet again.

I have no regrets, for such is the world of this man's court. Such is the world in which we live. I am sad that I shall never see the lovely Bess Holland again. I regret that she must continue to endure intimacies with Thomas Howard, to submit to a man of such treachery that it cannot help but spill over into his personal relations with her. I suppose that we all have our sufferings to bear.

Do you wonder about my interactions with Brother Giles and Robert, the lutist? I have told you my side of the story and I will leave it for you to decide.

What shall become of me? I do not intend to live a life of transience and depravity, for I have grown accustomed to the pleasures and drama of a king's retinue. They say that the French court likes oddities. Ha! Am I not that? Their frilly tongue does not intimidate me for I am now practised in making myself understood. Besides, it would cheer me to please a noble lady now and then.

For what is life if we cannot use our talents?

Selected Bibliography

Borman, Tracy. *Henry VIII and the Men Who Made Him.* New York: Grove Atlantic, 2018.

Duffy, Eamon. *The Stripping of the Altars.* New Haven & London: Yale University Press, 1992.

Head, David M. *The Ebbs and Flows of Fortune: The Life of Thomas Howard, Third Duke of Norfolk.* Athens & London: The University of Georgia Press, 1995.

Jones, Paul Van Brunt. *The Household of a Tudor Nobleman.* Memphis: General Books LLC, 2012.

Starkey, David. *The Reign of Henry VIII, Personalities and Politics.* Great Britain: Collins & Brown Limited, 1991.

Stow, John. *A Survey of London.* London: Whitaker and Co., 1842.

Weir, Alison. *The Six Wives of Henry VIII.* New York: Ballantine Books, 1991.

Bilyeau, Nancy. "Thetford Priory: Murdered Monks and a Desperate Duke." Nancy Bilyeau. October 28, 2015. *https://nancybilyeau.com*

Wheeler, Heather Y. "Thomas Howard 3rd Duke of Norfolk 1473-1554." Heather Y. Wheeler. October 13, 2019. https://tudornation.com

Historic England. "Thetford Cluniac priory." *https://historicengland.org.uk/listing/the-list/list-entry/1017669*

Tudorplace. October 7, 2021. "Elizabeth Stafford (D.Norfolk)." *https://tudorplace.com.ar/Bios/ElizabethStafford(D*

Lordsandladies. December 28, 2020. "Daily Life of a Monk in the Middle Ages." *https://www.lordsandladies.org/daily-life-monk-middle-ages.htm*

English Heritage. "Thetford Priory." *https://English-heritage.org.uk/visit/places/Thetford-priory*

Wikipedia. "Sir George Howard." *https://en.wikipedia.org/wiki/Sir_George_Howard_(courtier)*

AUTHOR'S NOTE

Years ago, when I wrote the first draft of *The Alchemist's Daughter* (which, at that time, was a coming-of-age story), the character of Kronos played a major role. I spent years rewriting that manuscript, trying to shape it into a tale that would appeal to readers and publishers. Eventually I chucked the concept along with several characters and wrote a mystery set in Tudor London, the basis for my Bianca Goddard mystery series. But Kronos was too saucy not to create an entire world for him where he could ingratiate, contrive, and wheedle his particular self within the backdrop of 16th century England.

In 2024, I enjoyed the privilege of watching Patrick Page perform his one-man show off Broadway, *All the Devils are Here*. The play is Page's review of the evolution of Shakespeare's major villains—their circumstances and motivations. One theme eclipsed all others for me; in the 16th century, physical and mental disabilities were viewed as moral failings—either reflections of your soul or punishment incurred from your mother's sins. Genetics and environmental causes were not even a concept. Compounding an already challenging existence, one had to cope with society's inherently suspicious attitudes. Little can be done to alter one's physical appearance, and this fact was particularly true back then, but choice, how one navigates personal circumstances, is a conscious decision. *Fool* is my exploration of a man—how he reacts to the prejudice of his era and his choice to either rail against others' preconceived notions, or embrace the physical and mental attributes that "God" gave him.

The best example of the struggle between noble families to preserve wealth and power during Henry VIII's reign is the rivalry between two of its most influential families: the Howards and the Seymours. In 1540, having engineered the downfall of the king's most trusted advisor, Thomas Cromwell, Thomas Howard (Norfolk) was, once again, rising in the king's favor. He had placed his niece, Katherine Howard, in Anne of Cleve's household not expecting the king to so strongly reject his new German bride. With the unexpected dividend of Henry's ultimate marriage to Katherine, Norfolk assured himself the political leverage of lead councilor.

The Seymours still held claim to the throne with Edward VI—Henry's young heir by Jane Seymour, but a potential second male heir—more robust and possessing Howard blood, posed a serious threat to the power of the Seymour clan. Through a series of indiscriminate choices, Katherine Howard inadvertently handed the Seymours the opportunity to spectacularly ruin her family.

No evidence exists that John Lascelles conspired with the Seymours to undermine the king's marriage. However, his statement proved immensely useful to the Seymours and the progressive council in bringing down the Howards. Lascelles was an ardent Protestant, a man once loyal to Thomas Cromwell. Lascelles was eager to see the conservative Howards usurped. In October of 1541, he sought his chance to speak with the progressive council which remained in London while the royal pair were on progress in the north. Upon their return, Archbishop Cranmer discretely passed a letter to the king outlining Lascelle's claims, begging he read it in private. At first, Henry denied the allegations, then within a week he directed an investigation into

Katherine's behavior. By November 14, Katherine was moved to Syon Abbey under guard. Less than a month later, Francis Dereham and Thomas Culpeper were executed for traitorous relations with the queen.

Thomas Howard did as he was prone to do. He denied knowledge of Katherine's indiscretions. As in Anne Boleyn's trial, he served on the commission to condemn his niece. Norfolk avoided complete ruin by abandoning his family at the first sign of trouble and he was capable of extreme malevolence. Accordingly, Lady Rochford and Katherine were executed on February 13, 1542.

During the final years of Henry VIII's reign, Thomas Howard still wielded some influence. He was, however, nearly 70 when the debacle with Katherine Howard occurred. Age was catching up to him as well as his less popular conservative stance. By the time Henry died in 1547, Norfolk was in the Tower waiting execution, and his son lay in a traitor's grave. Edward VI spared Norfolk's life, and ultimately, Queen Mary pardoned him in 1553. He died the following summer of natural causes. As for John Lascelles, he was burned at the stake for heresy in 1546.

I hold no illusions that I have created a perfect reflection of that time. My interest has spurred my education, and the result is my personal interpretation of the political, religious, and moral paradigms informing that era. To quote the late, esteemed Hilary Mantel in her wonderful Reith Lectures, "The writer of history is a walking anachronism, a displaced person, using today's techniques to try to know things about yesterday that yesterday didn't know itself." In depicting certain historical events, one often finds conflicting versions, and to those inclined to point out the faults in my interpretation, I apologize if I offend.

Fool is neither conventional historical fiction, nor patent mystery; elements of both are at play in a milieu of memoire. This work is a departure from my usual mystery fare. I have taken a chance in writing *Fool*, hoping that my readers will at least find Kronos's tale entertaining. And, ultimately, enjoyment and escape are why I read and write fiction.

Acknowledgments

I am truly fortunate to have had the support and recommendations from the following, without whom, I could not have completed this work: Dominic Wakeford, Tracey Stewart, Tom Feltham, Paula Keeney, Ann Whetstone, Andrea Jones, Joyce Turrell, and Eugenia Conte. Love and thanks always to Dave, and to our cabal of cats (which, by definition is a conspiratorial group of plotters or intriguers), Chloe and Kimba.

Mary Lawrence is the author of the Bianca Goddard Mysteries, a five-book series set in the final years of King Henry VIII's reign. Beyond reading about the sixteenth century, Mary runs a small fruit farm with her husband on a reclaimed gravel quarry in Maine, and creates specialty jams for sale. Her articles have appeared in several publications, including the national news blog, *The Daily Beast*. Visit her at marylawrencebooks.com